Rescuing a River Breeze

Rescuing a River Breeze

MRINALINI HARCHANDRAI

BLOOMSBURY
NEW DELHI • LONDON • OXFORD • NEW YORK • SYDNEY

BLOOMSBURY INDIA
Bloomsbury Publishing India Pvt. Ltd
Second Floor, LSC Building No. 4, DDA Complex, Pocket C – 6 & 7,
Vasant Kunj, New Delhi, 110070

BLOOMSBURY, BLOOMSBURY INDIA and the Diana logo
are trademarks of Bloomsbury Publishing Plc

First published in India 2023
This edition published 2023

ISBN: PB: 978-93-56400-27-6; eBook: 978-93-56400-29-0
2 4 6 8 10 9 7 5 3 1

Typeset in Sabon LT Std by Manipal Technologies Limited
Printed and bound in India by Thomson Press India Ltd

MIX
Paper from responsible sources
FSC® C010615
FSC www.fsc.org

Inspired by and dedicated to my mother, née Shirly.
To the rest of the Nathurmals—the original Pequeño Delhi settlers

There are no corals or shells on the sea floor of our soul
Just a smothered dream
And we don't really know what dreams are
Silent conductors faint songs
Which one day suddenly appear
On the broad flat patio of disasters

—Sophia de Mello Breyner, 'Transparency', *Log Book: Selected Poems* (Translated from the Portuguese by Richard Zenith)

On 18 December 1961, India invaded and annexed Estado da Índia, the Portuguese-ruled enclave of Goa, along with Daman and Diu, within the Indian subcontinent, in a war that spanned just one day. In the event that Goa was to surrender in defeat, its Governor-General had received orders from Portugal's prime minister to adopt a scorched-earth policy. However, the Governor-General disobeyed, risking the consequences, which included imprisonment. To date, no one knows the precise reason for that decision.

1

Goa, October 1961

The breeze wafted on to the land, tousling the hair of lovers on a riverfront bench, lifting the scent off buds too shy to open, mingling with the aromas of fish at the noisy market, transporting the purr of a stray cat, dancing on the tongues of hymn-singing nuns, coaxing trees to shed their colours and entwining with children at play in the gardens. It kept the buzzing company of bees as it warmed itself in a tropical evening sun that lit up rising woodsmoke, scattering its secrets at the windowsill of all who kept watch.

From her first-storey-high louvred windows, Shirly inhaled deeply as she looked out at the corner of the Palácio do Idalcão on Rua Vasco da Gama, the main road that flowed parallel to the muscular Mandovi, the river that defined the city of Panjim. Every detail of the evening was like the familiar groove of a fingerprint impressed deeply on Shirly. The audience on her tiptoes didn't need to wait long. On cue, like the punctual hands of time, four guards in uniform marched out from the Idalcão and came to attention at the flagpole on the riverfront. As one of the guards filled the air with the strains of 'A Portuguesa', another pulled down the colourful flag that waved its coat of arms overhead. As it reached the foot of the pole, the man unhitched it, wrapped it deftly, and handed it to a fellow guard.

Right after the flag lowered, signifying the dip of the sun across the horizon, thirteen-year-old Shirly's eyes fell on to the garden below. In it, the lone statue of Abbé Faria stood unmoving, unmoved. Then, hearing her mother Mamtu's call for a bath, she turned away.

In the bathroom, Goku, the maidservant, had left hot water ready in a steel bucket for her. Shirly latched the door and stripped off her clothes. With a small mug, she poured the water on herself, which splashed noisily on to the blue tiles. The sting of the water's heat felt comforting as it slapped her skin. The eddying whorl of sand near the drain led her to guess that Goku and Devika had been to the beach while she was rehearsing at Ana's house. Her throat was pulsating with soreness from the practice session, and she wistfully thought of the freedom she felt in the evenings on her beach outings. She promised herself to enjoy them fully after the musical was over, which was just another month and a half away, on Christmas day, as Dona Lisette had reminded her.

Freshly bathed, Shirly sat at the table in her cotton pyjamas. Goku set the dinner table for four, but only three seats were filled since Deepak was still away. This wasn't unusual for busy days before the Christmas month, and Shirly's mother trusted that the infinite goodness of the gods that gave her food on the table would as easily bring her husband back home to her. She set about ladling and spooning the dishes on to her daughters' plates, when the doorbell rang.

'Baba is here. Goku . . .' Goku didn't need to be told any further by her mistress. She too was glad that the master was home and that dinner would be complete in one sitting. The sooner she could wash up and head home herself.

Goku opened the door, but it wasn't the master of the house there. Instead, it was Deepak's business manager, Michael Cardozo. She led him into the salon.

'Bai, Michael is come,' reported Goku to the mistress of the house.

'Michael? So late?' asked Mamtu, not really expecting a reply from Goku. 'Eat while it's hot, okay, girls?' she instructed her daughters before wiping her hands on a napkin and gingerly pushing her chair back. Bracing the weight of her growing belly, she headed into the salon.

Michael was standing in the middle of the room, looking uncomfortable. He was a bachelor that Mamtu's husband could trust with the keys of his shop. Sometimes he was temperamental and tended towards laziness, but his trustworthiness was key to him being in the lives of the Quarachims. Very often, he would hold the shop open for delays caused by customers or when new stock had to be inventoried. However, everything was always accounted for, the till box was always even and the key was duly handed over whenever he worked overtime. 'Michael, please sit. Is everything all right? Is the shop closed?'

'Yes, yes, Senhora. The shop is closed.' He paused. 'Senhora, there is bad news, I'm afraid.' He seemed fearful of Mamtu's reaction. And Mamtu in turn had to coax him to speak despite her own misgivings.

'What happened, Michael? Please tell me. Has Deepak said anything, done anything? Where is he?'

'Senhora, the police came to the shop in the evening to inform me that patrão is arrested.'

'Arrested? Are you sure? But why?' Mamtu's confusion was expressed in a volley of questions. Her husband couldn't possibly be arrested. He was a beacon of trust and goodwill in society, always erring on the right side of the law. He never took, and in fact, always gave. So his being arrested was out of the question.

'Senhora, they didn't say why. The agente said that we can meet him tomorrow morning.'

'He has to stay the night in prison? How can he stay the night in prison? There must be something we can do! I don't understand why he would be arrested.'

Shirly heard the distress in her mother's voice and came to stand at the threshold of the salon.

'Senhora, nowadays they are arresting people and then asking questions. A few weeks ago they were arresting people from my village Assorem in connection with some propaganda flyers. Senhora, please, you must stay calm for the children.'

Mamtu, like the reflection of the moon buoyant in a lake, who navigated her little world through the watery surfaces of emotions, was already in tears. She noticed Shirly peeping from the doorway and held her arms out. Shirly didn't like seeing her mother so forlorn. She rushed to her. Holding her daughter tenderly by the shoulders, Mamtu wiped her tears.

'What happened to Daddy?'

Mamtu said, either bravely or helplessly, 'I don't know, Shirly. We will find out.'

'He's not coming home?'

'I don't . . .' Mamtu's quaky voice was lost in her sorrow.

'Senhora, it is no use right now. In the morning I am coming and we can go,' Michael repeated, hoping her tears would magically stop with his words. He too was worried that his impeccable boss had been arrested, for no reason that he could understand, since business had been on the upswing. There was no clue in the climate, physical or otherwise, that something like this could happen. He was sure that somehow this mistake would rectify itself with the grace of the Mother and the Holy Son. He rose to leave. 'It is my promise, Senhora. I will come in the morning and we will go to where he is being kept.'

Mamtu nodded tearfully, a little hopefully, yet feebly. She loosened her arms around Shirly as Michael stood up. But he gestured for her to remain seated and saw himself out of the front door.

With distracted heaviness, Mamtu went through the motions of getting herself and the girls to bed.

Under the mosquito netting of her bed, Shirly tossed back and forth a few times. She stared at the moon's fluid reflection on the walls. She could hear her mother's restless movements and intermittent sobs in her own chamber. Shirly looked over at Devika. Her sister was already asleep, her little belly rising and falling rhythmically. Prison was a faraway concept for Shirly. One that she had read about or was narrated to her in stories. Why was her father in prison? What did the prison look like? Was it small and dark? The thought that he would be alone and scared there saddened her.

As she lay wrapped in the echoing doom of her questions, the breeze gusted down Rua Vasco da Gama in short spurts, using its knuckle of branches to knock on the window with a sorrow older than desire.

2

If Shirly were to determine when it all began, she would reach across to a couple of weeks ago in the nautilus of her memory and pull out a day she had preserved within it like a perfectly intact seashell.

Goku gently squeezed the bread with her plump fingers. The bun was still warm, and it fissured delicately across its brownish crust, indicating its sojourn of freshness from the depths of a wood-fired furnace to her. As it gave beneath her fingers, signalling its soft, spongy insides, the bun released a farinaceous scent, sending a jolt of excitement racing through her.

It was an October morning in Panjim, still cool, before the sun cracked fully open into the sky. The city that was a jewel in the crown of Portuguese Estado da Índia, the only one planned in gridiron formation within the territory of Goa, was still waking up. Rightly given the appellation Nova Goa, or new Goa, it was the capital of culture and civilization, a finely suited fidalgo lording over the palm-thatched villages and small towns spread around it to the north and south. The commercial port town wore its well-cut livery with an intimacy of narrow streets, close-knit but colourful houses, squares, avenues and many gardens. It was hemmed in by the Mandovi River, which met with the Arabian Sea in the west and was looked upon by the white-garbed Igreja de Nossa Senhora da Imaculada Conceição on the hill near Altinho that regularly spilled its clergy on its grand interlacing steps on Sundays. Beyond the brickwork, however, like an aristocrat, Panjim wore a well-bred manner—a certain gentility and poise settled upon its neat rooftops like a velveteen hat.

For every one of its residents, the morning held different meanings. For the fisherman tying his boat at the Dona Paula dock, it meant a net full of slippery catch. For the midwife, it meant prepping linen for the at-home delivery of the latest wrinkly resident in the neighbourhood. For the devout, it meant forcing eyelids to stay open during the morning sermon at chapel. And for Goku the maid, it meant reaching the Quarachim household before breakfast to greet its string of early visitors.

The poder held out his wares in an open, cloth-lined basket for the maid to select the morning's leavened goods from his mud oven—pão, unnde or pokso, revdo or katre pão, kankon, poiee; all flaky, crispy, crusty in the right ways.

'Tasty and tender as the arms of a belle,' the poder crooned in Konkani, flirting with Goku, who blushed as she clutched half a dozen unnde against her generous breasts.

'Come tomorrow and make sure you give me the freshest ones again, yes?' she teased, heaving her body back into the doorway, scattering floury flakes around her.

The poder turned away, down the short flight of stairs, past the courtyard and vestibule to his bicycle on the street. He placed his basket on the rack behind the saddle as Goku continued to listen across the short distance. He tinkled the bell twice before riding away, and Goku knew it was for her. Beaming in rapture, she buoyantly retreated inside.

As she filled the bread tin, there was the doorbell again.

'Nustem!'

Goku opened the door to see the fisherwoman, with sharp and complex odours from several fruits of the sea wafting around her. Sukkoo and Bukkoo, the local cats that had adopted the Quarachim family, circled the seller's feet, purring and rubbing themselves against her deep-sea dark, salty ankles. She unloaded the basket from her head, and Goku, by now impervious to the snaking smells it threw at her accustomed nostrils, looked in eagerly. There were prawns, some still crawling with tickly pink legs, pomfret, kingfish, rockfish and more. Goku brought out a bowl where she placed her selection, splashing scaly drops on to the red-tiled floor of the landing.

Before they got to haggling, the fisherwoman gave her the neighbourhood news. 'I sold extra fish today to that Silva lady. She is too pregnant, gho. I think she will deliver by tomorrow. She gave me good business through her pregnancy . . . that Crispino is still having an affair with Couto's wife. He was standing at her door early this morning . . . Shoo, cats! Shoo! Mushu is so rude—tells me he knows fish better than me. I don't know who will marry him . . .'

Goku soaked it all in, punctuating the monologue here and there with 'Really?' and 'Saiba'. She disappeared inside and returned with money from Mamtu, who was setting the table for breakfast in the large, high-ceilinged kitchen. Goku offered up a crisp note to the fisherwoman, who tucked it into a pleat of her hitched-up sari. In return, Goku accepted some slime-coated coins as change and headed into the house with the vessel of fish. She hoisted the gilled creatures on to one of the kitchen sinks and began to de-fin, scale and gut them.

'Taaaaaaantem,' came another call from outside. Goku dropped the cleaver with a clatter, wiped her hands on her apron, grabbed another bowl, which she half-filled with water, and headed for the door.

'These eggs are the best, all the way from Tivim.'

Wordlessly, Goku peered inside the egg-seller's jute-lined wicker basket, pulled out an egg and placed it in the bowl of water. It sank to the bottom. The sign of a good egg, she thought, and left it in. She did this with the next and the next. None floated to the top today, which meant there were no rotten eggs. She knew the going rate for eggs, so she pulled the money from the bosom of her cotton housedress and paid.

'Bhorem mu gho?' Goku asked. 'All good?'

'Bhorem,' confirmed the egg-seller. 'All good.'

Leaving the door open, allowing the sunlight to infiltrate the cool, high-ceilinged hallway, Goku returned to the kitchen once more as a man's sophisticated voice floated into earshot.

'Devika, if you drink your milk you will grow to become big and strong, like your sister.'

'Tell me a story, Daddy.'

Deepak Quarachim launched into a tale in order to encourage his four-year-old to drink her milk and eat her sunny-side-up.

'What story shall I tell you? Okay, once there was a kingfish—open your mouth—aaaah—and he sat on his fish throne with a fish crown. All the fish in the kingdom came to him to solve their problems. But he thought, I need some breakfast. And just as he thought that, what do you know? A worm passed by!' Devika's eyes widened along with her mouth as Deepak fed her another bite. 'He thought, "Yum, yum, yum, I want to eat that worm." Open your mouth again, just have a bit of egg . . . good girl! So the fish opened its mouth and took a bite.'

'Goku, please give us unnde,' said his wife, taking a seat, 'and prepare the chai for Baba and me.'

Deepak asked, 'Where is that other daughter of ours?'

'Shirly!' she called out, while Deepak gently pushed another piece of eggy unndo into Devika's mouth.

On cue, Shirly padded into the kitchen from the depths of the house. 'Mummy, can we have ice cream?'

'Here is my star,' said Deepak, taking his daughter by the arm and leading her lithe frame to her empty seat. 'There is no ice cream for breakfast, Puttha. Come, eat your eggs and unndo, and I have a surprise for later.'

As Shirly joined in, Deepak continued to feed his daughters his story. Shirly had heard it over and over again but it was mesmerizing each time.

'Suddenly, there was a noise at the entrance of the palace,' continued Deepak with varying intonations that never failed to deliver gooseflesh on his captive audience. 'Two ladyfish were fighting. The kingfish went up to them and asked what the problem was. One ladyfish pointed to a babyfish and said, "This is my babyfish." Immediately, the other ladyfish said, "No, she isn't telling the truth. It is my babyfish!" The kingfish didn't know what to think.' Deepak paused. 'Luckily, he had just had his breakfast worm and could think clearly!'

Devika chuckled, flashing egg in her teeth.

'Aha!' continued Deepak, with added drama. 'The kingfish had an idea. He said, "Okay, simple. Let's just divide the babyfish in two and then each of you can have it." One ladyfish looked happy and agreed. But the other one looked worried. How could the babyfish be divided into two? It would die!' The girls became grim, concerned for the hapless situation of the babyfish.

'So,' Deepak continued, 'the second ladyfish, who started to worry, very politely told the kingfish not to hurt the babyfish and to give it to the first ladyfish. And you know what happened?'

Devika and Shirly recommenced chewing on their breakfast in delicious anticipation for the ending.

'The kingfish said, "This other ladyfish is the true mother. She has proven herself, since if you truly love something, you cannot bear any harm coming to it." And so, the kingfish handed the babyfish to the true mother, who was very happy!'

As Mamtu watched her husband charm their two daughters into polishing off their plates, a loaf of freshly leavened warmth filled her ladyfish heart.

The car horn blared over the muted roar of the ocean and through the surrounding thicket of greenery. Mamtu was at the wheel of their brand new silver Pontiac with Deepak next to her, while Shirly and Devika peered out of the backseat windows. They had come to a halt in the middle of an empty service road extending along the Gaspar Dias shore, with palm and casuarina trees jostling to reach the sun around them.

Mamtu pushed down on the horn again. A few feet in front of the car on the road stood a crow, nonchalantly ignoring all the trumpeting from the vehicle.

Deepak chuckled and turned to his daughters in the back. 'Unless one of you shoos it away, we will be here all day with this noise.'

Turning the handle of her door, Shirly stepped out and flapped at the crow, 'Booshaa! Boooooshaaa!' Her little sister followed, a little slower but no less enthusiastically, just in time to boo at the empty road.

The girls clambered inside the car as their father gave their mother a peck on the cheek before switching sides.

As the family of four drove back the short distance to their home, Deepak said, 'We will make your mother a good driver very quickly so that she can drive us all the way to America!'

'And honk at crows!' piped up Devika cheekily. Deepak laughed while his wife blushed, thrilled in that secretive pocket a woman has within her that she was adored by her husband.

The Quarachims pulled up on the road in front of the main entrance to their residence on the Mandovi waterfront. Everyone piled out, and Mamtu herded the girls into the gate.

'Aaoon Oilem Aravalem wanjan pyo,' Deepak announced. He used Sindhi as a way to communicate with his wife, as he often did to conceal any sensitive information from prying ears. This was usually in public, like in a market, when they would both agree to walk away from an expensive item without offending the shopkeeper. Or if they wanted to concur on the appropriate time to take leave of their hosts during a friendly visit, to preserve the gentility of the occasion. And ironically, even to conceal musings or plans from their daughters, who were being raised as English speakers. However, by now, Shirly had had enough Sindhi fall on her ears over the years to discern the meanings of certain words.

'Can I come, Daddy?' Shirly asked with widened eyes. If her father had simply said 'Oilem Aravalem', she knew that meant he would be visiting his iron-ore mines all the way across the river, several villages away. She immediately wanted to be part of the daytime expedition. Deepak was always at work at his store or visiting the mines, and Shirly frequently tried to find a way to accompany him. She adored her father, who was always gentle and indulgent with her inquisitive nature, so even spotting a spider resting on a wall was exciting if he was around to witness it with her. For her, he was the life of any party, the true north of her world, and everything seemed possible when his laugh pierced the mundane drag of time.

Deepak chuckled at his daughter for cracking the code. But Mamtu frowned, displeased with the idea of Shirly going away and shirking her homework.

'Yes, but ask your mother,' Deepak said, using his charm.

Mamtu frowned at the father–daughter duo imploring her with supplicating eyes and toothsome smiles. Deepak took his wife's hand in his and brought it to his lips for a kiss.

'Naughty, both of you,' she said, fondness entwined with her mock reproach, and added, 'Wait for two minutes.'

Shirly's heart leapt up, almost taking her slim frame with it. The Oilem Aravalem trip was already beginning to feel less like an errand and more like a thrilling father–daughter exploit. While Mamtu went up to their house, Deepak walked over to the Willys Jeep he usually took for longer road trips. Compared to the sleek, dancer-like Pontiac, it was pure bone structure, with a well-muscled frame in olive, bearing its identifying numbers painted on the exaggerated front bumper. Its removable canvas top and lack of doors and windows left its riders exposed to the elements.

'Can't we go in the Pontiac, Daddy?' Shirly asked, eager to experience their adventure with the new leather smell of Deepak's most recent acquisition.

'The Pontiac won't survive the rough roads, Puttha. The Willys is best for the mines.'

Ten minutes later, Shirly's mother returned with a rectangular tiffin box. 'There is a sandwich here in case Shirly gets hungry.' Her husband took the tiffin and pulled her in for a quick peck on the cheek. She shied away, blushing, both smiling and remonstrative, 'Shee, not in front of everyone.'

Shirly's mother wasn't comfortable with public displays of affection but was secretly glad for them, even though she protested too much whenever one came her way. Deepak then kissed his palm and placed it gently on his wife's stomach, protruding under her kaftan. Half a hemisphere with a whole new world within it. Deepak started the engine of the Willys and slowly drew out of his parking area.

The Jeep headed towards the jetty on the Mandovi river, where a ferry was making its way from the opposite bank towards a small crowd that had gathered. Families, schoolchildren and vendors bearing fish, eggs, coconuts and even flapping chickens were waiting to get across.

The ferry approached, dropped its engine and scraped to a stop on the sandbank. Two boatmen in square-necked uniforms unhinged two planks of wood from large hooks and laid them down wheel-width apart to serve as a ramp for the vehicles. Debarking was a chaotic process that delighted Shirly. Passengers hopped off in disorderly fashion, nearly being run over by a motorist or two making their way to the ramp. Three cars, one behind the other, began inching slowly backwards off the ferry, with passengers helpfully bellowing instructions at the drivers—'Rao re! Wait!'—so that the wheels wouldn't slip off the narrow ramp. Once all the ferry passengers were offloaded, the waiting commuters piled into its hold all at once, like an impatient wave. As the Willys ascended the ramp to station itself at the centre of the ferry, its weight caused the passengers' heads to bob, much to Shirly's amusement.

Once everyone was aboard, the boatmen shouted to the captain, at the wheel in his open cabin at the front, and pulled back the wooden planks. The diesel engine rumbled to life and the boatload of passengers started to slowly shift away from the jetty.

As the boat put-putted gently across the shallow waves, Shirly and her father descended from the Jeep and walked up to the bulwark overlooking the waters. Basking in the daylight, the river looked bedecked in strands of gleaming pearls. A lady bearing a nearly empty basket of tamarind made her way to Deepak. A slender woman, she wore a bright yellow sari and had a gentle air about her. Setting her basket down at her feet, she slipped with familiarity into conversation with Deepak. Shirly was too engrossed in the waves that extended outward from the ferry as it cut through the river. She delighted in glimpsing a stray fish jump above the water's surface in a silvered streak and the minty breeze brushing past her ears.

A half-hour later, the ferry reached the bank at Betim, and the car rolled off the makeshift ramp to the same cacophony. As Deepak gently inched on to the road, he spotted the tamarind lady and motioned to her to hop into the back of the Jeep.

The Jeep trundled down a narrow earth road flanked by plush paddy fields and groves of coconut palm. Egrets hitched rides on buffalo, while brightly hued kingfishers posed jauntily on rocks. The sun drenched the land with its morning heat, and Shirly soaked up the wind on her nose. Deepak and the tamarind lady fell into the local Konkani tongue, chatting at intervals along the way.

The road was fairly straight towards Mapuçá market, and as they neared, it turned dustier and more crowded. Vendors had laid out their wares on cloth or matting on the ground, shopfronts were open, ladies passed by taking refuge from the intense tropical sun under wide, black umbrellas, stray dogs wandered lazily between busy legs, and the sound of bargaining fisherwomen rose into the cloudless, azure sky.

Deepak threaded the Jeep through the busyness and parked near the main marketplace building, a one-storey structure lined with shops. The tamarind lady climbed out and walked around to Deepak's side. To Shirly's surprise, tears glistened in the woman's eyes, making her uncomfortable. She rarely ever came across it, but seeing an adult cry made the ground under her feet feel as liquid and unsteady as when the ferry was teetering on surging swells. Only another adult could handle such a situation, so she was glad to see her father immediately try to console the woman. She felt a clutch of relief and admiration for her father, with his self-assuredness and collected manner. She just knew from the marrow of her petite bones that he would make things better for that poor woman. As the tamarind lady raised her arm across her eyes, Shirly noticed that she had a brown mark, possibly a birthmark, on her forearm, and a few dots crudely tattooed near her wrist. She looked at her own skin, clean in its youthful suppleness. Another thing that adults had and she didn't were pocks or stains—symbols of life experience scored on to the body.

'Sunita, no tears, please. Don't worry about them, we will take care of it. Okay? Please, no more tears.'

Pulling out cash from his wallet, Deepak offered it to Sunita, whose sobs were stilted from controlling her emotions.

'Please take this.'

She nudged his hand away, but he insisted, pushing the notes gently into her palm. She relented, gratefully accepting the few escudos and tucked them into the waist of her sari. Then, braving a smile, Sunita raised her palm, both blessing Deepak and saying goodbye, 'Dev borem korum.' God bless you.

The tension melted away, and when the woman was gone, Deepak turned to Shirly and said, 'Come on, let's go.'

'Where to, Daddy?'

He ruffled the curls in her hair and responded, 'Someone wanted to have ice cream for breakfast, remember?'

They stepped out of the Jeep and entered a shop where an old lady stood behind the counter. She was tall and bony, with oiled black hair interspersed with a few silver-salty strands.

'Good morning! My daughter wants ice cream for breakfast.'

'I made some fresh this morning,' said the shop vendor, pointing to an ice cream churn in the corner.

Shirly and her father took a seat on wooden benches and the vendor placed scoops of cold, hand-churned ice cream—chickoo-flavoured for Shirly and sitaphal for Deepak—in brass bowls on their table.

In no time, they were licking their spoons and cups clean. They turned to make funny faces at each other, sniggered conspiratorially and headed back to their ride outside. 'Happy now?' Deepak asked Shirly indulgently. She responded by patting her tummy and nodding, with cream at the edges of her upturned lips.

They drove through long, narrow roads, passing neon paddy fields, hilly backgrounds, scattered villages, rivulets, mint-white crosses and bright, chalky churches. On the way to Bicholim, Deepak narrated stray facts to his daughter. About a branching route at an innocuous turn—'That's the road to Bombay. Dodamarg, or big road. So many Goans have gone down the road but not many return.' About the earth—'A long time ago, the sage Parashurama killed his mother on his father's orders on this soil, which is why it is so red. Don't worry, he received a boon from his father and so he asked for her to be resurrected.' About the next town—'The name Bicholim means "in-between". It's where the middlemen come for trade or travel between the large market towns of Sanquelim and Mapuçá.' There was no end to the things her father knew. In fact, Deepak had something to say about everything, and Shirly absorbed each fact through her pores. Perhaps these tidbits of fable-like information could be summoned to her fingertips sometime in the future when she needed them.

Nearing Bicholim, the roads and fields grew more peopled. Quite mysteriously, Deepak slowed the Jeep down near a herd of cattle crossing the road.

'We can go now, Daddy. They have crossed,' said Shirly to her father, pleased to offer him some information, however obvious. But instead of moving forward, Deepak let the idling engine fall quiet.

'I know. But we are waiting for my friend Sushant. When he found out that I would be passing by, he told me to wait here for him. He will show up from there.' Hardly had any time passed when they saw a figure on a bicycle coming up a narrow, worn track. Deepak gave a low whistle. 'He cycled for six kilometres to meet us,' he informed Shirly.

Greeting Deepak in Konkani, Sushant proceeded to unpack a sizable tin from the rear rack of his bicycle. 'These are kajus from the nearby Zantye factory. About a kilo.' Opening the tin, he showed the cashews to Deepak. Curled up against each other were perfectly formed comma-shaped nuts in their mottled, reddish peels. He placed a brown package furtively on top of them. 'For you and your family,' continued Sushant. 'All is well with you? And the missus?' Without even waiting for a response, he continued, 'Thank you, thank you, I appreciate. Borem, good luck.'

Shirly thought him funny and quirky, operating in his own tacit orbit, quite like most folks in the villages outside of Panjim tended to be. To her, they seemed freer, more relaxed about social graces than townfolk. This was another point she picked up about her father. He was equally comfortable with this villager as he was with the Governor-General of Goa at a tea party.

Sushant pushed the brown package deep into the tin, till it was covered with cashews, and replaced the lid deftly. He looked around furtively, hopped on to his bicycle, and just as quickly as he had arrived, headed back to wherever he had come from. Shirly wondered why he was thanking her father when he had himself made the offering, but quickly became distracted when the road began to move under them again.

In the centre of the Bicholim square shuttered houses sat so closely connected that their verandahs merged with each other. A guddi-soda vendor looked busy behind rows of green glass bottles stoppered at their rims with marbles. Business was good in the morning heat and he had a small number of thirsty men in uniform around his stall. They all turned to look at the Jeep in appreciation as it took the narrow turn past them. Further ahead, Portuguese soldiers patrolled in their classic uniform of side cap, khaki shirt with rolled-up sleeves tucked into belted khaki shorts, calf-high khaki socks and black lace-up shoes. They seemed laidback, coming from or returning to the barracks on the right. On the left, a sign on the police headquarters read 'Prisão', prison. Shirly stared at the men with curiosity, since this wasn't a scene she was familiar with within the civilian lines of Panjim. Deepak slowed the vehicle and good-naturedly saluted the army men, eliciting return salutes from some of them.

After crossing the Bicholim bridge and going beyond the town of Sanquelim, Deepak veered off the main road on to a red, unpaved, earthen passage through trees. A few kilometres down, they spotted a checkpost in the distance manned by two soldiers. Shirly's father killed the engine. He opened the tiffin box and turned to his daughter. 'Will you have your sandwich now?'

'I'm not very hungry now, Daddy. Can we have more ice cream?'

'More? We are quite far from any ice cream now, Shirly.'

Shirly grinned unabashedly. Deepak looked at her with paternal emotion. Even though he marvelled at how his teenage daughter appeared more grown-up with each passing season, she still had an unaffected spontaneity, allowing him to feel grateful relief that she retained a vestige of childlike spirit.

'Fine, we will have more ice cream later,' Deepak couldn't help relenting to his daughter, dearer than the earth to him. 'But you better eat your sandwich or your mother will give me an earful when we get home,' he mock-reproached her.

Shirly knew all too well that this day of treats was not over yet and felt a lurch of familiar exuberance in her father's company, just as the foliage around them shone energetically in emerald tones. In Deepak's presence, she could be plain with her emotions, secure in the subconscious knowledge that her father would safeguard them. She never knew humiliation with him, the way she learned the edges of that unwelcome feeling from the nuns at school.

As Shirly chomped through her sandwich, Deepak reached behind him to fish within the tin of cashews before lidding it again. He placed the neat brown package into Shirly's emptied tiffin and put the box on the seat between them.

The engine of the Willys drummed back to life and Deepak began to cruise towards the checkpost. As they approached, one of the soldiers raised his hand, motioning them to stop. Deepak pulled up near him and his compatriot, and cut the engine once more.

'Good morning, Senhor. Where are you headed?' the soldier who stopped their car asked in a pleasant tone.

'To Oilem Aravalem,' replied Deepak.

'Ah, the mines. That is not far from here.' The soldier noticed Shirly chewing her sandwich thoughtfully and said, 'Not to worry, Meninha, we won't stop you long. We will just quickly check the car if that is okay?' Shirly nodded slowly and deliberately at the friendly guard who had a smile in his words.

'Be our guest,' responded Deepak, throwing his hands up in mock surrender.

The guards approached the Jeep. The first one opened the glove compartment in the dashboard, saying, 'Pardon me, little dona,' to Shirly as he did so. The second guard went to the rear to scan the space behind the front seats. Noticing the tin at the back, he motioned to Shirly's father. Deepak stepped out, raised the lid and removed a handful of cashews for the guard. The guard picked up the tin and shook it, causing the contents to jumble.

'These are really good quality. Do try them,' Deepak coaxed the guard, who accepted. He popped a few in his mouth as Deepak closed the lid and returned up front, sliding back into his driver's seat. The first guard eyed Shirly's lunchbox as she sat there. 'You aren't going to share, little dona?' the first guard said, and Deepak froze like a brahminy kite when any sign of danger lurks near the young in its nest.

'All seems fine. You may go,' said the guard, giving the engine top of the Willys two quick slap-bangs with his palm.

'Thank you, Senhor,' said a relieved Deepak, giving a casual salute and starting up the engine once more. The

Willys began to roll forward. However, a few feet ahead, the first soldier called out to them once more.

'Hold on!'

Deepak's heart braked. Hesitating, he stopped the vehicle. He was about to reverse, but the soldier had already jogged up to his side.

'Anything wrong, Senhor?' he asked the soldier quietly.

'Just, you know, be careful. There are many unsavoury elements out here and you aren't too safe in this Jeep,' said the guard, referring to the lack of closed doors in the car. 'You never know.'

'You are right, Senhor, one never knows,' Deepak agreed.

'That's all, safe travels,' said the guard. Deepak restarted his engine, nodded silently to the guard, and started to push forward down the rough red road.

When they were moving along, out of sight of the guard post, Shirly's father looked across at her and reached out to pat his daughter on her head with affection. 'Good girl, you finished your sandwich. Your mother will be happy.' He added, 'You know, when our family was in Pakistan before we became India and Pakistan, we lived on a farm outside Karachi. The earth there was brown. But in Goa, the earth is this deep red. It is nothing like the earth you see in most places. Do you know why it is so red?'

'You said it's the blood of Parashurama's mother.'

Deepak chuckled. 'That is just a story. It's red because there is something known as iron oxide in it. Do you know even our blood has iron in it? There is something about the iron connection between the soil here and our blood that makes Goa very special. Anyone who comes here feels good . . . and happy.'

'Is that why you moved from Pakistan?' From her father's stories, Shirly had only heard of the country that was simultaneously far away and yet within her DNA. And even though the only roots she knew were that of Goa, somehow she had imbibed a floating mote of her father's nostalgia for his lost homeland.

'No, Puttha.' But Deepak didn't have to answer further. Shirly had heard from her father that at one time in the recent past, the land had been split into two, and since her family believed in the kind of gods that were in her mother's altar, worshipped by Mamtu every full moon, they were supposed to cross to the other side of the border. Since her father already had a thriving trade with Goa, it was natural for him to move there with his new bride, and within a year, Shirly was born.

Deepak changed the subject, 'Do you know what mining is?'

'Yes . . . no . . . I mean, I think so.'

'Well, in our mines, we separate the oxide of iron from the soil, so that we can get pure iron ore. The world needs iron; it is how many things, including this car, can be made.'

'But then if we take the iron out of the soil and give it away, there won't be a connection with our blood, and we won't be happy, no?'

Shirly's father laughed at the green sagacity of her words. 'No, Puttha. It's not like that. We mine only in a specific area allotted to us, not all over the place. And also, we do it with respect. We only mine a certain amount each year. And it is all done by hand mostly.' Shirly ruminated on this, unsure of her verdict on what she just learned about mining and thoroughly enjoying how her mind could form its own questions and conclusions. Deepak went on, 'You know, the labourers that we employ are Mahars. They are considered untouchable outcastes in society. But in this way, we give them employment and respect.'

Shirly was engrossed in her father's educative chatter and the view as Deepak led the Jeep up a narrow, winding road on a hill which had a forest draped along its side. 'We are here,' he announced when they reached the top. Shirly looked around and saw that they were high above sea level on the flat plain of a hilltop. On one side was a grand, sweeping backdrop of a virginal emerald valley. But her eyes were pulled towards the raw earth across from where they stood, freshly terraced to resemble bright crimson benches stretched wide. It was a magnificent and terrible sight. On the ground, different gradients of red stood piled in heaps. Off to one side was a manmade pool, surrounded by a few workers, and some handpans and shovels. Under a few trees near the cliff's edge to the other side, two men who didn't seem to be workers were sitting on their haunches and looking out at the valley.

Deepak killed the engine and pulled up the handbrake. He turned to his daughter, 'The sun is too sharp and you will feel hot. You can wait in the Jeep.' He opened Shirly's tiffin, winked at her, pulled out the brown package, and beelined to the two men. Shirly saw her father greet them and hand them the package. They hung around for a while chit-chatting before disappearing into the forested slopes. Deepak was left standing, looking off into the cradling lowlands. Bored with sitting in the Jeep, Shirly dismounted and walked over to him.

'See those men with buffalo there?' Deepak pointed to small and distant roving figures among the green swathes of the valley. 'That is Chorla Ghat. They are passing through it to go across the border to Karnataka in India.'

Fatigue suddenly crept up on Shirly—from the heat bearing down on her, the time-stretched trip and the many facts she was still to learn that were hiding everywhere around her in the trees, the breeze and the hearts of all creatures. 'Are those men you met going with them, Daddy?' She missed the fact that her father felt a puff of amazement at her intuitive perception as they watched the faraway troupe, small as ants, file forward through the valley below towards a broad pass between the hills.

'Maybe they will, Shirly,' he responded with deliberation. 'Come on.' He walked in the direction of a man whose hands seemed less dusty than the workers he was instructing near the pooled water. 'We have the contract to sell the lumps to Mina Goa. Japan is buying it up for steel . . . meantime, yellow bentonite clay . . . high silica content . . .'

Shirly tuned out her father's mine talk with his engineer and wandered over to one of the red mounds. She reached down to touch it, and when she looked at her finger she saw that the russet earth clung back. She tried to lick the colour off, but it stayed.

'If you eat a pinch of this earth every day you will be able to do anything you want.' Shirly nearly jumped out of her skin and into a fiery pile near her foot. She looked for the source of the voice. It was a woman crouched on the ground, looking like a maroon mound of earth herself. 'Like this,' the woman took a pinch of the reddish soil, placed it in her mouth and smiled with church-white teeth. 'It is how I can lift my load here,' she said, holding out her raw, forged bicep. 'Here, take.' The woman, who seemed to be a mine worker, quickly removed a small cloth that was tucked into her waist from a hitched-up sari. She placed the flushed earth in the cloth and tied it into a neat bundle. 'Here,' she repeated, handing it over to Shirly, who shyly accepted the hanky-sized item before wandering off to find her father. She would have to investigate the claim that the earth had strength-giving properties at home some other day, since the tiring heat finally had her flagging a little.

Shirly climbed into the Jeep, clutching the pouch of red earth. The workers and the engineer stopped to wave them off on their journey as though they were royalty. Deepak and Shirly waved back as though they were all old friends.

'You have been very patient. Thank you, my darling,' Deepak said indulgently, noting his slumping daughter, glad once more that she'd insisted on accompanying him. 'We're going back home now. But I think you deserve another treat. Some more ice cream?'

Shirly let out a whoop in affirmation, her energy quickly topped up at the thought of brightly cold excesses. And, of course, after a day across water and roads and forest, she was well and truly on her way to being a full-fledged adventurer. Today it was the mines. Tomorrow, who knew? But first, some ice cream.

3

'Shirrrrrrly,' Mamtu's sing-song voice suffused through her daughter's fog of sleep as she tugged at her blanket.

'It's too early, Mummy.' Still a captive of the deep lethargy that accompanies young limbs at the cusp of waking, Shirly pulled the cotton coverlet back over her head to resemble a corpse in the foetal position. If she couldn't see the morning, perhaps it wouldn't notice her either.

'Come on, good girl. Brush your teeth and get ready for school.' Shirly could hear her mother's coaxing voice through the thin blanket. She held on to its inside edges even more firmly until she heard the slap-slap of Mamtu's slippered footsteps disappear from the room. She stayed underneath the cover for a few minutes, until it became too stuffy to breathe, and then pushed the blanket away from her face to inhale the musty smell of her room, which was both familiar and comforting. Wiping the sleep from her eyes, she looked across the bedchamber to her sister's wooden four-poster. The toddler was up already and playing with her Thumbelina doll.

Shirly lazily slipped out from under the gauzy cosmos of the bed's mosquito netting and walked over to the window. She swung the wooden shutters of the half-open window fully inwards and unlatched the windows. The room lit up with dawn's halcyon light reflecting off the Mandovi River, which lay to her left. Her view overlooked a narrow side street that ran perpendicular to Rua Vasco da Gama, an artery at the heart of the city, grandly named after the sailor who linked the nerve centres of the subcontinent with the West, adding fresh blood to the history of these lands, although he never sailed the river that lapped gently against the road bearing his name. Shirly's view directly under her window included a tiny garden—*her* garden—with a statue in it. Beyond lay the Idalcão palace, also located on Rua Vasco da Gama, with its face to the river. To her right, running parallel to the main road, Rua Afonso de Albuquerque—named after that other ambitious sailor who added Portuguese flavour to the western coast of the subcontinent—carried on its path behind her house.

Overlooking the road on her right was a two-storey building that belonged entirely to one family, the Mhamai Kamats. On its flank was a building whose lower storey at the street corner bore a sign that read 'Loja Paraiso', referring to the general goods shop that carried everything from toys to groceries and vessels.

Then, on cue, four men in uniform came marching out from the Idalcão and crossed the empty street to the flagpole that stood in front of the main administrative building. Even though she had awoken every day to watch this event, it always felt new and entertaining to Shirly. She looked on keenly from her vantage point as one guard held a folded cloth and two others carried bugles. They marched right up to the flagpole; the cloth was handed to another bearer, who hitched it to the halyard. Simultaneously, the buglers put their gleaming horns to their lips and blew a brassy staccato of 'A Portuguesa', the national anthem, into the moist air as the flag rose along the length of the pole. While it flapped its way up majestically, deigning to look down on its kingdom, Shirly drank in the colours of its two uneven-sized rectangles of green on the hoist and the red on the fly. A yellow sphere sat evenly where both met, and was the bed for a red coat of arms. She never missed the detail of the five mini coats of arms in blue that sat in cross formation within the white space of the main coat of arms. It was grand theatre for its young audience, who propped her face in her hands at the open window to watch while ardent flutters from her depths rose outwards and alighted on her skin as goosebumps.

However, she wasn't the only one raptly watching the drill that day. She looked to her right and saw the Loja Paraiso shopkeeper in front of his shop's shutters, standing at attention and saluting the flag, his little contribution to the ceremony in this tiny corner of the world.

Once the flag was seated at the top of the pole, the two hoisters saluted it, the buglers finished with the last tan-tan of their horns, and in silence the foursome proceeded to march away.

Shirly looked to the right at the shopkeeper absently. She watched as it suddenly started to drizzle on his head and a dark stain grew down the front of his shirt. He turned his head upwards, squinting, checking the weather, and saw droplets streaming down from overhead. They caught the morning sunlight as they hit the pavement. His expression was of mild bewilderment till he saw the source of such cloudless rain—a little boy who lived on the first storey of the building, peeing off the balcony directly above the shopkeeper's head. The shopkeeper's cheeks steamed earth-red as he hopped aside with a shout, startling the cat napping on the kerb.

The shopkeeper shook his fist at the little boy, who simply responded with laughing impudence, his high voice full of naked mischief. Soon enough, the fountain that arced gracefully through the grillwork of the balcony withdrew doggedly to its owner. Then, with his penis still sticking out through his shorts, the little boy stuck his tongue out at the livid shopkeeper and ran back inside. The man railed and cursed the brat to hell while opening up his shop shutters. Shirly found herself rooting for the little fellow. What a stroke of good luck to have watched two riveting shows first thing in the morning. She turned away from her vantage point—the centre of the world as far as she was concerned—and all the entertainment it held to get dressed for school.

Shirly sat at the kitchen table, staring at the glass of milk in front of her. Deepak was across her reading the *O Heraldo* newspaper, while Mamtu, with a fulsome belly, fussed with the logs for the fire, where she would cook the meals of the day in a large iron pot. Goku was busy alternating between answering the door for various vendors and helping Shirly's mother in the kitchen. As usual, the unmistakably sharp smell of feni, the fermented alcohol made from the cashew apple, wafted about her as she moved around. The spirit commonly found in every self-respecting Goan's stash was their housemaid's medicine of choice for all ailments—and the solution to any problem. Goku would rub it over an aching belly after having overeaten or to soothe a stiff joint. She had even offered Deepak her bottle to pour into the engine of his car. 'It working better than petrol, I tell you. Cheaper also.' Deepak had politely declined the experiment.

'Cha chari ai!' What madness, he had countered confidentially in Sindhi to Mamtu, who acknowledged him with a tickled look. The Quarachim kitchen was a crucible of languages by now. Sindhi, Konkani, English and Portuguese. Shirly was intimately aware of the nuances of the word for lunacy in all of them. Besides chari, there was pishem in Konkani, nutcase in English and louco in Portuguese.

'Not chari!' It was no use. Like Shirly, Goku had wised up to key phrases used by her employers too and promptly rejoindered.

Shirly was distracted by gulping sounds and turned to see her sister avidly drinking her glass of milk. She was still too young to latch on to the polylingual banter. When Devika finished, she placed her glass back on the table, turned to Shirly, who was now taking in the sight of her small mouth rimmed with milky foam, and burped in satisfied innocence.

'Good girl, Devika. Shirly, if you finish your milk in the next minute, I can give you an extra unndo so you can feed the crows,' Mamtu bribed her, glad to change the subject. In her excitement to move on to the next bit of divertissement—tempting birds to collect around her feet—Shirly glugged down the milk and dabbed her mouth on the sleeve of her uniform. Mamtu put Shirly's tiffin into her satchel and handed it to her, along with an unndo from the bread basket. 'Bye, Puttha,' she said, slathering Shirly's way out with concerned motherliness.

Shirly couldn't figure out where all the crows came from. One minute the road outside the main gate was empty, but when she tore doughy bits from the unndo and scattered them around her, to her delight, one by one, her customers flap-landed and pecked at the food. She made the pieces smaller so that the feed would last longer and watched with pleasure as the crows, two or three at a time, dove for each morsel, crashing into each other.

One excited fellow flew towards each appetizing lob, picked it up in his beak, flapped his wings in the face of the losing competition, then shot away to a perch where the bread disappeared into his blackly iridescent throat. When all the bread was over, he sailed back to the top of the statue in the garden and sat on its head in anticipation.

Shirly looked up and squinted. The sun stuck its fingers directly in her eyes, creating a bright aria around the crow and the statue's head, filling her vision. The entire sculpture, made of dark stone, depicted a man who looked like he was reaching out to a woman figure who lay at his feet, perhaps to strangle her since she didn't seem too happy. The man had a wide-set jaw and looked intense, while the woman's features were, quite literally, petrified. This scene atop a pedestal was the centrepiece of the small garden between the side of Shirly's building and the Idalcão Palace. The crow flapped its wings on top of the man's head and cawed out for more bread, giving the intensely focused statue a ridiculous air. And then a memory reached out to Shirly.

She was around five at the time. Her mother was seated on the bench fringing this garden, doing some needlework. It was early evening and they'd stepped out for fresh air. Shirly was on the grass, playing with her plastic doll that had big blue eyes, pink lips and brown hair. She was pretending that the doll was her child, and she was cradling and protecting her from the evil-looking statue. She noticed that even though he was made of stone, everywhere she moved, his eyes seemed to follow.

'Stop looking at me!' she said defensively to Statue Man as she roamed about the garden she considered exclusively hers because of its location under her bedroom window. Statue Man may have been there before her, but now he was in *her* territory, no doubt hoping to find a way to trouble her too, like he was doing Statue Lady.

It happened quite suddenly one evening. As is only possible in the fluid imagination of a young child, Statue Man straightened up from his position and spoke directly to Shirly.

'I'm only looking at you because you are looking at me, Meninha.'

Shirly shrieked inwardly. She definitely hadn't expected this stone adult to talk back to her. She clamped her eyes shut and held out her doll at arm's length in front of her. In case the imperious Statue Man tried to reach out and wiggle his menacing fingers at her too, the doll would get zapped first.

'Don't be scared, Meninha, I'm not going to eat you.' Statue Man was really speaking to her. Shirly unclenched her eyes and peeked out from behind the doll she held out as a shield or a cross. Statue Man's robes still had their stony appearance, even though his head had turned to look at her. Then, braver than she had ever been in the entirety of her life, she dared to ask him what was uppermost on her mind. 'What are you doing to that lady?'

'My dear, I am a hypnotist. I am famous all over the world, don't you know?'

Shirly slowly shook her head no, a little less terrified. The figure sat down on the pedestal, his face quite close to Statue Lady's, and swung his legs back and forth. The lady, with her perfect chignon and the long dress with puffed sleeves, remained lifeless as ever in her pose of distressed cowering.

'Aaah, it feels good to sit. I'm José. What's your name?'

Shirly came closer and sat on the grass, nervous but curious as well.

'I'm Shirly, and this is my dolly,' she said, holding her doll out so that José could not miss it.

'She looks like a very nice doll. She can't talk to us, can she?'

Naturally, it didn't occur to her that her five-year-old mind could be so arbitrary as to infuse chatter into a statue, but the plastic toy stayed silent. However, to keep up appearances, Shirly furrowed her brow and held the doll's face up to her ear before responding curtly, 'She said she only talks to me.'

'So, Shirly, what does your name mean?'

Names had meanings? 'I don't know.' Five-year-old Shirly hadn't been confronted with this question by anyone so far. 'It means nothing.'

'Not possible. It must have a meaning.' Now that her thirteen-year-old self was thinking about it, was it her imagination or had this statue been a little pushy back then?

'I'm named after Joseph, the father of Jesus. Jesus was one of the most magical men in history. He was like a god, but on earth. Joseph taught his baby Jesus the alphabet and how to fish, making him into a strong young man.' Shirly knew the characters in his story, recounted to each child at Christmas mangers in every parish. She lost her shyness around this odd, talking Statue Man named José.

A few days later, there was an invasion in her garden. One evening, while debating the colour of the sky with José, an elegant Portuguese woman arrived with three children in tow—two boys and their younger sister. Mamtu, seated on a bench, invited the woman to join her. The trio of kids pointed excitedly at an old cannon on one side of the small garden. Shirly turned to look at Statue Man and saw that he had resumed his original place and position. Suddenly, she feared she was alone again. She held her doll behind her back protectively. The boys began to balance-walk on the stones skirting the garden while their sister came to stand in front of her.

'Hello,' said the girl as Shirly stared at her. 'My name is Ana, short for Analise,' she continued in her high voice. 'What do you have there?' She reached out to the hand behind Shirly's back.

Shirly was annoyed that these three children had encroached on *her* garden and were doing as they pleased, disrupting her peaceful absorption with a new-found friendship. 'Nothing,' she mumbled.

'My mummy says we should share our things,' Ana announced expectantly.

Shirly looked back with defiance, so Ana gave up and went over to join her brothers, who were zipping around the stone and trying to push each other off the cannon with boyish gusto. Shirly then looked over at José, who came back to life and turned his head to her.

'Tch, tch. Do you want me to make them go away?' he asked her. Maybe it would be all right for her to share her garden with him after all. Shirly nodded her assent. 'Very well,' José said, still on his pedestal. He turned away from Statue Lady and began to wave his fingers hypnotically in the direction of the unruly siblings disturbing the order of Shirly's garden. Shirly was highly entertained by this. She shifted her gaze from José to see where he was hocus-pocusing and saw the trespassing trio looking back at her and at José. Then, as suddenly as they appeared, the intruders inexplicably stopped their play and ran to join their mother. Shirly was highly tickled with the show put on by her new friend José, who winked at her. The interferers were gone, and good riddance.

Thinking back, Shirly was sure that it wasn't her imagination that could change events like that. Could it?

A loud cawing pulled Shirly back to the present. The crow on top of José's head complained and flapped for more unnde. 'Boosha!' she shooed him. Then Shirly reached for her bicycle and turned away from José, who remained motionless and unblinking as ever.

4

Shirly bicycled down a back lane tightly knit together with yellow-, green- and blue-walled houses in the Fontainhas bairro. They were lined up gloriously with their red-tiled roofs, shell-encrusted window shutters and lacy grillwork balcãos. Their keystones ensconced on arched windows or doorways benevolently watched the girl zipping past on her two-wheeled mode of transport. An old man sat bare-chested on his balcony reading the morning *O Heraldo* while puffing on a pipe. A violin squealed into the neighbourhood from another house, causing the old man to look up in disgust from time to time. Shirly took care not to run her wheels too close to the drains—although dry and protected with stone slabs—that ran parallel to the street on either side.

On the smooth road that passed through the neighbourhood, Shirly glided by the interlacing steps leading up to the Liceu, which stood grandly out of reach on the Altinho Hill to the west. She knew it as the school where girls and boys sat together for lessons. She wondered what that would be like since she was only familiar with the all-girl classes in her convent school, but was glad not to have to climb the Liceu's steep and numerous stairs to find out. As her wheels spun down the windy road, she took the detour on to Rua 31 de Janeiro, where the warm scent of fresh baked goods reached out to her.

Shirly's nose guided her now, and she slowed her bicycle outside Confeitaria 31 de Janeiro to avoid the bumpiness of the cobbled path. The shutters of the bakery were still down, but she caught a glimpse of the baker through the window. Placing both feet on the ground, she halted just in time to see him retract a shovelful of biscuits from the open brick-kiln furnace featuring a very burnt cross on the wall above it. She made a mental note to return for some lemon Swiss rolls or doce or patties or bolinhas or flower biscuits . . . Reluctantly, Shirly stepped on her pedals once more and cycled onwards through narrow lanes and finally reached the rear entrance of her school.

Leaving her bicycle outside the school gates, where a board over the arch proclaimed 'Our Lady of the Ocean of Providence Convent School for Girls', Shirly walked in with her satchel on her back. The bell dinged with a thick sound as she entered the school, which was a large, charming villa that had been converted by Franciscan nuns. English was the medium of instruction here, and so it was predominantly full of Goan students of native descent. There were also a few mestiças—those who were a mix of European and indigenous descent.

The clanging bell incited the schoolgirls, uniform in their white shirts and blue pinafores, to drop their games of hopscotch in the courtyard or scurry out from a corner here and there, and enter the two-storey villa. The girls sieved themselves by age and size—with the smaller children below grade four slipping into the rooms on the lower storey, while the older lot up to grade ten flowed up the staircase.

Shirly, now in the eighth standard, headed towards the wide porch for the grand wooden staircase with its sweeping balustrade, a graceful invitation to the higher storey crowded with rushing girls. As she waited at the bottom for the onslaught to reduce, Shirly spotted a befuddled chicken clucking on a step, trapped between the jumble of socks and shoes, and scampering calves. She knew it had escaped from the poultry coop in the front of the building that lay outside the kitchen and dining area, and the school sweeper would find it soon enough to return the fugitive to its cage. Once the coast was clear, she shooed it out of her way and hot-stepped up the staircase, which was split halfway to ascend in a conch-like spiral on either side to meet in a bright landing on the floor above.

The landing space was bare, with just a couple of large paintings of the school's beneficent-looking founders. It led into the second-floor corridor that lined up classrooms and a new music wing to one side, a chapel in the centre, and a visitor's lounge, dorm rooms and the elusive Mother Superior's suite in a wing at the other end. Shirly cast her glance out an east-facing window to see the Ourem Creek, a branch of the Mandovi, moving in prayerful silence past the school. The October sun was hypnotic as it danced on the water's skin, giving it the delicate shimmer of a mermaid's tail. All the students were in their classrooms already and the sound of the nuns' singing from the chapel across the corridor meandered around the school like incense from a censer. In that perfect moment all to herself, Shirly could have stood for ages but was soon disturbed.

'Time for class, girl!'

The sound of Ana's voice greatly vexed Shirly. What troubled her even more was that she felt a rude pull on her plait. Argh! She would not put up with this pestilence. Shirly forgot the beautiful day, running behind Ana, tugging at her skirt. Soon, the girls were in an all-out hair-pulling, skirt-lifting, biting fight on the landing, heavenly lit with sunlight, the air doused in hymns, under the beatific gaze of the school's founders.

It was only a matter of minutes, however, before Sister Olga separated the girls. They had to look upwards to meet her eyes and appeared puny in front of her wide frame. Their hair was dishevelled, one of Shirly's plaits had come totally undone, with the red ribbon lying on the ground a few feet from her, while Ana's hem was ripped and hanging unevenly near her knees.

Breathing heavily and red-faced, the girls found themselves fixated on Sister Olga's quivering upper lip, made all the more dramatic in its hirsute luxuriance. She wore the nun's habit, which consisted of a loose, grey-blue tunic, bearing long sleeves, its length draped to the ground. On her head she wore a white coif—a cotton cap and a white guimpe or wimple of starched cotton—from which her cheeks rebelled puffily. Over this was a grey-blue veil, hiding away any good spirits the Sister may have, along with her hair. She wore the cross in brass on a chain around her neck that gleamed menacingly when her lip quivered.

'Fix your hair, Shirly! And get to your classrooms! If I see you two being naughty again, I will take you straightaway . . . to Mother Superior.' Sister Olga dipped the boom in her voice with holy subservience at the name of her senior. When the two had turned down the corridor towards their classroom at the end, out of sight of Sister Olga and her quivering moustache, they stuck their tongues out at each other.

'Naughty girls, I see you!' They turned back to see the nun's hulking frame blocking the corridor and fled faster than chickens in pursuit.

The rest of the morning was mostly uneventful. The two girls were seated in the last row of the class at wooden desks that lay still while the sunlight moved across the room. After the first lesson in English, they took science, and right before the near-noon break, a choice of music or physical education. Shirly decided on the less insufferable of the two. Sister Olga of the bewitched lip was the music teacher. So she opted for physical education with Sister Agnes who occasionally allowed them to play with the school's lone football in between a routine of callisthenics.

She saw Ana head for the music room, a new addition to the school in the last couple of years. The music students would be lined up by Olga, and each one made to sing in the nun's ear, which was muffed behind her wimple so one really had to exaggerate their voice for her benefit. Only when her furred lip quivered in pleasure or abject disappointment would she move on to offer up her hidden ear to the next girl.

Shirly was glad to escape any potential sternness from Sister Olga and skipped downstairs to the courtyard where she caught up with Nancy, who was a mestiça classmate. She stayed in the dorm room on the school premises and looked mostly unwashed, since the girls were only allotted bath time once or twice a week. She definitely looked very different from the rest of the students with her short, curly, mud-blonde hair. Her skin was light but coarse, and the bones in her body were wide, giving her a hefty physique. Her nose sat wide on her plump face. Shirly lived mostly in her own head, but Nancy would reach out to her, including her in conversation matter-of-factly, whether by choosing her for the football team or talking about other things.

Sister Agnes had put Nancy in charge of the callisthenics that day and left the courtyard as she sometimes did to do 'God alone knows', as Nancy put it. However, since Nancy strung the words so fast, Shirly heard the first and last words and filled in the middle herself. So in her head, it sounded like 'God-all-does-knows'. While

Nancy stood at the front and earnestly did the exercises and kept count, most of the girls, Shirly included, took the occasion as a cue to daydream or chat.

When Sister Agnes didn't return after a long time for the session that day, Nancy picked up the ball that lay in the corner of the courtyard and started a game of football. This was one of the rare few instances in Goa where girls were given the opportunity to play football.

Lygia, another student, had once said that her boyfriend who attended the Liceu would often play football on the grounds near their church with a motley group. But girls were never invited to be on their teams or on any of the several fields that dotted the towns and villages in the Portuguese estado.

However, the all-girls Our Lady of the Ocean of Providence Convent School had begun its gender usurpation of the sport a few years ago when Sister Agnes discovered Eusébio, the Brazilian who played for Benfica football club in Portugal. She had seen his photograph in the newspaper and fallen in love—secretly obviously, since her soul was sworn to Jesus. In a bid to be closer to her idol all the way in Lisboa, she brought the football to sessions with her students. She would interject the foot-play with trivia about the player. 'Did you know when he was young, he would stuff socks with newspapers rolled into spheres?' And then she would press into motion, raising her skirts, lifting her foot behind her dramatically, yet kicking the revered ball with immaculate mildness in the direction of the nearest goal.

Oddly, that day, some of the music students came trickling downstairs and sat at the foot of the stairway, watching the game. One of them said that Sister Olga too had left class. Shirly noticed immediately when Ana came and sat down, attuned as she was to her prickles being raised by an aggravating presence. The sight of that irritating girl made her more ferocious with the ball that was moving purposefully between her legs and the other players', with the favourable consequence of improving her defence and passes.

The mid-morning break bell rang in the middle of the rowdy match, and subsequently, the players disbanded with gradual entropy. With thirst finally catching up with her, Shirly headed for the stairs. On her way, a chicken crossed her path, again on the loose from the school coop. Though flush from all her football exertions, Shirly changed tack and began to chase after it. 'Chick-en, chick-en . . .' she called.

'You think you can catch it?' Ana had a snide way of provoking her. That sneaky, two-faced . . . Then Ana's voice melded with hers, 'Chick-en, chick-en, chick-ennnn.' Shirly saw in consternation that Ana too was trying to goad the unsuspecting bird into the poultry coop. 'God-all-does-know why this chari-pishem-nutcase-louco girl has to do everything I do!' Shirly's angry thoughts swooshed through her veins, and she decided that she was going to be the one to catch the chicken and restore it to its cage, just so Ana wouldn't. She could even picture it in her flash of rage—Ana standing empty-handed, watching Shirly outmanoeuvre her to place the bird in the cage and lock it with accomplished magnanimity and grace.

The two girls chased the harrowed bird from the courtyard to the left of the building where the coop was housed. Two pairs of shoes and socks haphazardly tracking the wayward, scratchy quickness of chicken feet. The girls stopped once they realized the scared fowl was cornered. Breathing heavily for one suspended moment, both lunged forward at the same time to capture the poor creature.

Shirly elbowed Ana, 'It's mine. I saw it first!'

'Who says so?'

The next minute was a blur of feathers, squawks, flaps, scuffles and shouts. Finally, they both grasped hold of the annoyed chicken that beat its wings in their faces, escaped upwards and scurried towards the courtyard again.

'This is your fault!' Shirly said, feathers on her hair and uniform.

'Phtoo!' Ana spat a feather out of her mouth, which landed on Shirly's foot. Shirly pulled Ana's hair for this deliberate, insolent slight. Ana, quickly spotting a small egg that had rolled away from the coop, picked it up and rushed at Shirly. She dove into her and crushed the egg with a splatter on top of Shirly's head. Ana stepped back, and both girls stopped to assess the moment. The greasy yolk sat heavily on Shirly's hair and ran down her arms and uniform, dripping on to her lace-up black shoes. A shooting fury for the cretinous creature in front of her filled Shirly, and she scrunched up her face, opened her mouth and let out all the raging gales in the sky and ripping tides in the ocean. It lasted a little over a minute, sending seismic waves in every direction. Ana shielded her ears while the chicken ran for cover behind the coop. Shirly's grand siren carried to the courtyard, across the creek, upwards to the roof and around the neighbourhood.

When Shirly finally stopped for breath, she looked up. A crowd of Sisters had huddled their wimple-cramped faces in the window frame of the visitor's room on the first floor, seeking the source of the hell cry that would have shaken Satan's mansion itself. In a jiffy, Sister Olga reached the girls downstairs and pronounced her disgust. 'God alone knows!'

She took each of them by the arm and roughly led them upstairs to the bathroom, bare apart from blue-and-white azulejos and a tap. She turned on the faucet to fill a bucket with cold water that trickled slowly as her upper lip quivered. 'What will your parents think? Chickens and chicken eggs are not to be played with. Take off your clothes!'

The door of the bathroom creaked open and Sister Agnes entered. Shirly's face was bound in a tight scowl. She didn't feel as embarrassed at her nakedness but was sore that she was being stripped and disciplined in equal measure with Ana, who was now smiling as annoyingly as ever! However, she didn't dare do anything else to further the wrath of Sister Olga.

'Mother Superior would like to see them when you are done,' said Sister Agnes with a tinge of sympathy for the sodden girls whose dripping hair lay flat against their heads. She hung two loose, bag-like dresses on the inside of the door, borrowed from a couple of the dorm girls.

Scrubbed and clean, with damp hair and sulky faces—even Ana's usual mirth seemed to have dried up—the girls, dressed in borrowed robes, were ushered past the visitor's waiting area, where all the nuns watched them pass by. One of them made a quick gesture of the cross with her hand, forehead to chest to left shoulder and right, and then kissed the brass cross around her neck. Sister Agnes took over from Sister Olga and led the freshly washed girls into the Mother Superior's chamber. She shepherded them in, curtseyed and exited. The girls heard the ominous click of the office door behind them.

The Mother Superior sat behind her desk but Shirly noted that her presence filled the entire room. A slim, straight-backed woman, she was distinct from the other sisters at the school by her completely white robes and veil. The chain she wore had a bigger Jesus-on-the-cross than the rest. Her office was sparsely furnished with a large teakwood desk and a couple of framed photos of Mother Mary. Seated opposite her was a woman, familiar in her elegance, with reddish-brown hair, dressed in a floral frock. It was Ana's mother, Shirly realized when mother and daughter exchanged unsmiling looks with each other. There was a nervous silence as the two girls stood in front of the head nun, whose cushiony face bore complete grimness.

'We've come to a decision.'

'I didn't do it! I was just trying to get the chicken in the cage. She started all the trouble!' Shirly felt as if she had stepped out of her body, witnessing her outburst from afar. A mortified Ana was met with questioning eyes from her mother.

After an astringent silence, the Mother Superior continued, 'As I was saying, we've decided to stage a musical during this year's Christmas festival. Ana's mother Dona Lisette has very kindly written it out and all of us read it during the last period. We're quite delighted with the piece and are now looking for the leads.'

To Shirly's consternation, the holy Mother Superior wasn't chiding them or praying for their damned souls. Instead, she turned to Ana and went off-topic. 'Sister Olga suggested your name for the second lead, since you have been doing quite well in music class. No doubt you are your mother's daughter,' she said. Ana turned to Shirly with a look of decided smugness.

'And you,' the Mother Superior turned to Shirly. 'Dona Lisette seems to think that you should play the lead in the musical.'

This was most unexpected and had nothing to do with the chicken incident. Shirly deepened her scowl. And there was another problem to consider.

'But I don't sing!' said Shirly.

'What? Why her?' asked Ana at this new injustice.

There was bedlam, with Ana and Shirly objecting at the same time.

'I can't do this,' said Shirly.

'But she doesn't sing!' protested Ana.

'I don't want to,' sputtered Shirly.

'Who decided this?' asked Ana.

'Silence!' said the Mother Superior. 'This was Dona Lisette's decision.'

'But . . .' said Shirly.

'How?' asked Ana.

The Mother Superior raised her hands and there was immediate silence. Lisette took a deep breath and said, 'I heard your voice all the way up here, Shirly. It is perfect. Just what we need. Your sound carries quite well.'

'Mãaaae!' protested Ana.

'But . . .' Shirly repeated. 'I don't sing!' She desperately wanted a familiar punishment, like swabbing floors for a week or collecting all the hymnals after morning prayer. Anything but this.

The Mother Superior's clipped tone settled it. 'Either you sing the lead as Dona Lisette here suggests, Shirly, or we'll have to do something about all the ruckus you created with the chicken coop. Your parents would be very displeased if you had to stand in the corner of the classroom for the next month.' Shirly certainly didn't want that trial. She would be mortified if her mother or, heaven forbid, her father, her dear, dear father, knew who she really was—an errant cannon of a daughter. Shirly and Anna slipped into disgruntled silence. 'That is that. You can begin your training with Dona Lisette,' the Mother Superior announced with finality.

Ana folded her arms vehemently, while Shirly's eyebrows knit together in wordless defiance, both sullen in their frustration. Shirly was sure she saw the older women's shared wink of epicaricacy.

5

The surf washed away from the shore, and Goku's feet sank deeper into the wet sand. Another couple of waves rushed forward and danced around her plump ankles before pulling away and sinking her further into the shifting ground. White skeleton crabs scuttled here and there, nipping around broken bits of coloured shells before dropping into burrow holes in the powdery earth. The four o'clock sun was too violent for Goku's liking, but Mamtu preferred that Shirly and her sister get enough time at the beach to tire themselves out and return home before it got dark. The early October weather was pleasant, and the breeze at the Gaspar Dias beach was heady. The surf was frothing healthily all the way till the eye could see at the rocks near Dona Paula in the distance.

Shirly's clothes lay on higher ground along with Devika's—the two were in their skivvies, rolling around in the surf, using their tiny palms to catch even tinier silver fish darting in the shallows. Goku belched serenely as the gambolling, good-natured sea breeze made her wide skirt billow about. She leaned to one side and then another to take her sunken feet out of the wet sand, but her weight only took her further down. Unsteady yet unable to free herself, she flapped her arms awkwardly.

'Ai gho!' she exclaimed plangently in Konkani, drawing the attention of the two sisters, who came splashing through the wavelets to assess the situation. Free from the complex burdens of insincere sentiment, the young girls giggled. The hapless Goku's reproach for their aggravating schadenfreude only tickled the girls, further causing them to howl with laughter and splash around their captive keeper.

'Catch the fish, cook the fish, eat the fish . . .' Shirly started and was joined in her limerick by her younger sister as they both pranced around the wide sculpture of an awkwardly rooted and flailing Goku.

Goku turned livid and began flapping even more, trying to reach out and cover their mouths in an attempt to silence them. 'Shut up, you! Stop laughing or I'll tell your mummy!'

Still giggling, Shirly and Devika finally took pity, and each of them took an arm and pulled at her. Goku allowed her insubordinate charges to help her out. Unfortunately for her, they pulled in opposite directions and she soon resembled a very portly saviour on the cross while being drawn apart. 'Ai gho!' she protested. A large wave suddenly washed in as the tide was mounting inland. The girls tumbled away squealing and reeling uncontrollably, and Goku finally lost her balance. She fell sideways into the surf, her feet uprooted at last from the sand, and her impact sent out a tidal wave, causing more excited squeals from the girls.

With her hair clinging like seaweed around her face and salty water in her eyes, Goku picked herself up and, panting, dragged herself to the drier ground near Shirly's and Devika's clothes. The girls ran up to her. 'Wait, wait,' Shirly said, as they unfolded and spread out the towel under Goku. The housemaid collapsed on to it heavily like a walrus, sending water droplets everywhere.

'Aiiiiieeeeeeeeee!' Goku shrieked. She rolled over and patted the towel under her. Wheezing and panting, she fished out a conical turritella communis shell planted into the sand like a drill bit, sharp tip up.

'Awwwwoooooo,' Goku howled, rubbing her rear and feeling sorry for herself. 'Don't make me get up,' she threatened, and the girls fled, whooping and shrieking, into the water as fast as their skinny legs could carry them.

Happy to have some distance between those devil girls and herself, Goku watched them splash water on each other and soon enough felt the tranquillity of the evening sun on her face and the wind on her skin.

But the peace didn't remain for long. A babel of shouts had begun behind her. All three of them turned to look in the direction of the sound, where the beach met the road.

A bronze of the curly bearded Afonso de Albuquerque in chainmail and a sword stood vigilant on the traffic island in the centre of the road, overseeing a large procession of people trooping past. It definitely didn't look like a wedding party to the trio watching from the beach, the usual reason for so many people to be walking on the road. There weren't any European faces, only natives. A few were carrying placards, and they looked like they were on their way to Dona Paula. On the same road where Shirly's father had given her mother driving lessons, a palm-lined avenue that held for her the breeze of dulcet memories.

Shirly and Devika approached Goku, shivering as the evening had become cooler. On the horizon, the sun engorged itself in orange, recasting the cirrus clouds overhead in a salmon blush. The trio, however, was focused on observing the crowd in the distance. Goku helped wipe the girls down with a towel and held up cotton sheets between which they removed their wet underwear and changed into a fresh set of dry clothes. With excitement and curiosity, the girls then rocketed off towards the road, kicking up sand behind them.

An irate Goku yelled after them but of course they had dropped their ears along the way.

Nestled between the trees near the road was a life-size, oceanic-blue, concrete whale, hollowed out at the centre. It was large enough for people to pass through its yawning mouth and emerge at the archway near its tail. Visitors of all ages to the oceanfront, including Shirly and Devika, often delighted themselves as they traversed the belly of this curiously large beached sculpture. The girls stepped in from the rear and stood in between its open fish lips at the mouth, looking out at the procession. The men were chanting slogans, and some of them had placards which read 'Right to Free Speech' and 'Independence for Goa'.

This went on for a few minutes, till a couple of Jeeps roared on the scene and stopped with a lurch by the kerb. A few policemen stepped out of the vehicles and, quite out of sync with the tranquillity of their surroundings, began to use their batons on the protestors. Shirly watched in horror as she held Devika's shoulders protectively.

In the midst of the absurdly violent kerfuffle, a red Standard slowly pulled to a stop, and a dark-haired man of medium height stepped out. As the police were aggressively landing blows on the protestors, two of them broke away from the crowd and began running in the direction of the sea.

The girls jumped when they heard a thumping echo from the bowels of the whale. Goku had caught up with them and was panting wildly, holding their belongings as well as a stitch in her side. She padded on to the tongue, where they were standing, her wheezes ricocheting around the insides of the whale, but before she could say anything, they pointed to the scene outside. Two of the men who had separated from the crowd were being chased by the policemen, who followed them all the way into the surf. Before they could get too far into the rising tide, the policemen caught up with the runaways and tied their hands behind their backs. A moisture-laden grimness spread with the sea winds everywhere. Goku held the girls back protectively as they peeped from their open-lipped lookout, 'Ai gho!' Her whisper rebounded and magnified, echoing in the whale's belly.

As the policemen were bringing their haul back to the road, one of the men looked in the direction of the trio standing in the gaping mouth of the giant fish. His eyes caught Shirly's briefly, and in that moment she became sure she had seen the man and his companion before but couldn't recall exactly where. It was all too much, too close. Fear gripped her and she looked down. The men were roughed up with batons and pushed into a Jeep. The rest of the group was disbanded, their placards taken from them or broken, and they too were shoved into Jeeps.

After the official conveyances drove off with their cargo, the evening breeze picked up, whistling through the whale. The statue of Afonso de Albuquerque stood alone once more.

'What happened?' asked Devika, who was pressed against her charge's thigh.

'I not know, baby. Some fighting,' Goku replied dolefully in her cobbled English.

Once every trace of the protestors and police had disappeared, leaving a hollow gust blowing leaves around the statue on the stark road, Goku, Shirly and Devika gingerly left their hiding place. As they started to make their way home, Shirly saw a familiar face step out from a cluster of palm trees adjacent to the whale. It was Ana! She had been hiding behind a tree and was running to reunite with her guardian, who had come up from the shore looking for her with a very worried expression which soon turned relieved. As Ana and Shirly caught each other's eye, Shirly felt a strange kinship with her nemesis—a brief bond of having witnessed something that made their small world wobble on its axis.

6

The sun melted into the horizon, and its blaze rippled through the estuary where the Mandovi met the sea at Gaspar Dias. Further upstream, the buglers kept up with their tooting till the flag with Portuguese colours came down the mast. From her window vantage, Shirly as usual caught the second flag show of the day. Those who were out and about stopped whatever they were doing and stood at attention. Some, like the shopkeeper, stood frozen in salute. Only José, or more fully José Custòdio de Faria, tenaciously kept up with whatever he was doing to that poor lady he shared the pedestal with, overlording the scene around them. The flag was wrapped up and then all four of the flagmen marched back into the Idalcão Palace, not to be seen again before the next day's hoist.

With ritual satisfaction, Shirly stepped back from her window when she heard her mother's summons. She was ushered into the bathroom where Devika stood naked with her eyes tightly shut while Goku lathered her hair. A water bucket for Shirly stood full next to Devika's, so she stripped and started to bathe herself, washing away all the grainy textures of their evening dip.

Once she was fresh and desalinated, Shirly sat at the kitchen dinner table to finish some homework under Mamtu's supervision. She was so distracted, trying to process the events she had witnessed earlier, that an exasperated Mamtu had to repeat each of her questions twice. Devika seemed relatively unaffected and doodled on some rough paper, feeling as important as her older sister while she feigned concentration on her pretend homework.

'Awooooo,' moaned Goku softly. She had lifted her skirts and was rubbing feni on to her sore backside, the part that had met with the prickly end of a gastropod earlier that evening on the beach. Her back was to the earthen fireplace along the wall near the sink.

'Goku, one day you are going to catch fire with all that feni on you,' Mamtu looked up from the homework and said in consternation as the sharp, vinegary odours of the local fermented cashew apple spirit hotly jabbed her nostrils. Secretly, however, she was grateful to have Goku's assistance in the kitchen and to keep her own growing belly, which weighed her down more and more these days, away from the heat of the flames.

'Bai, I putting feni on your stomach, you understanding. All pain going. In my village we do massage on baby, make strong bones, like fighter. Even cows drinking, giving more milk,' Goku responded with gusto. She picked up a pipe and blew on the flames to get the coals glowing, causing Mamtu to hold her breath in case a spark fell on her alcohol-soaked maid, igniting her into a firework. But Goku calmly alternated this fiery act with stirring the pot of mutton gravy balanced on a grill over the coals. Mamtu could only lean her aching back on her chair and send a prayer up to Saint Jhulelal to save her kitchen from any accidental infernos.

When they heard the main door opening and closing, they knew that Deepak had finally arrived home. Goku started ladling the cooked gravy into a large bowl that was placed on the table along with steaming rice. Deepak pecked each of the girls on the cheek and took his seat.

'Daddy, did you get me a present?' asked Devika hopefully in between mouthfuls.

'Of course I did,' her father improvised gamely. 'I'll give it to you after you finish your dinner.' Deepak was a well-known merchant in town and had a large showroom on the shop-lined Afonso de Albuquerque road which ran behind their house. His shop, Loja Mamtu, named after his wife, stocked many fine things from all around the world. There were batteries and saris from Japan, scented talcum powders and tinned biscuits from England, pens from the USA, watches from Switzerland and perfume from France, among other delights. Before the great divide of India and Pakistan, he had set out from the port in Karachi in search of new business ventures and was led to the bright shores of Goa. There was an appetite for expensive goods here, and he broke away from his family business of tending the land and ended up a middleman. Just a year before Partition, he acquired a new bride and decided to settle in the place that was already buttering his bread. The locals started referring to him simply as 'Karachi', which to them meant someone who originates from Sindh, a nebulous place somewhere northerly on the subcontinental map. Out of convenience, he was even referred to as 'Karachi' on official documents, softened on paper with a passport of Portuguese phonemics to Quarachim. And so, as he made a life away from the land of his roots, he dropped his last name, Devchand, his father's name, and ironically came to bear the name of the city from which he took the boat to his merchant life across the border. And just like that, his became the first Sindhi family in Panjim, followed closely by a few others when the new nations of India and Pakistan were born in 1947. His brothers, who had fled to Bombay and Hong Kong after he settled in Panjim, narrated the horrors of Partition in their telegrams and how a new local government had appropriated their father's fields forcefully.

Despite all his trademark optimism, Deepak sensed in his bones that he never had any hope of seeing his ancestral lands again. This was one of the few secrets he kept from his wife, since he knew she harboured a desire to return to her roots in Sindh someday. However, Partition wasn't the final occasion for the Quarachim family to learn that time could be a slippery river, where once you choose to shift downstream the path behind you vanishes to the point of no return.

'A customer has placed an order so Monkar will come over in the night,' Deepak informed his wife. His shop of treasures also included jewellery, made of gold from Beirut and crafted by a local jeweller, Monkar.

Deepak looked over at Shirly, who was chewing distractedly, shrouded in her complicated thoughts. He turned to Mamtu questioningly, a bit amused at the seriousness of his young daughter who suddenly seemed so grown-up in her moody silence.

'Did you know that Shirly has been selected to sing as the lead in the Christmas show at school?' Mamtu said brightly, in a buttery attempt to bring her daughter's attention back to the table while helping Devika flitch meat strips off the bone on her plate.

'Oh really?' He looked genuinely surprised and delighted at his older daughter, who seemed to have matured an inch more in his estimation. 'That is wonderful! We had no idea you were a singer. Acting, you can do,' he added playfully, recalling the several times she had feigned pain or discomfort just for his attention. Shirly blushed. 'But singing . . .'

'But . . .' Shirly said, feeling muddled about the entire affair. So many thoughts ran through her mind, causing her speech to short-circuit and switch off. She found her new role with singing and music at odds with her on-ground abilities. Plus, it was simply getting in the way of her ambitions to have grand adventures. Every second person in Goa was a singer, but how many were blue-blooded adventurers, sailing across the Mandovi to the oceans and lands beyond? If the great Abbé Faria was a singer, history would have been very different, and he wouldn't have done all his hypnotic travels.

'Congratulations, we are so proud of you.' Deepak's expression was filled with parental enthusiasm. 'You have really become a Shirley Temple.' When his eldest daughter was birthed in the red-earthed land that magnetized his blood to it more and more, Deepak had held his tiny infant in his arms and couldn't stop marvelling at her delicate head of wispy curls, which reminded him of his favourite child actress. Shirley, he had whispered in the small whorl of her translucent ear, while Mamtu was asleep, spent from childbirth, in their bedroom. After the midwife cleaned up, she recorded the birth in her scrawl, mistakenly dropping the 'e' from the original name for baby Shirly.

'What is the play about?' asked Deepak.

Shirly's brow somehow unfurrowed at the ease with which her father could feel pride for her. 'It's a musical, Daddy. I still don't know the story. I have to go to Dona Lisette's house to practise,' she answered with her most grown-up nonchalance.

'Dona Lisette?' questioned Deepak.

'You know,' responded Mamtu, 'Lisette Lucilia de Araujo, wife of Eugenio. You know him, I think. They have three children, two boys . . .'

'Yes, yes. Eugenio works with the government. Something with finance, I think, the fazenda, the bank. Ah, yes. This is good, Shirly. Who knew you had these hidden talents tucked away?'

Shirly hung her head sheepishly. She was enjoying the attention from her parents so much that she decided not to get into how exactly she had got the lead in the musical.

'Beach fighting today,' interjected Goku, changing the subject as she added more hot rice to the pot on the table.

This triggered Shirly to open up about what was preoccupying her beneath all the musical chitchat. 'Oh yes. There were a lot of people on Gaspar Dias beach, on the road, with signs, and two men ran into the ocean, and there were police with sticks and guns . . .' she blurted out chaotically.

The moment Mamtu heard 'police' and 'guns', concern transformed her features. 'Thank god you are all okay,' she said.

'Sounds like a protest march,' Deepak said with seriousness.

'What's a protest march, Daddy?' asked Devika.

'It's when people want to tell the people they work for or more important people—like the government—something they are upset about. They march together so that they can bring attention to their issue,' said Deepak. 'But the important thing is you are all okay.'

There was silence at the table for a while. Then Shirly said, 'Where did the police take them, Daddy?'

'I'm not sure, Shirly. Maybe they wanted to talk to them.' Shirly was thoughtful. There was something familiar about those two men, but she still couldn't quite place where she had seen them. Deepak changed the subject to unload the heaviness off the table. 'Uncle Monkar is coming. Who wants to show him their palm? He will tell you your future.'

Monkar was a jeweller who came all the way from Margão. He would go door-to-door to take orders for various kinds of gold jewellery, create his designs in his workshop, passed down to him from his father, and bring back the newly fashioned treasures after a week. However, he had a unique facet to him that intrigued Shirly and her sister—his penchant for divining the future by looking at the palms of his clients. What they didn't know was that he had a hidden facet too—a small habit of keeping a little extra gold for himself, which he'd slip into his pocket. Clients usually found a little loss here and there on occasion after a meeting with him but passed it off as their misjudgement.

As they were speaking of the jeweller, the doorbell rang, which Goku went to answer. Monkar could be heard greeting her amiably, while she responded in grunts, informing him to 'Wait salon'. Deepak wiped his mouth and rose to join Monkar.

As Goku re-entered the kitchen, her mood had darkened. Monkar was too greasy for her taste, but since the master liked to do business with him, she couldn't throw him out with the gills and fishbones to Sukkoo and Bukkoo. 'Goku! Light!' Monkar boomed his order.

'Heinh!' Goku snarled. She returned to the living room shortly, where Deepak and Monkar were already talking shop. 'Light,' she announced. Deepak stopped mid-sentence, and Monkar's ocular nearly fell off. Goku stood in front of the two men holding a tong with an inflamed piece of charcoal from the fireplace. 'Light?' she repeated, holding the tong forward, shoving the smouldering scarlet coal dangerously close to Monkar's walrus moustache, nearly singeing it, scattering a few hot sparks over his pants.

'Ah, fire!' Monkar shrieked in a high, delicate tone. Deepak leaned back to avoid the sparking flare radiating from the end of the tong. He was sure Goku was deliberately trying to antagonize their guest. Once his housemaid decided she didn't like someone, there was little he could do to control her.

'Goku, er, don't we have any matchsticks?' Deepak asked carefully.

Shirly passed the doorway and watched from the threshold as Monkar gingerly held out his tobacco pipe while Goku dropped the coal into the open end and walked away smugly. An embarrassed Deepak watched Monkar trying to get his pipe going, hoping its wooden body wouldn't burst into flame.

When Monkar realized they had company, he looked up. 'Oh ho, Shirly, come come! Your father is giving me all his gold. You want some?' he said with bombastic flair. Shirly shook her head shyly. 'No? Okay, then I will keep it all,' he jested. 'This is very fine gold, all the way from Bai-root. Come over the sea in a boat. Very fine, very fine. Come on, show me your hand.'

Shirly went closer because of the way he said Beirut. She didn't know where this faraway, over-the-seas locale was but it certainly was now pinned on her map of places to discover. She held out her palm to Monkar. He held it, balanced his pipe on the crystal ashtray on a side table, adjusted his ocular and peered into the lines on her hand. 'Oh ho,' he said enigmatically. 'Oh ho ho . . . hmmm . . . ah . . . good, good . . . very rich girl. Lots of money. And see here, you are very strong. Good, good. Two children, one girl, one boy. Good marriage. Before marriage boyfriend also!' With the last comment, Monkar looked up with twinkling eyes at a blushing Shirly and her father. He peered into her hand again, then closed her palm into a fist. 'You are a very important girl, especially for your Daddy. Be good, okay?'

'What about . . . will I travel, see the world, will I have adventures?'

'Oh ho ho! Quarachim, your daughter is ready to leave you already!' Monkar joked before peering into her palm again. 'Ah . . . I see . . . yes, yes, you are going to have adventure and travel. I can see it in your luck.' Whether or not he could read the timelines etched in Shirly's young palms, now that she had heard the words, she believed that they would be self-prophesizing. Devika came running up towards Monkar for her reading, while Shirly, feeling light-hearted at the evening's copacetic prognostication, skipped away to work on her Stomachion before bedtime. She'd have to figure out how to keep that pesky Ana away from her garden while she was off discovering the world. But that was a problem to deal with at a later time.

When tucked in bed, Shirly saw her wall shimmer. It was the reflection of the moon on the Mandovi projected into her room through the window. She forgot the rest of the day as she stared at the glimmering light, finding the imagery of boats, flags, mermaids and unknown faces morphing into each other in oneiric seamlessness until sleep overtook her in its blanket.

7

Goku sat down mid-afternoon with a steel thali in front of her, piled with a mountain of rice and streams of fish curry running down its peak. She dug into a steep side with her hand and fed herself. She slurped up each fistful between her fingers with deep, glopping sounds and generously used her tongue to catch stray ribbons of juice that rolled down her forearms. Seated on the ground in a corner alcove of the now-quiet kitchen, this was the best part of her day, and Goku savoured every second of it, knowing that a delicious afternoon siesta was to follow. So she was mildly irritated when Devika came running up to her asking for some newspaper. With her mouth too full for words, she motioned to Devika to wait till she finished eating and that she would give it to her when she washed her hands.

Devika retreated from the kitchen and past her parents' room where they were napping. She returned to her own bedchamber. A serene and unseasonal early November rain had washed in during the night and for most of the morning. So the drain that ran around the house was full and flowing.

After Goku finished slopping up the last bits of curried rice off the thali, she relished the feeling of fullness in her ample belly. She belched with bovine satisfaction, then after rocking herself from side to side lifted off the floor to wash up. She removed some old issues of the *O Heraldo* from the pile in a recessed wall cupboard and went to look for Devika.

Excited, Devika took her newspapers to Shirly, still in her pinafore after returning from school, and now curled up on her bed with *The Seven Voyages of Sindbad the Sailor*. Big sister was a role that came with duties like responsibility and superintendence that Shirly was still raising an eyebrow at. However, Devika had pleaded her case with doting liquid eyes that filled her innocent little face. And as annoyed as she was to be snapped back to her room from Baghdad and beyond, Shirly had reluctantly let her little sister, who was clutching as many newspapers given by Goku as her tiny hands could carry, lead her outside.

Beyond the front gate, the open drain channel skirting the buildings on the street wore the sounds of rushing liquid. Clean rainwater was swirling and moving in liquid grace through the stone-lined drain, coming from the back roads and moving westwards to meet the sea at Gaspar Dias. Devika dropped the newspapers on the ground. Both sisters sat down on the damp kerb, Shirly ripping out pages and showing Devika her role in the production line. The first boat Shirly fashioned quickly drowned when she set it afloat, so she made another, larger one, with a wider base and three layers to make it sturdier. Shirly watched it float downstream gleefully and proceeded to fold another one. In a sisterhood of sailor girls, Devika's hands were driven to keep up with page-tearing while Captain Shirly folded and launched. First mate Devika clapped in adoration as her older sister fulfilled her afternoon wish.

They weren't the only ones sending paper boats down the drain. Clusters of children around most buildings were doing the same. And two houses down the road, much to her chagrin, so was that silly Ana. The presumptuous usurper of her territories and peace, the outsider who now wanted to take over *her* neighbourhood with her own paper boat. She was reminded once more of all her feelings towards Ana. She would have to show that girl her place.

When Shirly's next boat was set afloat, she ran down alongside it in case there were any blocks. It caught up with Ana's boat, and soon she and Ana were elbowing each other, running alongside their boats till the paper craft were whisked away by the current faster than they could keep up. The girls craned their necks, each hoping that their boat would have beaten the other's, but beyond a point, they couldn't tell the specks floating downstream apart. By now, Shirly's competitiveness was contagious, and Ana, deciding to no longer be a pushover to this rude, unfriendly neighbour, kept her guard up and her elbows out. Once their boats disappeared, they cast dagger eyes at each other, then ran back to their gazettes to bend and crimp paper for their next boat.

Each of them set fresh craft down in the water and ran alongside like belligerent cockfighters, goading their newsprint contenders to move faster.

'Move! Move, boat! Move, swim!' Shirly coached her contestant vehemently, backed up with equal enthusiasm by her loyal younger sibling.

'Mine will win! Mine will win! Faster! Faster!' Ana shouted at hers.

During the next round, Shirly's boat swiftly overtook Ana's but further down was waylaid by a stray pipe jutting into the drain. Shirly surged forward to free it. 'Boat, don't get stuck!' she roared from a distance.

Before she reached the trapped vessel, a motorcycle rode up and came to a stop on the service road. A man in khaki pants and black shoes stepped off the bike and stood next to the drain in front of the wedged boat. Her eye still on her paper craft, Shirly watched with surprise and indignation as the policeman deliberately reached out with his foot and stepped on the boat. The newspapery hull filled with heavy wetness and sank. Devika clung to Shirly who looked over at Ana, whose eyes were as shocked at what just happened. They stood there wordlessly. And then a clammy shiver went through Shirly as she recognized the man. He was the arrogant policeman at the protest she had witnessed by the beach. Why was he here? In her little paper-boat corner of Panjim.

The policeman flecked some water droplets off his shoe with his handkerchief and smirked at the girls. He passed them and kept walking. Where was the awful man headed? Shirly wondered; after all, there was only her house at the end of the street.

The policeman turned exactly at her front gate and rang the bell. Shirly and Devika saw a sleep-saturated Goku answer and then disappear back inside. Within a minute, their father popped out and invited the policeman inside. Shirly forgot her boat race and went closer to her gate, her younger sister at her heel. She wondered why adults were so polite to each other even when there may not be any reason to be so—her father should just kick the horrible man out. So Shirly was a little relieved when the evil boat-drowner declined Deepak's invitation. Instead, her father stepped outside the gate.

'Bom dia, Senhor,' the policeman said.

'Bom dia,' Deepak responded with a serious face. 'How can I help you, Agente?'

'Senhor, as you know, these days there are terrorists running loose. They can threaten the security of our government, our lives, our families . . .' the agente looked over in their direction, meeting Shirly's eyes.

'What exactly is this about, Agente?' Deepak asked, a little sternly.

'Well, I will be frank, Senhor. I am here today because we recently arrested two men who were causing trouble to our peace. When I questioned them, er . . . with my methods, they said they received some arms from you. I want to ask you, Senhor, is that true?'

Yes, it's true, Shirley sensed. The two men he had arrested were familiar to her for a reason. She had seen them with her father on their visit to the Oilem Aravalem mines. Shirly feared for her father. How would he get out of this horrid mess with this awful man?

Shirly's father was quick to reply. 'Agente Monteiro, I do not own or supply any firearms or bombs to anyone. Yes, we do use a small amount of plastic dynamite to unearth some stones in the mines, but those are too minor to be of any use to anyone else. There must be some mistake.'

There was a long silence. 'Well, if there is anything you wish to tell me, you may contact me at the headquarters, Senhor Quarachim.'

'If I know of anything, I will surely contact you, Agente.' There was her father being polite again for no reason. She wanted to scream out on his behalf, 'No, we will never call you!'

Deepak and Agente Monteiro stepped out of the gate. 'This is a very beautiful car, Senhor Quarachim.' The policeman ran a finger over the family's new Pontiac parked near the gate, gleaming from the sunlight trapped within raindrops. 'Clearly your business is doing well.'

'Yes, it has been good, Agente.'

'I'm sure you wouldn't mind passing your good fortune around. It would be nice if I pulled up to my meetings at the headquarters in something like this on occasion. It would make the troops quite excited, I think.'

Deepak waited a blink before answering. 'Yes, of course, Agente. A man of your stature deserves the adulation. I shall send my driver with the car to your residence in the morning for your use,' agreed Deepak, much too easily to Shirly's boiling anxiety.

Monteiro walked slowly and deliberately back to his motorcycle, surveying the neighbourhood, as though he owned the earth under his feet. He started his motorcycle noisily and rode off. As Shirly's eyes followed him, she noticed Ana working on another boat on the drain, occasionally looking her way. But Shirly had more important matters on her mind. She had just heard her father deny knowing those two men who were arrested. Was her father a liar? No, it couldn't be. Could it? A terrible sinking feeling entered her stomach, drowning out any of her earlier zest like a sodden paper boat.

8

With each plant he watered, Mushu felt his heart squeeze until a dollop of love fell into the pot. He felt grateful, and even lucky, to be handling these plants in this very house. He made sure that he wasn't wetting them too little or too much, just as his senhora had instructed him. After attending to the pots that lined the stairway at the entrance, he made his way to the small green space at the side of the house.

Hedge-lined with purple and pink bougainvillaea constantly in bloom, the yard that flanked the house was his oasis. He often spent time sitting on the red-tiled steps leading down to it from the kitchen, surveying his domain with calm satisfaction, keeping a lookout for stray weeds. Every blade of grass that sparkled fully with the green within it was testament to his good fortune, and he was eager to protect the colour of his luck. In the corner of the garden grew some wild touch-me-not. He itched to get rid of them lest they spread and overtake the soft grass. However, the senhora's children, Ana, João and Tomas, delighted in the way the toothy viridian leaves folded into purplish closed books. They would tickle the blades with their index fingers or else swish over them with their open palms and watch in fascination the way the plants reacted in shyness. Although Mushu kept a close eye on the shy offenders, he let them be. After all, they gave the children of his dear mistress happiness. And he too remembered the simple joy he received from them in a similar time of innocence.

Back home in his village in Mornem, bushes of touch-me-not grew without any effort, lining unpaved pathways. Lush, tended grass wasn't a luxury to be found there. The road leading up to the village bore ferric red soil that was too acidic to grow much besides grain. The dwellings were so close together that you could hear the arguments in the adjoining hut as though they were taking place in yours. The homes were cobbled together from stone and brick, unpainted and unwashed for years. Tin roofs fluttered noisily with the wind and banged around ears during monsoon tempests. There were cracks in the walls and on the four steps that led up into the dark womb of his family's home. He shared it with his three brothers and their kin, where each family took up a corner, with only a couple of saris strung across hooks in the wall for any semblance of privacy. On the rare occasions he went to visit, he slept outside at night on a woven-mesh cot, on which the womenfolk jiggled babies, sorted rice or peeled vegetables by day. Meat was a rarity, usually enjoyed only on festive occasions—when scrawny village chickens were sacrificed to the gods to honour an occasion like birth, marriage or one of several festivals.

Most of his community found work in the fields of villages outside Mornem. When he was very young, the sweat of sinewy labour was written into his future—he would duly accompany his mother and help her out, along with his brothers. The man they worked for was a bhatkar, a landowner. He owned a wide acreage of paddy and hired labourers during the sowing and harvest seasons. Mushu's mother was employed to collect the discarded rice husk to burn as well as to sweep the grounds around the bhatkar's house. She also had to pick up the dung droppings of his cattle and arrange them to dry. The dried cakes were later used as fertilizer or fuel as required. In addition to wages, she was usually given small portions of the harvest to take back for her family. On the return to Mornem, Mushu and his brothers liked to spend time at the stream they passed and catch some freshwater crab or fish. So their stomachs were never empty, thanks to Devi Parvati, the mother goddess of their local temple who watched over them. But it was the big event that followed the little events that made Mushu question his existence.

He noticed that every time he passed by residents of other villages, they would cross to the other side of the road, even if they were returning from the temple or heading to church. His unworldliness hadn't allowed him the fully formed thoughts to ask his mother about this. On the bhatkar's land, they were never allowed to draw water from the main well and instead were given a bucket of water that had been filled for them. That didn't seem so out of the ordinary. Until one day when the bucket ran out of water and one of his brothers decided to let it into the well. The next day, new ropes were affixed to the well and a Hindu priest was chanting mantras to purify it. The bhatkar's daughter-in-law had noticed the defilement from her window but since she was tending to her infant at the time she couldn't do anything to prevent it.

On another occasion, a cassock-wearing priest all the way from the Basilica de Bom Jesus church in Velha Goa had come to visit the bhatkar and survey the spiritual needs of his village. Once he left, the steel vessels that he was served in were given away.

'Why?' Mushu asked his mother.

'Look, Mushu, there are four types of people,' she responded without a blink, as if she were explaining the theories of heliocentrism or gravity or any other well-accepted scientific law governing the universe. 'The brahmins, who are the agents between man and god; the kshatriyas, who fight and defend honour and society; the vaishyas, who are the merchants; and the fourth class, who are below all of these three.'

'So which are we?' Mushu asked, fascinated at the layered integument of a world that seemed beyond the unschooled ken of his child's mind.

'We are the fourth class, my son.'

'Why?' Mushu asked, despondent at his genes for not having made the cut towards a respectable social class without his knowledge or consent.

'Because it is the karma of man, his actions in previous births, that decide his fate.' His mother's resigned response was uttered as though she had recited these answers to herself several times over her life. But Mushu was sure in the recesses of his being that he or his mother couldn't have done anything to deserve being untouchable.

'So, Ai, was the priest an untouchable?'

'No, my son. He was a brahmin. He was a Catholic brahmin.'

'So was it because he has a different god?'

'No, my son. It is because his god allows him to eat beef and pork. His touch is not clean to the bhatkar's Hindu brahmin code, but he and his family didn't want to offend the priest, or make him think that his spiritual services were needed, so they politely fed him. Only later, once he left, they discarded his plate and water tumbler.' Saying so, Mushu's mother placed the plate and tumbler in a ditch by the side of the stream they passed on the way back home.

'Why are you throwing it away, Ai?' For someone inured to poverty's starkness, the waste of such materiality felt like throwing away a treasure they could barely afford with their year's wages but could have such potential for being well-used in their lives.

'It has been touched by one who eats beef and pork.' Mushu's mother didn't even have a hint of remorse. 'We may be unlucky Mahars, only fit to clean up after others, but in our family we do not eat beef and pork. If the bhatkar is not touching it, maybe we also should not.' She washed her hands in the stream's cool water and took the name of the family deity under her breath. Mushu understood caste that day as a human circle of touch-me-nots. But these were still little events, mere seeds.

One day, his mother doubled over in pain. The verdict: rotten fish or dirty water. The bhatkar's doctor didn't want to lay his hands on her and instead offered some medicine. But fate was impartial, and as Mushu watched the breath leave her body, turning it into stiff clay, he suspected he wouldn't feel the loving touch of his mother from that day onwards. It was the biggest event in his little life, falling on his path like an uprooted tree. Grief-stricken and unanchored, he wandered for a few years. And somehow his feet took his untouchable, wrung and broken heart far away from the saturnine future his roots held and found another by the Mandovi River with his European employers.

In his Senhora Lisette's garden, he felt safe from that vicious circle of untouchability. Thankfully, the Araujos, with their European orientation, were oblivious to the cruel nuances of other local societies beyond their backyard and didn't concern themselves with them either. Yes, the White people were not just good people, they were his angels. As long as they remained in Goa, there was hope yet.

9

Shirly daintily parked her bicycle at the gated door to Ana's house. Today she would have her first lesson for the musical with Dona Lisette. Now that her parents were fussing over her being the lead in the musical, Shirly didn't mind having to sing so much. Even the new reverence that Devika bore for her older sister brought in a sweetness of emotion that she didn't expect to feel for her little sibling. She still didn't see the reason, but if Dona Lisette wanted to use her voice—and God-all-does-knows why—then so be it. But she wasn't too pleased with having to share her time with Ana. If that irksome mosquito caused any more trouble, she would pull her hair first with a war cry and run out of the house. No matter what. She would be fine not to be in the musical—familial pride or not.

Shirly took a few moments for herself outside the door, dreaming, planning her escape with a suitable defence against any Ana-related attack before venturing into enemy territory. She pulled back the large knocker on the front door and let it rap a few times into the quiet afternoon. There was a pause before Mushu, the caretaker at Ana's, opened the door.

Shirly was led inside the Araujo home. It had high ceilings, elegant furniture, blue china vases and an impressive azulejos panel depicting Panjim on the wall. An upright piano sat at one end of the living room near tall windows that let the ripe mango sunshine fall across the space.

Three boys sat in one corner on a settee, with the boy in the middle plucking on a guitar. A most heavenly exotic sound wrapped around Shirly's ears; she had never felt as charmed by the dulcet timbre of a classical guitar or its boyishly fetching player. She wasn't used to feeling uncomfortable around a lad, and this day was certainly appearing to be a turning point in more than one way. Watching him strum, with a brown lock of hair fallen across his downturned, sun-soaked forehead, she felt a bazaar of complex sensations stir up within her, ranging from being transfixed, to feeling like an intruder, to numbing bashfulness. She tried to stand still, not breathe, become a part of the furniture. She hadn't even noticed that Mushu had left her side and disappeared.

Shirly didn't have to wait long before Lisette entered the room. 'Shirly, my dear,' Lisette greeted her daughter's classmate eagerly. She walked over to the piano and pulled up a chair next to the piano stool. The trio on the settee, now noticing their audience, took the presence of Lisette and Shirly as their cue to leave. As the boy with the guitar walked out, he locked eyes with Shirly for a brief second that spiralled and stretched time in her world.

'Come have a seat here, dear,' Ana's mother broke Shirly's spell by patting the chair next to her. She had a kind face and wore a cream satin blouse with a long, brown cotton skirt. Shirly gingerly took her place while Lisette appeared to read her mind.

'I understand that you have not been to singing classes with Sister Olga. But that is no matter. Let's begin.' Lisette didn't waste any time with niceties. She pushed down on the middle C ivory with her long index finger and demonstrated by singing it out. 'Laaaaaa!' Lisette's voice was full and round with an undulating river in it. 'Think you can do that too? Let's try.' Lisette played the note once more as a cue for Shirly.

'La . . .' Shirly's voice was weak and unconvincing. She wanted to run and hide underneath the settee.

'That is not the voice I heard the other day at school,' Lisette said cheerily. 'Okay, here, how about you sit straighter, keep your back upright and your shoulders . . .' Lisette placed her hands gently but firmly on Shirly's shoulders to relax them.

'Now,' she said, 'breathe . . . like this.' Lisette then placed her hand on her belly, and with every inhale and exhale, Shirly saw Lisette's hand being pushed out and in by her stomach. 'Now you try.'

Shirly placed her own hand on her belly and felt her stomach move her hand back and forth like Lisette's. They kept up breathing like that for a few minutes.

'Okay, and now let's try,' said Lisette again. 'Laaaaa!' she sang out.

'Laaa . . .' Shirly sang a little louder.

Lisette smiled at her. 'Much better.'

Shirly already felt fatigued from breathing so consciously.

Every day after school, Shirly headed over to Lisette's for a singing session. For a couple of weeks after her first lesson, Lisette only had her practise breathing and voice exercises. Shirly found this mostly boring. Until she could hear the difference creep into her own voice.

'Maa, meeeyy, meeee, mawww, mooooo!' They went up and down the scales with different solfège sequences, strengthening the confidence in Shirly's vocals. Shirly was grateful for one thing—there was no Ana to be seen. Until two weeks later, when Lisette decided to have them in a session together.

Ana was already seated at the piano when Shirly rang the doorbell that day. The two of them looked at each other, guarded and sceptical.

'Girls, today I want to give you your scripts. You will both be playing major roles, even though you are the lead part, Shirly dear.' Lisette fluttered busily around the piano, rifling through some typed-up papers. She handed the girls stapled pages of a script entitled *Zulekha* in a bold font and launched into an explanation of the narrative.

'The story is about a gypsy girl called Zulekha—you'll play her, Shirly. Once upon a time, a king and queen have a baby girl—we'll have two of your classmates play them and get a doll for the baby. The queen swaddles the child in fine muslin, and she is gifted a silver ring by her parents, which they put on her little toe. One day, a gypsy woman who works in the palace gets angry with the king and decides to teach him a lesson in humility. She takes the newborn girl and swaps the child with her own newborn son. The gypsy woman raises the princess in captivity and has her son become the future king—the heartbroken king and queen are consoled by the little boy they find in their baby's crib and they decide to raise him as their own. So little Zulekha grows up to be a gypsy girl, and a wild and free woman. One day, while she is singing in the forest—this will be the song we train for, Shirly—the prince—that will be you, Ana—finds her and falls in love with her beautiful song. They romance each other and grow to love each other.' Shirly could feel a concentrated pout take over her face.

Lisette continued, 'The gypsy woman meanwhile falls ill, and while she is on her deathbed, she reveals all to Zulekha. She tells her where to find the little clothes she was swaddled in as a baby, and the silver ring, and tells her to take this to the queen mother. So Zulekha finds the articles and shows them to the king and queen, who believe her. The king and queen are so happy to be finally reunited with their daughter. And the ending is happy for them when she marries the prince and they rule the kingdom.'

Yuck, thought Shirly, marry Ana? Even if it was make-believe it was nauseating. Ana was doing a better job as an actor since the unresponsive look on her face appeared to hide any misgivings she certainly had.

Shirly and Ana blinked back at Lisette. 'That is the story, girls. It is quite easy. So, let's begin with the songs.' At that moment, Lisette went alert when the phone bell began to ring in the alcove adjoining the living room.

Shirly heard Mushu's voice as he picked up the receiver. Lisette's eyes went far away as her ears sharply tuned in. 'Hello? Yes, Operator . . . yes, I will call Senhora Araujo. Please, one minute.'

Mushu walked into the salon to let Lisette know there was a phone call, but she was already off her seat. She told the girls to start reading the script while they waited for her to return.

When left to themselves, the girls didn't look at each other. Shirly pretended to pore over her script. After a few minutes, Ana broke the tense air. 'Come on, let's go see what my brothers are doing.' Ana stepped out of the room and looked back at Shirly from the doorway. 'Come on, it's okay. It's probably my father on the phone, so Mãe will take a long time,' Ana reassured her.

Curiosity overtook her wariness, and Shirly put her script on the table to follow Ana. They went up the stairs and stood in the doorway of the room where Ana's older brothers were playing with miniature toy racecars. Shirly felt shy in front of the boys, especially when she saw that one of them was the guitar player from her first session with Lisette. 'May we join in?' asked Ana fearlessly, walking into the room and motioning Shirly to follow.

One of the brothers, who looked younger than the guitar player, said, 'Girls are not allowed. Only boys can be racecar drivers. Girls can only watch. Those are the rules.'

Shirly thought he sounded rather churlish. She had never experienced this sort of sibling sexism and was glad when Ana piped in, 'Only a dumb boy would need these rules, Tomas.' The older brother remained calmly silent, while Tomas further maintained his hostile stance by crossing his arms and standing between Ana and the toy cars. Ana shot back, 'Are you scared that we're better at racecars than you could ever be?' Ana defiantly looked up into her brother's face. Wordlessly, Tomas unzipped his fly and pissed near Ana's feet. The two girls screamed—'Eeeeeeeee!' 'Muth!'—running out with Tomas's fiendish laugher trailing them.

'Run, silly girls. Go make us some cake! Maybe then we'll let you join us.' Tomas's mockery followed them down the stairs.

Mika whined as he shat on the grassy patch behind the house. The pet canine of the Araujo family turned around to sniff the lumpy blobs of his creation, raised his leg to piss on them, and kicked up some dirt on to the pile with his hind legs. Then he trotted past Ana and Shirly with an air of self-satisfaction.

The two girls had just finished their first lesson together, which had ended quickly since Lisette became preoccupied with other responsibilities. Their experience with Tomas had struck an immediate unspoken kinship between them that only those who have been discriminated against on the basis of gender could relate to. Some of their barriers had melted away, and after the session, Shirly agreed to join Ana in the yard to tickle the touch-me-nots into clamming up. Then Ana ran indoors and brought out a unique gift that she said her father, who travelled often to Portugal on work, had brought back for her on a previous trip.

'A doll?' Shirly asked contemptuously. Weren't they a little too old for dolls? She knew she was anyway.

'Not any doll, silly. It is a mama–papa doll,' said Ana. 'See, I bend it like this . . .' When Ana tipped the doll over, it said 'Mama' in an electronic voice. She tipped it over again and it said 'Papa'. Shirly was fascinated. It was more than a doll. It was a wonder of physics or a piece of magic. She hadn't ever seen a talking effigy like this, it was truly a marvel of modern technology. Then, conspiratorially, Ana added, 'If I make her drink water, she can do muth—pee-pee. We can make her do muth on Tomas and João, all over their dumb racecars.' Ana used the Konkani word for piss effortlessly, which melted the last thin film of separation between her and Shirly—her skin might be European but her gumption was definitely Goan. The adolescent girls sniggered candidly in the comfort of their new bonhomie. As Shirly looked again at Mika's offering on the grass, she was struck by an idea. She shared it with Ana, who green-lit it with a whoop of excitement.

Within the next few minutes, the girls were huddled together, hard at work on a project that completely absorbed their attention. The sound of pencils sharpening punctuated their giggles and whispers. 'You need more glue for that,' Shirly said to Ana. She handed the tub to her new friend. 'And for the final touch,' said Shirly, looking critically at their handiwork, 'the "cake" needs chocolate icing.'

Shirly used a twig and a leaf to pick up Mika's dung and carried it back to a pair of dark blue slippers that were smeared with glue and pencil shavings. She allowed the mephitic offering to fall on a rubber slipper, and, using the twig like a spatula, spread the dung on both the upper soles. The girls fell over themselves, snickering and cackling.

'Good boy, Mika!' said Ana, laugh-tears in her eyes, to the pooch who had flopped belly-down on the kitchen step, suspiciously watching the girls handle his excreta.

A while later, Shirly headed back into the salon to collect her script and take it home when she heard the doll's robotic voice say 'Mama'. Ana had just tipped her doll over, and they both snickered again. Just then, Tomas entered the room and began to conduct a search.

'What are you doing?' asked Ana nonchalantly.

'Can't find my slippers. Have you seen them?' he asked distractedly, peering under the settee. Shirly took the doll from Ana's hand and tipped it over so it said 'Papa'. Then, feigning control of their infectious sniggering simply didn't work.

'Are they blue?' asked Shirly innocently.

'Sim,' Tomas replied in the affirmative, standing up now and looking expectantly at the chuckling girls.

'Then it was probably the ones we saw João holding. He went outside with Mika and took them with him,' said Ana, mustering up her most skilful angelic tone.

Tomas stormed out of the room, which made the girls guffaw from their bellies. Before they knew it, they heard a thump. Tomas had returned with the slippers, dressed up in pencil shavings and iced with ochre dung, and he dropped them to the floor. He stood over them masked in an expression of purple anger, similar to the shade of a freshly shied-up touch-me-not. The girls did their best to suppress the peals of laughter that threatened to explode the situation. And then, things got more interesting as João strolled into the room from the kitchen, munching on a banana. He noticed everyone staring at him and then looked at the slippers on the ground.

'Wha—?' Before João could complete his sentence, Tomas came lunging at him.

'Why did you do this?' Tomas headed for his older brother, who stood his ground in bewilderment. Tomas crashed into João but his skinny limbs were no match for his older brother and he simply bounced off him.

'Estàs louco! You are the one who cannot keep your pants up!' The annoyed João retaliated by holding his younger brother away from him while being swiped at. This was the first time Shirly saw him ruffled, and she was definitely glad he wasn't directing his ire at her or his sister. Meanwhile, the half-eaten fruit in João's hand became a banana mash on the floor. The two brothers rolled and scuffled before the tables turned and it was Tomas's turn to be charged at by an annoyed João, who chased him out of the room. The sound of running footsteps was punctuated by their caveman yells and yelps, and a couple of smacks, which could have been slippers meeting flesh. Shrieking guffaws filled the room as the two freshly forged friends failed to contain themselves, falling off their perches on to the ground and tipping the doll over, who chimed in with 'Mama'.

10

The next few days were filled with Shirly and Ana's lessons with Lisette, and in school their amity grew like a surging wave, which resulted in their sense of mischief multiplying. Once, when the grade two teacher Sister Boniface took off her wimple to splash her face in the late morning heat, she forgetfully left it in the washroom. During their break, the girls found a pen and made some stars on the forehead bit. After the break, when Sister Boniface rushed to put her wimple back on before class, she didn't notice the additional handiwork. Right through the class, she couldn't understand why the students were tittering non-stop until she caught her reflection in a glass-fronted bookcase. True to her name, however, she just joined in with the laughter.

Sister Olga once heard loud squawks from inside her piano during choir practice. When she raised the lid, a chicken leapt out and began running around the room clucking wildly, sending all the girls into a squealing tizzy. Among other things, Shirly and Ana also became quite good at squeezing through a small hole in the gate to break out of school between classes—against the rules. Once, they ran down the road in the direction of Rua 31 de Janeiro. The girls scurried as fast as their skinny legs would carry them and showed up panting at the tiny shop selling ice fruit—frozen, fruit-flavoured treats on sticks. Pooling the few escudos they had between them, mostly from any pocket money their parents gave them that week, they purchased their ice fruit of choice. Then they sat on the steps of the shop, numbing their tongues on the delicious coldness while gazing up at the magnificent structure of the Liceu crowning the Altinho Hill in front of them.

'My brothers go to that school,' said Ana in between licks.

'Muth!' said Shirly when a ribbon of ice fruit melt strayed down her arm and she chased it with her tongue all the way to her elbow with a slurp. The girls giggled hysterically at the memory of getting even with Tomas. Somehow, the flavours of the ice fruit were enhanced so much more while dodging class, giving the nuns the slip and being engrossed in their palavering drolleries.

When they finished, they ran back through the narrow lanes to their school. They assisted each other through the hole, only to find themselves standing in the courtyard face-to-face with Sister Olga, who loomed up over them with her quivering lip.

'Where did you go?' she asked them in her most dangerous tone, her cross flashing angrily.

'Nowhere,' replied Ana breathlessly. Shirly turned to look at her new best friend. How easily she could defuse a tense situation with her laissez-faire style. It was thanks to her breezy brushing-aside of the messy hillock of resentment Shirley had once kept between them that their sisterhood flourished. If this sweet, kind girl, whose puckishness perfectly complemented her own impishness, were to visit her Abbé Faria garden now, she would have full rights. After all, what was Shirley's belonged to her best friend, did it not?

'Oh, really?' asked the imposing nun, crossing her arms over her ample chest.

The girls nodded unconvincingly.

Olga oh-reallyed again, uncrossed her arms, placed them on her hips, and said, 'Have you madams seen your tongues?'

With the strength of their number, which mostly felt more manifold in their hearts than in reality, the girls staved off any shamefacedness. They turned to each other and stuck out their tongues for the sake of examination. To the Sister's irritation, they remained unrepentant and snickered peskily while pointing at the other's exposition. Both their palates were stained bright orange, while Sister Olga's neck and face went sunset-purple.

It was finally on one day when Sister Olga came across the girls trying to wash away a line of ants with the garden hose that she put the fear of god and gypsies in them. They had created a pool of water in front of the chicken coop, causing rivulets to stream all the way to the courtyard. When Olga came to investigate the source of the roving runnels, she found the two girls being their usual annoying, obtuse giggly selves. She wrenched them aside by their arms to give them an earful.

'I will not tolerate any more mischief. You girls had better pull up your socks,' she said, swiftly turning off the tap that was feeding the hose. Her plump cheeks, cut into by her wimple, were particularly carmine now. She looked over at them with a face full of monsoon thunderstorms. Her lip wasn't quivering this time and the girls implicitly understood that she meant business. 'I will hand you over to the gypsies.' It sounded like an anticlimax. 'You don't believe me, do you?' She continued with dangerous calm, 'Have you seen the dhows on the water? They are filled with gypsies who have come from Arabia. They are always looking to catch young girls and boys when their families aren't watching. Then they keep them and raise them to work. You don't go to school, you don't play, you don't do anything you want. You are made to work, and if you don't, they beat you. I know some gypsies who are looking for young children. I think I am going to let them know that I have two children here whom they can take.'

Ana and Shirly both stopped laughing. Shirly recalled the dhows on the Mandovi, and suddenly their presence was more sinister. She imagined being pushed into the hold of a vessel, bound and gagged, her family unaware of her whereabouts. She would never meet her new sister or brother who was yet to be born. This was not the adventure of her imagination at all. She wanted to travel the world and do something wonderful, like discover a new continent as a free bird, not as a gypsy slave. Could this mean-spirited Sister Olga really do that to her? Shirly's greatest fear washed over her—if she was trapped in an oubliette by an evil gypsy, how would she be able to tell her parents where she was? She'd never be able to see her father or mother ever again, the two people who represented home in the truest sense for her. For once, her face turned serious.

'Now go to your class and sit there the whole day. I don't want to see you in the courtyard at all!' the nun barked in her deep voice.

The girls scooted upstairs to their class. Shirly was quite shaken by Sister Olga's intimidation; it felt real and visceral. She sat at the desk clutching her stomach in fear. Her newly developing insubordination still had her retain an innocent belief in the face of threats from an adult where her well-being was at stake. She couldn't understand why Ana seemed as relaxed as she did.

'What's wrong?' asked Ana.

'I'm really scared,' said Shirly in a small voice, 'I don't want her to give us to the gypsies.'

'She's only joking, she won't do anything,' said Ana confidently. Shirly was grateful for her friend's kind response, but clearly she didn't have the imagination to foresee the possibilities of a very real peril. Had she learnt nothing from the narrative of their musical?

Shirly wouldn't be consoled that day. Even though Ana suggested they go to the courtyard in the second break, she sat at her desk, clinging to it for life, like to driftwood in an open sea, obediently waiting till the school bell released the students for the day.

11

For a week, the main topic of conversation in the Quarachim household was the upcoming dinner party at the Araujo residence. Deepak and Mamtu had received hand-delivered invitations and decided that Shirly and Devika could accompany them. While the grown-ups mingled, the children could play with each other. It was going to be a grandiose gathering with a mix of important people in society. Even the fish-seller gleefully recounted to Goku the extra business she received that week. Meanwhile, Mamtu was busy on her sewing machine, the roar of her foot treadle filling the air as fabrics were stitched together to shape the clothes that she and her family would wear. For Deepak, it would be a well-tailored suit with a black smoking dinner jacket and a bowtie. Mamtu would wear a peach chiffon sari, and the girls had matching frocks in different colours. Shirly wasn't pleased about this, but it made Devika very happy to be like her older sister in any way.

Even though Ana's house was just a block away, Deepak's hired driver drove them there in the Pontiac. They were ushered by uniformed help into the large living room that Shirly was now familiar with. However, evening had transformed the Araujo living room with soft, warm light waterfalling from two large ceiling chandeliers. The tinkle of clinking crystal punctuated the murmur of conversation in the room. A liveried and white-gloved Mushu came around aristocratic guests bearing amuse-bouche delicacies on fine, gilt-edged delftware. With the effulgent chandeliers overhead casting a shimmer on every surface, the best table linen and crystal on display, and the elegantly dressed guests gliding around the room, the familiar place appeared like something out of a fairytale. Shirly and her sister stuck close to their parents' legs.

Spotting the Quarachims, Lisette came up to them with characteristically sincere amiability. She was dressed in a long powder-blue ballgown that accentuated her tall, slim frame.

'Bem vindos! I am so happy to see you all.' She shook hands with Shirly's parents, gave Shirly a light hug and, bending down, said obligingly to Devika, 'You must be the little princess of this family,' which made Shirly's younger sister smile and blush. Shirly couldn't help noticing the way Lisette's form was outlined by her close-fitting gown and the heady perfume that wafted from her. These had such a grown-up tangibility to them. For the first time, Shirly felt conscious of her own body, still lacking the girth of maturity, but not without some of her angles softened and a waist delicately chiselling itself into her torso.

Lisette steered the Quarachims in and introduced them to clusters of guests, most of whom appeared to know Deepak. Mamtu was the only woman in the room attired in a sari and was immediately surrounded by a few ladies admiring its fine embroidery. Portuguese Europeans were stocky and mostly burnished in complexion, so the present gathering of European and native residents was an assortment of biscuit shades from a butter-cookie tin united by their citizenship on the banks of the Mandovi.

Shirly wondered where Ana was. She walked across the room along with her mother to take a seat, passing through mists of varied conversations.

'We are just so busy from now on. There will be the Feast, then Christmas and, soon after, preparations for Carnaval next year. I just don't know how we will be able to take care of our house guests adequately,' said Irma da Costa, a woman who prided herself on being a descendente, born in Goa itself with European parentage. 'Who do you think the next King Momo will be?'

'No, it's not true. Goa is most definitely not a colony. We are an "overseas province". Think of it like an overseas Portugal,' said Christian Menezes, a plump, well-dressed man of native origin, with a walrus moustache. He was accompanied by his wife, Maria Menezes, who was dressed in de rigueur fashion from Lisbon.

'Well, what's the difference?' asked Clara Lopes, a descendente in Menezes's conversational circle.

'The economics of a colony is to take wealth away and enrich the country. But the entire revenue from Goa, which is around 24 crore escudos per year, is utilized to pay for the import requirements of Goa-Portuguesa. Nothing goes to the exchequer in Portugal. We are, after all, every one of us in Goa, Damão and Diu, Portuguese,' Christian responded loudly, as though he wanted to be heard by all present. The people around him clinked their wine glasses in agreement.

'Thankfully, the slave trade is abolished. Ghastly business that was,' Teodoro da Costa, Irma's husband, was saying in another conversational orbit with the Quarachims. 'Our housemaid Bistui told us the story of her grandparents who were brought from Mozambique. You will never guess where they were harboured. In your home, Quarachim! Your house used to be a storage unit for slaves, can you believe it!'

'Is it true?' asked Mamtu incredulously.

'Yes, Bistui herself told me,' said Teodoro. 'She was told by her mother, who was told by her mother. No matter now, she is Portuguese like we all are, and the first one in her family to receive a salary.'

Shirly tried to imagine her residence as a site with slaves in clanking chains. The gypsies may have had some hand to play in it too. She felt relief that she lived in this present time, where everyone was fully free in this city of her birth.

'Our city has a lot of history, it is true,' agreed Deepak, sipping on a glass of gin.

'Yes,' said Eugenio, Ana's father, joining the group. 'I recently came across some documents alleging there was a secret tunnel between the Palácio do Idalcão and the fazenda.'

'What for?' asked Mamtu.

'Well, it was at the time of the Mughal ruler Adil Shah. Then of course there was no fazenda, only a building. The harem was probably located there. A good idea for someone who may have needed to make a secretive trip.' Eugenio winked and received a light slap on the arm from his wife. 'A harem in the fazenda and slaves in your house, Mr Quarachim. Our Nova Goa isn't as exciting as it once was, it seems.'

Ana appeared through the guests and came up to Shirly, whose spirits visibly lifted, grateful to be rescued from the conversations that had no consequence on the world of her adolescent preoccupations. Would she get a glimpse of João once more?

Mamtu nodded her approval for Shirly and Devika to accompany Ana. Devika clung to Mamtu's knee and stayed behind while Ana escorted her very willing friend upstairs to her bedroom. It was a broad, spacious room, with Ana's postered bed on one side, and her school things, toys and davenport on the other. An adjoining door led to her brothers' shared room, which appeared empty at the moment. Shirly was drawn to the window as she always was and looked out through the open panes to the building opposite.

Music from the two-storeyed building across the road wafted in. Shops concatenated with a portico at the lower level were shuttered closed at this time. On the second level was a wooden verandah that fronted it with several arched doorways framing a ballroom where women in dresses and heels swirled around with men in dapper suits. This was a building at the rear of her own home, but she had never paid attention before and was mesmerized by the scene.

'What is that?' she asked Ana, who joined her at the window.

'Oh, that's Clube Nacional.'

'What is that?' she found herself repeating.

'It's just a place where people go dancing,' said Ana, who was used to this sight every Saturday evening.

Shirly's eyes travelled with one couple, the woman in a cobalt gown with matching cobalt dancing heels moving backwards as her partner led with quick steps, turning her around every so often. As she searched out the bright blue that disappeared behind the columns and then reappeared within the openings of the archways between them, another couple captured her fancy. The woman wore a knee-length red dress with stockings and black heels and was led by a man in a white smoking jacket. Shirly had never witnessed such glamour at close quarters in one evening and was delighted with all the twisting and turning well-heeled feet. She found herself noticing the way the men had their hands on their partners' waists, cognizant of the way their bodies kept a yearning distance between each other and yet moved in unison.

'You want to play marbles?'

Shirly turned around to see João leaning against the threshold, looking directly at the girls. The sudden sight of his attractive, intelligent eyes and smooth, sun-browned skin over his nascent, ridging cheekbones had the involuntary result of her breath catching in her chest.

'You want us to join you?' Ana's thoughts echoed Shirly's.

'Yeah. You want to or no?'

'Yes . . . Shirly, come, let's shoot marbles,' said Ana without hesitation, unaware of the new sensations her friend was experiencing.

Shirly was thrilled and terrified when João's eyes lingered on hers for a long second before all three headed to the adjoining room the brothers occupied. Negotiating one's upspringing hormones is an intricate and perplexing business for the emotional body.

'Where is Tomas?' asked Ana, remarking that her younger brother was amiss, accounting for why it was so quiet.

'He must be sulking somewhere else around the house,' said João. 'He still suspects me for the slipper trick you naughty girls pulled.' The grin on João's face told Shirly and Ana that he was a sport and didn't give the girls away to Tomas. Shirly felt safe around his good-humoured balance. João extracted a pouch from his school satchel and released its contents on to the floor gently. A few marbles came rolling out on the tiles noisily. Shirly picked one up and held it to her eye. They looked like the washers that stoppered guddi-soda bottles, but somehow with more swirls and bubbles entombed in the transparent glassiness. Shirly was mesmerized by some that looked like they had a 'cat's eye' enshrined within, which she found as enigmatic as they were hypnotic.

João showed them how to place a marble on the ground and then to fire another one using a stretched-back thumb or forefinger. That marble cannonballed forward to hit the stationary marble on the ground. Whoever got the most hits got the most points. On the first try, both girls misfired so João carefully showed them again. He held the marble against Ana's hand first and, using his own, pulled back the 'trigger' finger.

'Like that,' he said. With a cracking sound, Ana's marble hit the target, and she whooped. He turned to Shirly, who felt a shyness cloak her from head to toe. João's eyes were hazel, with swirls of kindness in them. She somehow felt at home and a fizzy excitement to be here with him, learning the intricacies of how to flick a marble. There was an unaccustomed intimacy with his hands touching her own, his face so near hers—concentrating on the marble before them, she could see his breath through his slightly parted archer's-bow lips. The noise of marble on marble splitting the air jolted Shirly and she let out a small shriek of delight. With their new ability, she and Ana picked up marbles randomly and started flicking them at each other.

'Ow!' said João when one struck him on his knee, and he joined in the fray. Soon, they were flicking anything they could get their hands on. Pencils, erasers, toy soldiers, dinky cars . . .

'Not the cars, they'll break,' João said protectively.

'Will a slipper break?' asked Ana, holding up one of his as if ready to flick, with a cat glint in her eye.

'I'm . . . going . . . to . . .' João slowly picked himself up and moved stealthily like a panther, 'tickle you!' He lunged at his sister with this threat. Ana was ambushed and wriggled under her brother's attack. She screamed here and there till uncontrolled tears of laughter rolled down her cheeks. Shirly stood on the sidelines in amusement. When Ana couldn't take any more, she broke away from João's grip and rushed out the door, as though drunk, and down the stairs. João looked at

Shirly for a moment, both grinning conspiratorially at each other. Unexpectedly, João gently touched the side of her head and her cheek. She didn't flinch. Outside first, and then within. They held the quietude between them till he said, 'Let's go find Ana.'

Shirly followed João's lean shoulders leading the way down the stairs. She made out the back of Ana's head at the foot of the stairs, which was in the alcove between the kitchen and the archway to the living room full of guests. She was sitting to the far left of the stairs, her shoulder to the wall, and out of view of the crowd outside. The two caught up with her and joined her on the stairs, peering into the other room from where the sounds of a poignantly melodious voice came drifting in.

Lisette was seated at the piano, her hands gently rising and falling on the keys, singing. The song was in Portuguese and its mood sounded so profound and mournful, evoking a faraway feeling, as though something or someone was lost. In the marble of Shirly's emotional world, she held the recent memory of João's delicious touch to her cheek like a coloured swirl as Lisette held the room entranced with vocal tones that seemed to emerge from the depths of the earth itself. As the song slinked to a gentle ending with a final chime of piano notes that was pure pathos, the room was enrobed in reverent silence.

'Viva!' A guest started clapping appreciatively, which began a wave of applause through the room.

'Que saudade!'

'Viva Lisboa!'

'Viva Dona Lisette!'

Lisette stood up and gave a little curtsy to her guests before placing the lid on the piano keys. Shirly watched her move gracefully through the room with new eyes and understanding for her friend's mother and her teacher.

'So beautiful,' she said to Ana and João. 'What is that song?'

'That one is "Ai Ai Lisboa",' responded Ana. 'It is fado.'

'Fado?' asked Shirly.

'Yes,' said Ana. 'My mother loves fado, a special type of song everybody likes to sing in Portugal.'

'She is a very good singer,' said Shirly humbly.

'Yes,' agreed João. 'Even Amália wanted to sing with her.'

'Amália?' Shirly asked.

'Amália Rodrigues, the most famous fadista in Europe. Amália was planning a programme and wanted her to join.'

'What happened?' asked Shirly.

'She was getting married to my father at the time. And they were preparing to move here from Lisboa for his work,' João explained.

Shirly didn't know how to respond so she silently looked over at Lisette once more with renewed respect. Then her attention wandered over to a man of medium height in the centre of the room, who now commanded several eyes on him. He was in ordinary clothes and yet Shirly recognized him immediately. He was the police agente at the beach and the one who had drowned her paper boat. Shirly bristled on the inside and hid herself further behind João's frame.

'As I was saying earlier, he is a genius of economics. Our only exports are wine and olive oil. And yet, we are one of the greatest nations spread all around the world, truly a pluri continental country. Neither capitalist nor communist, the Estado Novo is the greatest idea. Private ownership of the means of production while the State balances this out with regulation. So let's all raise a toast to the finest leader for Portuguese glory—viva António de Oliveira Salazar!'

'*Viva*!' Everyone in the room raised the glasses they were holding following the agente's cue. There was silence at first, then the gentle murmur of regular conversation resumed.

'Who is that?' whispered Shirly.

'That's Agente Monteiro,' said João in a hushed tone. 'He's not very nice.'

'Yes, I know!' Shirly exclaimed in a whisper. 'He was arresting men on the beach. I saw him a while ago.' She caught Ana's knowing look and remembered that she had been there too.

At that moment, Agente Monteiro stepped closer to a group where Deepak was standing. 'A successful business is the sign of the times,' said Monteiro. 'Isn't it, Mr Quarachim?' The agente looked directly at Deepak.

'Peace among the citizens is a sign of the times,' ventured Deepak a little boldly, inviting loud silence.

Christian broke in to defuse the troubled quiet with amiable punchiness. 'For a businessman to be successful he must have the three M's—motorcar, mines and mistress! Eh?' He looked at Clara Lopes, who just rolled her eyes.

'Why is he here?' whispered Shirly, back at the staircase in the alcove.

'Well, our parents are not really his friends. Don't you know?' asked Ana.

'Know what?' asked Shirly.

'Anytime there is a gathering of several people, we need to take permission. It's the law,' explained João.

'Permission?'

'Yes. After Mãe printed out the party invitations, we had to send them to the police station for approval. Anything and everything that is printed for distribution has to be checked. Just like our newspapers. Nothing goes through without first sending them to the corpo de polícia. And just to make sure there is no trouble, the police drop in. He was not really invited, but he has invited himself and no one can do anything about it.'

'He sounds like a . . . bad, bad . . . man,' Shirly spluttered for lack of an adequate way to express how she felt about the agente. Her world tilted off-centre. She looked out at the sparkling party, with the shiny crystal glasses and beautifully dressed people; the cream of society gathered in the crowning city of Estado da Índia. How could something be so wrong in a world that appeared right?

'Clearly there is one person in the room who doesn't think so,' João nodded in the direction of a young admirer by the agente's side. The younger Araujo brother was holding a glass of port, poured by his father from a carafe on the liquor cabinet. As Tomas handed the drink to Monteiro, the policeman mock-saluted him.

'You want to be an agente?' asked Monteiro, pleased with the attention from his young devotee.

Dazzled by recognition from his hero, Tomas proudly stuck his chest out and saluted back. 'Yes, Agente.'

Ana rolled her eyes at João.

12

Deepak tipped his head back deeply and drained the last drops of guddi-soda. He handed the empty green bottle back to the vendor and headed for the Willys, parked on the side of the intersection. The passenger seat was empty this time. Even though it was the weekend, Shirly had a music session with Lisette for the upcoming Christmas show and couldn't accompany her father on this trip. Deepak was headed to the mines as usual to check on operations. As the Willys bounced through rough macadam, he could hear the metallic sound of the cashew tin's clasp in the back. Deepak had decided it would be a quick visit; he wanted to return home before the sky would be obliterated of light and well in time to have dinner with the family. Beyond Sanquelim, he turned off the main road and trundled down the familiar forest dirt track. Dreaming about the fragrant and steaming chicken curry waiting for him at home, he remained oblivious to the lengthening shadows of the thicket closing in, grasping at him with hungry fingers.

'No, Shirly, no,' said Lisette. 'Try again.'

Shirly looked at the lines on her sheet once more, reading off them to sing out. 'Water droplets on leaves, dance like diamonds for me . . .'

'Não, your timing, Shirly, on the count of four. Okay, again. One, two, three, four . . .'

'Water droplets . . .'

'That was too early now. Try again.'

'Water droplets on leaves, dance like diamonds for me.'

'Better . . . keep going . . .'

'The light on the river, valuable silver . . .'

Shirly stopped abruptly when she saw Lisette wasn't looking pleased at all.

'Now what's wrong? I started on time . . .'

'Yes, you did, dear. But maybe we need to go back to some basics. Follow after me,' said Lisette and playing the notes on the piano, sang out, 'Ma, mey, mi, mo, mou!'

Shirly hesitated. And then repeated without conviction, 'Ma, mey, mi, mo, mou.'

Lisette ignored all the faults. 'Good, again.' And again they repeated. 'Let's go higher now, up the scale. Ma, mey, mi, mo, mou!' she suggested a few tries later.

'Ma, mey, mi, mo, mou,' Shirly wasn't out of tune but she just didn't have the resonance of Lisette's voice, which inhibited her further. Lisette wasn't dissuaded.

'Good,' said Lisette. 'Higher.'

'Ma, mey, mi, mo,' Shirly tried to muffle her giggle before finishing these notes—mostly sounding like gibberish to her and making her feel like a village cow.

'Oh, dear, is this funny to you?' Lisette certainly wasn't infectiously laughing along with her as Shirly hoped she would. In fact, to add to her pupil's overstrained state, Lisette wasn't easily amused at all. 'Perhaps we should end for today?' Lisette's terseness surprised her. Her own parents would have found a way to indulge her, but Lisette seemed to be a different kettle of adult. Polite, kind and yet firm when required. She even respected her more for not putting up with her gaffe. 'The show is just a month and a half away and you think that this is the time to laugh? Do you not like the play?'

Shirly didn't like being chided by Ana's mother. Or anyone else's mother. She shook her head.

'Do you not like the songs?'

Once more, Shirly, resolving to be more grown-up than ever, shook her head.

'Would you like to go straight for the play without practising?'

Once more, no.

'Okay, then, young lady, let's try to practise properly?'

Yes, she was a young lady and would prove it. Shirly nodded her head yes, vowing to be more responsible with their time, to focus.

'Okay, once more, and . . .' Lisette nodded at Shirly to join in with her.

'Ma, mey, mi, mo, mou!' their voices mingled up and down the scale.

After the trying lesson with Lisette, Shirly walked home slowly through the narrow streets, unable to savour the delicious falling light of the sky, the hour right before dusk took over. There was too much noise in her head. So many thoughts snaked and hissed in her brain and she felt that she needed so much more practise with Lisette before she could have the gumption to get on stage and deliver her performance. She was simply unable to hit the notes in her solo song. Every time she sang them, she sounded flat to herself. She wasn't a singer, and this Sisyphean role wasn't ever what she would have chosen for herself. So it wasn't fair that she was feeling so punished by the process. But now that she had got the part something in her didn't want to let go. Perhaps the pride she had seen in her mother and father's eyes when they found out she was in the musical. It was cause enough for her to skip out on an outing to the mines with her father. She had to fix her song somehow. But how was the question, to which she didn't quite know the answer.

Mamtu rubbed the masalas on the chicken breasts and thighs, exactly like her grandmother had taught her. Goku, who sat on the floor shelling peas, stood up when she finished her task and, collecting the spiced chicken from her, put all the ingredients into the pot on the woodfire stove. As the dish simmered on low heat, releasing its aromas, Mamtu was transported to her grandmother's kitchen in Karachi as a child.

She remembered running around the grand old lady, who was usually seated on her kitchen floor chopping ingredients or at the stove tending to a meal. The youngest of five sisters and a brother, Mamtu never lacked company or games to indulge in. And being the smallest, both in age and size, she could easily hide under her grandmother's underskirts and evade being caught out by the rest during hide-and-seek sessions.

Mamtu had lost her mother just a few years after her birth, during the plague. As a result, she was raised by her doting grandmother, who was fiercely protective of her. The matriarch had given nicknames to Mamtu and her siblings, each one inspired by a local Sindhi food. The eldest brother, Doulatram, she called 'pakwan', a crisp bread, for being heavy and strong but fragile at heart; her eldest sister after him, Mehek, she'd call 'alu tuk', fried potato, for her wide girth but universally adored character; next was Nandita, whom she called 'pallo', a quick and quiet river fish; Indira was known as 'karela', a bitter gourd; Chitra was 'bhee', lotus stem, watery and full of holes, referring to her daydreaming nature; and finally, Mamtu was 'thadal', a sweet and cool drink.

Mamtu's father was a moneylender who was usually too busy for his children. When he wasn't working on his accounts, he tried to forget the sadness of the loss of his wife by attending Sufi concerts, usually hosted by one of his several clients. As time went by, one by one, he arranged to have his children married and, one by one, they left Mamtu's life. Each of them went on to settle in different parts of the world with their spouses.

When she turned twenty, Mamtu's grandmother found it difficult to arrange a suitable match for her. 'Saint Jhulelal will give you the best husband, don't you worry. Anyway, what will I do without you, my thadal?' she'd say, dragging on her beedi with her chai and releasing a plume of smoke in front of her.

Mamtu always responded the same way. 'I'll take you with me, wherever I go.' This usually delighted the old lady and she'd pull out a neatly wrapped, saffron-scented boondi laddoo from the pocket of her skirts and watch as her granddaughter smacked her lips. The hearth fed Mamtu's soul. Food and love and home were interchangeable ideas for her. This was her grandmother's legacy to her, which she tied to herself like apron strings and sought to recreate in her Panjim kitchen.

Mamtu walked over to Goku, stirring the pot. She spooned a small amount of the curried Mughlai gravy on to her open palm and brought it to her lips. It needed salt and more cream. Deepak definitely preferred it with the heaviness of cream to counter the cooler nights and feel fuller. He would be famished on returning from the mines.

The Mughlai chicken was the first dish they had ever eaten together, she mused, a slow smile spreading on her lips. Deepak had first seen her when he came to visit her father as a new client. He was exiting the outer compound of her haveli as she and her grandmother were returning from purchasing fabric at the market on their horse-drawn carriage. One passing glimpse of her was enough. Deepak began to stand at the corner of her street every day and knew exactly when she left and when she arrived. Then, one day, as Mamtu was returning home, her carriage came to a sudden halt in the middle of the road. 'What's happened?' her grandmother asked the driver. Mamtu craned to look in front of the horses, and that's when she first saw her future husband. Lying on the road, blocking her carriage, was young Deepak, pretending to be asleep.

The carriage driver and her grandmother were furious when he simply jumped up, dusted himself off, winked at her mischievously and walked away. But young Mamtu found it funny. And more flattering than vexing. That night, she thought about the attractive man who had tried so hard to get her attention. To her happy surprise, he was a guest of her father's at their haveli the next evening. She was so pleased to see him she didn't pay attention to the reason he was there as they all tucked into her grandmother's Mughlai chicken curry. Something to do with his new business in a place called Goa.

Deepak won her and her family over easily, even the old lady, who made sure that Mamtu learnt how to make his favourite dishes.

They were married in a few months' time, and she had to move away from her grandmother, who refused to leave her natal city. 'Return to me whenever you can,' she instructed her in a quaky voice. But her soul slipped out of her body a few weeks after Mamtu, her heart, left.

And then the next tragedy struck. Within the year, Partition took place. Every year, Mamtu promised to return to visit her father, who was ailing and alone in their sprawling old house until he was finally taken abroad to live with her eldest brother, who had settled with his family in Gibraltar.

Together, she and Deepak had decided to be modern and have a small family—only the five of them, with the last one on the way. In the swirl of her family life, she enjoyed the process of losing herself to her maternal instincts. But she had one desire that flamed up strongly within her like the rising sun: to return to the familiarity of her home. After all, her family's large property was probably still there. Perhaps, one day, they could all move back and she could show her children the Karachi of her youth. One day, she promised herself, as the spiced scent of her grandmother's kitchen filled the room.

13

As they approached the Aguada prison, the driver parked the Pontiac under an Indian laurel tree and turned the key to switch off the engine. Mamtu's eyes appeared veined and red from crying. Even in sadness, Shirly found her mother beautiful, with her soft, framed face and the fresh wetness on her long lashes. She knew her mother hadn't slept much the previous night and had instead sat in front of the altar in her room, sending strings of prayers up to Saint Jhulelal.

They stepped out of the car, and the sound of its doors shutting was deafening in the picturesque silence. On their left, the ocean lay like a glittery blue suspension, spreading itself all the way to the sky-blue horizon. Waves crashed on the boulders under the palisade they stood on, and the breeze tangoed aggressively in their hair. It was a bright day, and nature was full of mirth. It definitely wasn't a day to visit a prison.

The prison lay at the foot of a scarp that had a lighthouse where sentries bearing rifles and bayonets stood in front of large iron gates. Overhead, an arched sign bore the name of the jail. Any visitor here would have trouble accepting the graveness of the situation, with the sight of artillery juxtaposed with the balmy air and wild scenery.

The gates were opened for Michael, Shirly and her mother. Before they left the house this morning, Mamtu had decided that Devika was too young to come along and so she was left in Goku's care at home. Mamtu knew she couldn't keep her older daughter away and was, in fact, glad to lean on her in her fragile state. To the right were the offices—Luso-Goan style with lateritious earthen tiles, complete with porticoes and verandahs. Spotting the mother and daughter, who fidgeted quite nervously, looking out of place, a European-looking soldier in khaki shorts walked over to them from his desk. Michael introduced them as the family of Senhor Deepak Quarachim and said that they wished to meet him.

'Please wait inside.' The soldier, noticing a very pregnant Mamtu, gestured to the three to step into his office and take a seat. Then he headed to another bureau at the end of the long row of offices that lined the entrance to the prison. He returned after a minute with a logbook. 'Do you have the letter?'

'Yes, from the Panjim Police Station,' Michael said to the officer, handing him the official letter authorizing them to visit Deepak in prison. He had hastily procured it that morning. Mamtu gave him a look of relief and gratitude.

'Please write down your names,' the officer handed Michael a pen and tapped on a line with his finger. Michael scribbled all their names in the book and handed it back to the officer.

'Please, what is he arrested for? We don't even know.'

'Senhora, it is for sedition,' replied the officer calmly, as though he were announcing the price of cashews.

Sedition. Mamtu wasn't even sure what the word meant, but it sounded so bold and treasonous that she inhaled sharply and held her hand to her faint heart.

The officer motioned for all three to follow him out. He led them past the offices that opened out to a small courtyard on the right with a jackfruit tree and a well. They walked towards a building block that ran perpendicular to the sea on the left. The first storey had offices that belonged to the prison commandant so he could survey everything around him on land and sea. The row of offices stood like an overhanging bridge, below which was a wide tunnel with several archways. The officer asked them to wait on a bench there and disappeared down a long, open-air walkway into the bowels of a gated door.

After about fifteen minutes, the officer reappeared out of the sunlight, tramping back with a second person in tow. 'Daddy!' Shirly exclaimed, a shuddering echo boomeranging under the chambered arches. Mamtu pulled herself to her feet, her full stomach rising first, her tears reflecting a sea in spate within her eyes. As Deepak drew nearer, he came forward hurriedly and held Mamtu in his arms. He bent down, gave her belly a kiss, and then opened his embrace to scoop up his daughter. Shirly felt scrutinized by the officer who stood just at the edge of the archway. She also noticed that her limbs were getting to be too long and weighty to let herself be picked up in her father's arms, but she allowed him to hold her up off the ground.

'I've missed all my girls,' said Deepak with his usual warmth in a steady voice, as though unaffected by the circumstances. When he released both of them, he turned to Michael. 'Thank you for bringing them.' Deepak drew them to sit in an arched alcove and nodded in the officer's direction, who now turned his back to them, arms crossed, facing the ocean. 'He said I have only ten minutes.'

'What happened, Deepak? Why do they think . . . why prison . . . what is . . .?' Mamtu's anguish came tumbling out like a landslide, without a semblance of order. She desperately wanted to know why her husband had been arrested like a common criminal—or worse, an uncommon one.

'Mamtu, please don't worry. It is all a mistake, they will find out soon,' Deepak tried to reassure her, hoping to keep the emotional barometer in the big-little world of his family calibrated to normal.

Mamtu's breathing reverberated through the echoing chamber. After a minute of silence, more composed, she spoke, 'How can they make such a mistake? You wouldn't hurt anyone. I don't understand, Deepak.' Then, with grim intensity, she added, 'They said that it is sedition.'

'I know,' he said quietly. 'Do you trust me? I promise I will be out soon. In the meantime, I need you to be strong for the girls.'

'Is there anything we can do, Patrão?' asked Michael apprehensively.

'There is nothing that needs to be done. It is all a mistake and they will realize it soon. I am innocent and have done nothing. I suspect that there are suspicious activities and people who must harbour ill will. It will all wash away soon. Just yesterday when I was put in the prison cell, the other inmates informed me that another man had vacated the place in the morning since he was found to be innocent.'

'But who could harbour such ill will?' Mamtu asked insistently, her lashes wet and fluttery.

'I don't know, my dear, but I will find out. In the meantime, smile for me?'

Shirly watched her mother manage a weak upturn at the corners of her lips through streaks of tears and vicariously did the same, for her father's sake. Her wonderful, strong, kind, good father. This was all surely a mistake, and nothing would happen to him. He would return in a day or so and they would once again gallivant off the track for ice cream and adventure, perhaps to the Oilem Aravalem waterfalls. The officer strode towards the family. 'Time is up. Please say goodbye.'

Mamtu motioned to Michael. 'I brought you some sheets and a few changes of clothes, and your shaving kit, and your toothbrush and your comb and . . .' Michael handed over the bundle of cloth he was lugging around under his arm to Mamtu. She opened it to show her husband and the officer its contents.

'Senhor?'

The officer inspected all the goods and okayed them but pulled the razor out. Mamtu retied the four ends of the cloth, which contained all the basics for her husband's use, to resemble a washerman's bundle. Deepak rose, and so did Mamtu and Shirly. He hugged them once, shook Michael's hand and let the officer lead him out into the sunlight, across the leafy pathway on the other side of the archway towards the great big door with multiple heavyset iron bolts.

Once he left, Mamtu's sniffles ricocheted off the stone walls and ceiling. The visitors stood there together in silence till Deepak was out of sight and then ambled towards the sunlight on their side of the arched bridgeway. They stood looking at the waves crashing against the boulders in front of the crenellated fort walls lined up with stone cannons, and Shirly felt an ocean of helpless sadness within her till the officer returned and led them out the gate.

Deepak carried his bundle of sheets and toiletries under his arm and fell in step shoulder-to-shoulder with the officer who had taken him to meet his family. They walked in silence past rusty cannons that pointed out from the embrasures of the fort walls, all trained on the glossy ocean. He could see the Gaspar Dias estuary where the Mandovi met the Arabian Sea, where all his happiness with his family lay, out of his reach. It was a clear day, and if he concentrated enough he believed he could see the Mormugao harbour in the pearly distance, where the ships came to dock with goods and ferried the ore of the land beyond Goan shores. The breeze came in intermittent gusts. It played in his hair and soothed the growing despondency in his soul. If one had to be in a prison, this would be the most beautiful one they could be trapped in. In fact, this could easily be the venue for a soirée or a music festival. However, the stories he would find out over the next few days were far from breezy.

He would learn that the only reason he was at the Aguada prison was because the Panjim prison was full to capacity. The inmates who were transferred here after suffering the lashings of Agente Monteiro would show him the disfiguring scars they had received all over their bodies. They would insist they were the lucky ones, since they weren't tortured to death. Monteiro's goons would hold down a prisoner they were interrogating while he took his shots and swung at them with various truncheons and sticks. The inmates were sure he enjoyed having such absolute control over the pain another human experienced and would swear they saw him smile from his dark eyes every time baton violently met flesh. Some would openly admit they wished for freedom for Goa from Portugal, just so Monteiro wouldn't have any more control over them.

Deepak's fellow prisoners would turn out to be a ragtag bunch. A few unfortunates who had found themselves in the wrong place at the wrong time or in the wrong company. Apparently, one fellow had been arrested simply for shouting loudly while he walked past the Portuguese flag, mistakenly believed to be abusing the government. Once suspicion was cast, there was no escaping the wary omniscient eye of the agente, and the target would be hooked and booked in a flash. Agente Monteiro wasn't above accepting a bribe here and there, and some lucky fellows who had the means could buy themselves a less severe punishment. Word got around that the agente didn't gain as much pleasure from prisoners involved in non-violent movements as he did with those who took part in armed movements; just so that the crime could justify the increased ferocity of punishment.

Some prisoners were new. They could be distinguished by the fact that their spirits were still buoyant, like Deepak. Some had been languishing there for years, like the prisoner from Daman, another territory under the Portuguese flag along with Goa and Diu. He was simply forgotten. Even he didn't remember the real reason for which he was jailed. So every month he invented a new felony to his credit. In October it was for being a satyagrahi. In November it was for indecent exposure.

One of the inmates Deepak befriended was a young fellow named Clinton. However, since trust is a rare earth in prison, neither of them asked each other about their political leanings. They spoke about everything else.

'Aguada means "watering place",' Clinton would say on one of their open-air rounds in the outer courtyard of the men's prison, where Biblical phrases were painted on a shabby brick wall, 'Ask and you shall receive', 'Seek and you shall find', 'Knock and the door will be opened unto you'. High walls spiked with broken glass separated the courtyard from the ocean below and freedom beyond. 'This place is named for the freshwater spring within it, which passing ships would use to replenish their stores.'

'If someone wants to get us out, that's the way,' Clinton would point to the fort walls on the cliff above, but Deepak's eyes would sweep past them to the lighthouse. Deepak knew it well, as did all of Panjim since its beam of light swept the coast every few minutes on ink-steeped nights. Deepak would now find the silent swish of the rhythmic light strobe reassuring as it lit up the water. A small mercy to ensure that this corner of the world wasn't forgotten. He shuddered to think of being shut away in the one room that every prisoner dreaded: the Dark Cell. With a small square of iron bars on a padlocked door, it was as black as a matchbox inside, utilized to condemn prisoners if they got on the wrong side of the fort's highest authority, the commandant.

On some mornings, new inmates would be trundled in via a Black Maria. They were mostly transfers from the other overflowing prisons in Panjim, Altinho, Mapuçá or Bicholim. Deepak realized how little he knew of what the government was hiding under its coattails. For each of these 'law-breakers', there was nothing soft to break the fall from honourable society. There was no mat or bedding available, and inmates had to depend on the kindness of their families, if they could visit. The cold stone floor was literally the only comfort they had while trying to rest.

Deepak realized that the jail had women prisoners as well, but they were in separate quarters.

Deepak walked past the courtyard through a warren of stairways to his cell block. He didn't know how much longer he would be in this aberrantly briny situation. He gripped his belongings as the cell door clanged shut and was padlocked again, the quiet eyes of other lonely strangers within the prison on him.

14

'Very good! You are hitting the notes so much better. Have some water and let's break for five minutes.' At her mother's insistence, to maintain some semblance of normalcy, Shirly was adhering to her daily routine. And so, she was at her music lesson, with Lisette at the piano. However, although her solfège was much improved from when she first started to practise, she felt like a jet-black flat note on the inside. Ever since she heard about her father's imprisonment two days ago, a big piece of iron ore seemed to have lodged itself in the pit of her stomach. And seeing her father the previous day, dishevelled and unshaved, had shaken Shirly's world. Life took on a surreal inconsistency now, as though anything dreadful was possible—the fan might unhinge and fly around the room like a propellor, or the grandfather clock could melt and completely annihilate any sense of time.

At school, she didn't fully seem to inhabit her body as her mind flitted like a paper boat in the stream of several thoughts. She imagined her father in prison, then imagined her whole family in prison. Not one to rein in her imagination, flaming like a petromax lantern, she visualized them being tortured, then paraded outside, hung upside down on the flagpole for all to see, and sold off to hungry, grubby-looking gypsies. Ana simply couldn't persuade her to relax and join in the game of hoops downstairs. The nuns noticed her distraction but were kind enough to let her be. Even Sister Olga used her most tender voice when calling out her name for attendance.

After school, Shirly and Ana walked over sombrely to Ana's house for her voice-training session with Lisette. The play was only a month away and soon there would be longer rehearsals with the rest of the cast. Lisette had said that this week Shirly would focus on her solo song, the one in the forest where she was secretly spotted and watched by the prince before he fell in love with her. Shirly had misgivings about being ready for it. She still had a long path ahead of her to sound even a notch above respectable, and the song would only really work if she sang beautifully. No prince would easily lose their heart to someone with a monsoon frog in their throat. Especially a flat one.

'And one and two . . . water droplets on leaves . . . follow me . . .' Lisette began Zulekha's solo, nodding at Shirly to repeat after her. Shirly was far away in her thoughts once more, this time considering if she too were imprisoned then she wouldn't need to sing at all. 'Repeat after me, Shirly . . .' Lisette tried to bring her back.

'Waaa-ter dro-op-lets on leaves!' she followed, snapping to sudden attention, causing her voice to spill out of tune.

'Well, let's try once more,' said Lisette patiently and prompted her again.

Shirly struggled to keep up with her session. The lump of ore in her stomach was weighing on her too heavily and at the end she couldn't help bursting into tears. 'Maybe I shouldn't be in the play. I'm not very good!'

'Oh minha querida, come here, my love,' Ana's mother cradled Shirly to her chest and held her till she stopped sobbing. 'I know, I know. It must be very confusing for you. But you mustn't worry. When Ana's father returns from Lisboa, we will make sure to see what we can do to help. Shhh. Don't cry.' It was wonderful to be held by Lisette as though she was a precious thing, but somehow it wasn't enough.

Shirly could only repeat, 'I'm not very good and I don't know if I can sing well in time for the play.'

'Of course you will, my dear. I will make sure of it. Please don't worry,' she said to her student, who remained unconvinced but only sniffled in response. 'Ana! Ana!'

Ana popped her head into the room. 'Yes, Mãe?'

'Ana dear, take Shirly to the beach. Both of you girls need some fresh air.'

'Dona Lisette, my mother will worry, I should go home,' said Shirly lamentably, wiping her face on her sleeve.

'Okay, then, Ana, walk with her home, will you?'

'Yes, Mãe,' said Ana, with a sombre mix of obedience for her mother and worry for her friend.

Ana decided to take her companion home the long way. They walked first in the opposite direction, then crossed the road to the waterfront. On the return, they walked upstream to the Mandovi on the main road that led to Shirly's house. The water lapped gently on their left and twinkled in the late November evening light. Across the river on the other bank lay the Betim ferry point, beyond which stood the Aguada prison with her father in its recesses. Even the waterway's ballet of lustrous, glinting and leaping mackerel to attract her favour didn't lift Shirly out of her dull spirits.

'D'you want to sail boats?' Ana asked with a generous dollop of enthusiasm, hoping to jump-start her friend's way out of her dolorous pit.

Shirly remembered how Agente Monteiro had stuck his foot out and drowned her paper boat before meeting her father. 'There is not enough water in the drain. It hasn't rained recently,' she responded glumly. New thoughts began to swim through her mind. Was her father really capable of being a criminal? Was he on the wrong side of the law, causing Monteiro to seek him out that rainy day?

'There was another dance yesterday. I saw it from the window!' Ana tried again, skipping a little, but Shirly barely mustered a weak smile in response.

They passed by skiffs docked in the water by the customs house. Shirly wondered what exactly took place there—she had never thought to ask her father. She made a mental note to do so when he got out, when they would go on a walk along the waterfront or maybe even if they passed by in the Pontiac on their Sunday outing to the Gaspar Dias beach. Unless he wouldn't be released, and then . . . Suddenly, Shirly stopped.

'What's wrong?' Ana asked.

'Gy-gy-gypsy,' Shirly said, pointing to the water.

There was a small canoe with a young boy sitting in it. His hair was slightly bleached in the sun, and his skin was the colour of coconut husk. He wore an unbuttoned beige shirt over a cotton vest and loose beige trousers that were rolled up. He wasn't wearing any footwear, and his face looked like it needed a good scrubbing. The boy wasn't doing anything, just sitting and waiting. As she pointed him out to Ana, his eyes met Shirly's, which made her heart leap into her skull and throb fitfully at her temples. They stared at each other for half a minute. The boy stood up and called out, and the two girls screamed and dashed down the road all the way to Shirly's house.

On arriving at her gate, they bent over, huffing and puffing from being winded, and between breaths, discussed their near escape from being kidnapped by the gypsy boy.

'I'm sure he was calling out to the other gypsies. They would have come very quickly and . . . and . . .'

'Put gunny sacks over our heads!' Ana completed Shirly's sentence.

'And kidnapped us!'

'And . . .'

'Girls?' Mamtu, hearing the duo, popped out on to the sidewalk. 'What happened?' she asked, and without waiting for their reply added, 'Goku is breaking some coconuts in the courtyard, go and have the water.'

Mamtu went out for some evening air to the Abbé Faria garden while the girls went in to guzzle from green coconuts, the tops lopped off by Goku with an iron sickle. With one efficient swing, Goku then split the drained coconuts into two. She made them a wooden spoon each from the edge of their coconut shells, which they used to scoop out the milky flesh. And Shirly felt gratitude lurch its slim head into her leaden heart for moments, however transient, of translucent sweetness in the coconut cream and the osmotic exchange of trusting sisterhood with Ana.

15

The mosquitoes were out and looking for meat, so twenty-four-year-old Aphonso Kamat went inside and shut the door and windows. Within his little kitchen, he lit a palm-sized piece of wood and, shuffling around his tiny house located at the edge of the village of Anmod in Karnataka near the border, let the grey smoke choke any buzzing in the air.

He stepped towards one corner of his living room and turned the big knob on his metal and wood transistor radio. A faded 'Phillips' was etched in cursive penmanship at one edge of its steel frame. The radio crackled to life with white noise, and he adjusted the volume with the small knob to save his senses. The temple down the mud road from his house was clanging with the evening aarti bells. He lifted the antennae from its case, swivelled it upwards and gently pulled it till it was a metre high. Then he fiddled with the big knob to find the right station.

He was on time for the news scheduled at 6:20 p.m. Most of Goa wouldn't be able to hear this station since it was jammed by the local authorities. However, he could access it since he was close to the border. At a precise turn of the knob, the crackling died and he could make out the words of the reporter. 'Kssssssrrrr . . . There is talk that the USSR will be showing solidarity with India to overthrow any trace of colonialism left in the country. This follows on the heels of the prime minister's visit to Moscow two months ago. Perhaps it is the start of a beautiful relationship between India and the Soviet Union. Maybe the Russians will leave their snow-cold climate to visit our sunny sands one day. In other news, just last month the Indian Council for Africa organized a four-day seminar on colonialism, specifically Portuguese rulership. Let's listen to the words of our leader . . .'

The British English of the Indian prime minister came through the webbed speaker, carrying a short fragment of his speech at the seminar. Despite the strong accent, Aphonso could make out what he was listening for—that new strategies were being considered and that Goa would soon be free. There was a moment of silence before the reporter started again. 'If you are listening out there, have courage, be brave, and God be with you.'

16

'Oh, I forgot to wear earrings,' Mamtu said without slowing her pace. She and Shirly were walking through the narrow streets and past the colourful houses in Fontainhas, headed towards Frederick Baptista's home. He was an unassuming, light-boned native son of the soil but was known to be a heavyweight advocate in the Panjim court.

'Your father highly trusts Senhor Baptista to help him with the legalities of his trade. He says he has a silver tongue,' explained Mamtu, panting slightly as she walked. 'He can find the right way to argue any case. But he isn't a rogue and will do so only if he believes in his client. Your father has said that he is known not to take on the cases of wealthy mining families whom he believes to be corrupt and who have the government in their pockets. But Deepak, he knows him to be a fair and honest man who wouldn't let greed dictate his business.' To Shirly, it seemed almost as though Mamtu was trying to convince herself. 'I'm so glad he made time to meet us. This advocate is a busy man . . .' Nevertheless, Shirly was glad that they had someone to turn to, and had insisted on accompanying her mother.

The sign outside his door stated his name simply: Frederick Baptista, Advogado. Mamtu and Shirly were let into the door by his housemaid and made to wait in the living room while she disappeared past another door. Mother and daughter gingerly sat on a peach sofa and looked around the room, which was sumptuous with wooden furniture and objets d'art.

Just as quickly, the maid reappeared. 'Senhora, you may go inside,' she said, holding the door open. Mamtu and Shirly entered a room full of shelves stocked with books. The smell of leatherbound covers and dust reminded Shirly of the smell in the public library, to which her father took her on occasion to borrow her fill of books and comics. He had encouraged her to pick up *The Old Man and the Sea* and *A Christmas Carol*; she had discovered the precise detective mind of Sherlock Holmes and wandered far from home with *Gulliver's Travels* and *The Lion, the Witch and the Wardrobe*. It was, however, years before she would read *The Count of Monte Cristo* and fully understand how a local Goan would travel so many miles from his doorstep and inspire the imagination of the world. How José Custódio de Faria, a languishing prisoner at the Château d'If, would guide a young Edmond Dantès to his true fortune. She remembered these as the seed of her spirit of adventure but surely hadn't imagined the way it would play out. The book of her life should have titles like *Shirly Slips Through the Looking Glass* or *Shirly Takes Over Oz*, not *Shirly Meets the Criminal Advocate*. The prolepsis of her days seemed like fragments from a book of disquiet.

Nonetheless, this was where she inevitably found herself. A wide wooden table was centred at the back wall, and a man seated on a leatherbound chair was bent over sideways, frenetically digging in a drawer so only his green velour jacket could be seen.

Mamtu cleared her throat. Without looking up, the bent-over advocate said, 'Ah, come in, come in, be with you in a moment, I'm looking for a paper, it has to be here somewhere, I just saw it . . .' There was some scuffling before the corybantic advocate looked up at the two still standing there. 'Sit down, sit down,' he straightened up and gave his attention to the women. He was bald, with a fringe around the pate of his head, and he wore green cotton trousers that matched his green jacket, even though it was too hot to wear one in this tropical weather. 'Tell me, tell me . . . who is this? Is this your daughter, yes yes, Senhor Deepak has two daughters, lovely, she looks just like you . . . what's your name?' Baptista spoke fast, although not with any nervousness, simply with several thoughts all at once. Shirly answered the question directed at her, but he didn't seem to be interested in going much further with that and instead went straight to the point. 'Ah, yes, lovely . . . so, tell me, Senhora Mamtu, what can I do for you?'

'As I said on the phone, Senhor Baptista . . .'

'Please, call me Freddy. Ah, yes, you mentioned on the phone, your husband, prison.'

'Yes, Senhor Freddy,' Mamtu replied.

'Quite right, quite right. Was there any reason given?'

'I believe it is a case of sedition. How is it possible?' Shirly noted the edge of shakiness in Mamtu's voice as she addressed the advocate.

Freddy heaved in a deep breath and let out a whistle. 'It is pathetic what is happening. I have five cases of sedition that I am working on at the moment. You see, the government is feeling a little nervous, and with Salazar and all . . .'

'But what does that have to do with my Deepak, he is innocent . . .' said Mamtu with high-pitched impatience, cutting off the advocate's words. She had looked up the word in the dictionary Deepak kept on his study table since she first heard it and now understood its full import.

'Yes, my dear, I trust your words, however, the government is prone these days to make arrests based on whims and hearsay. Just a minute,' Freddy picked up the telephone receiver and dialled. 'Hello, hello, operator? Please connect me with Senhor Mario Crasto? Yes, I'll hold on . . . hello, Don Mario? Bom dia . . . I'd like to inquire about another sedition case, Senhor Deepak Quarachim. What is the situation? Yes, I am waiting . . . Hello, yes, I am here, hmmmhmm, okay, I see, hmmhmmm, okay, okay . . . Oh ho, I see. Yes. Well, muito obrigado, Don Mario.'

After hanging up the receiver with its delicate wayward bell and rounded click, Freddy turned to face Mamtu once more. 'Senhora, that was the Secretary for Legal Affairs in the Polícia. He has informed me that Senhor Deepak Quarachim, your husband, has indeed been suspected of sedition. He was arrested near Oilem Aravalem for possessing gelatin bombs hidden in a tin of cashews.'

'Near our mines . . .' Mamtu's mouth remained open.

The tin of cashews? From Sushant! Shirly immediately connected the dots.

'I believe so, and Agente Monteiro was present and personally saw to his being charged and imprisoned in . . . let's see . . . the Fortaleza da Aguada jail.'

'Yes, he is in Aguada now, I met him there.'

'Senhora, your husband didn't tell you any of this?'

This was too surreal for Mamtu. 'No, Doutor, he didn't mention anything like this. So, my husband . . . it is true? How can . . . there must be some mistake . . . sometimes bombs are used in mining, my husband is innocent.'

'Senhora, it seems these bombs were not authorized for mining use. These were gelatin bombs which are not recognized by the government. And it is suspected that he wasn't going to use them himself. He may have been operating with—I can't be sure, but this is what is suspected—a group of insurgents.'

'Insurgents?' Mamtu pronounced the word like she didn't like the taste of it, slowly and with questioning disbelief. She didn't know what else to say about the situation. Then she added slowly, 'Doutor, is there anything you can do?'

'Yes, we can try the easy route first. Would you be prepared to offer something in exchange . . . how should we say it, some escudos and a gift, to the agente?'

It took Mamtu a minute to process the advocate's suggestion. 'Yes,' she said unblinkingly when his words achieved illumination. 'Yes, escudo, yes, yes . . . I can get a bottle of very fine vinho do Porto. In exchange for my husband's liberation.'

'Ah, Senhora,' Freddy the advocate steepled his hands and added delicately, 'I understand that his tastes are rather closer to home. May I suggest feni?'

Mamtu knitted her eyebrows and thought that maybe Goku was right after all, feni was an all-purpose solution. 'Yes, of course, it is possible.'

'I will telephone you when required. Please don't worry, I will do my best to free Senhor Deepak.' Not knowing how else to erase the worry creases off the brow of the lady in front of him, Freddy resorted to the intangible, 'Have faith, Senhora, Jesus is watching. He will protect your husband.'

Mamtu exhaled a lungful of pent-up anxiety and donned a temporary mask of relief, 'Thank you, Senhor Freddy. Please do be in touch as soon as you know. I will organize what is necessary in the meantime.' Mamtu pushed herself off her chair, leaned on Shirly's shoulder and led her out.

As they walked back home quietly, hand in hand, Shirly felt the throb of Mamtu's heart from the veins of her fingers. She sensed her mother's pulsations of apprehension, but they were definitely lighter than before, even if slightly.

17

The flag fluttered its way down the pole, and Shirly waited till the final sound from the trumpets wound down before closing the shutter to her window. She was summoned for dinner, which was solemn, except for Devika humming a folk tune she had learnt from Goku.

'How is the musical practice, Shirly? Is everything all right at school?' her mother asked.

'Yes, it is fine. Dona Lisette is very nice, but . . .'

'Is anything wrong?'

'I just . . . I don't want to make a fool of myself in front of everyone,' Shirly finally admitted to the misgiving that sat inside her to her mother.

'Well, Puttha, whatever you want to do is fine. I just want you and your sister to be happy,' replied a lugubrious Mamtu absently.

Later that evening, as Shirly was working out a puzzle of woodland scenery on her bed, dusk descended on Panjim with its cacophony of sounds: the steady chirp of crickets, a windy breeze from the river wheezing through cracks in the window and relaxed, muffled chatter from passers-by taking a stroll. The puzzle wasn't too large, but the pieces were tiny and interlocking the right ones together was a meditative challenge she enjoyed.

During the course of her pondering, her eye fell to the top of her dresser. Sitting among combs and curios was the pouch given to her by the Mahar woman at the mines. It contained the strength-giving red earth. She contemplated sticking her finger into it and bringing it to her lips. What if it was true? Would her body change into a supercharged battery? Able to cross the seas for a grand adventure? Like the one Abbé Faria had, she too would have a statue erected in her honour, with all the fame she had garnered amongst her people back in Panjim. Yes, a statue of her right next to her old friend José. Shirly dropped another piece of the puzzle into place as she imagined what pose her statue would take. The doorbell rang through her reverie. It was probably Michael, who had come to drop off the shop keys as usual. She was looking for the right piece for the tree bark when her mother filled her doorway. 'Shirly, look, your friends are here.'

Shirly raised her chin, surprised to see Ana appear behind Mamtu's frame. And then she was flustered. João had arrived with his sister and was standing there, at her threshold. She sat up quickly and smoothed her hand through her hair. Ana wore a frilly red frock with white socks and shiny white patent shoes, and João was in formal navy blue trousers with a crisp blue shirt tucked in, a navy blue belt and polished black shoes.

'Shirly, you have to come with us! It's finally our chance!' Ana said excitedly. 'We're going to Clube Nacional! We are going to see the dancing!'

Shirly's heart surged, but she turned to her mother questioningly. 'It's all right, Shirly, you can go. João said Dona Lisette will also be there. Isn't it so, João?'

'Yes, Dona Mamtu,' said João, boyishly, respectfully and shy all at the same time.

'Thank you. Will you two wait in the hall? Shirly will be ready shortly.'

In front of the mirror, Shirly ran her fingers over the emerald locket on a delicate golden chain around her neck. Fashioned by Monkar, it was a recent gift from Mamtu, for her 'grown-up little lady', she'd said, placing it around her daughter's slim neck admiringly. Wearing a jade-green, knee-length frock, which had fashionable tiers of organza in the skirt, a matching green satin ribbon tied at her waist, and squeaky new black patent leather shoes with a slight heel, Shirly appeared before her friends waiting in the salon. They all trooped out the door with Devika and Mamtu watching, accompanied by Goku, who was recruited by Mamtu to drop them off at the Clube. It was a quick trip—past the palácio and the Abbé Faria garden, and right around into Rua Afonso Albuquerque behind their house.

Shirly loved her dress and she rarely got to wear it. It made her imagine that she was a fairy queen with wings, and she treaded in toe-heel fashion to suit her mood. She especially loved the tic-tic sound her heels made and she felt very grown-up in them. She didn't fail to observe that João was noticing her appreciatively too. Tic-tic-tic-tic, her back straight as she walked, one foot delicately, deliberately, in front of the other, into womanhood.

Some people were walking into a building across the road up ahead, vibrant music calling out to them. Crossing the road, the troupe accompanied by Goku soon reached the Clube Nacional building. On the lower storey were the Vaglo building's now-shuttered shop doors, and upstairs was the Clube Nacional hall, with a glorious verandah and a wooden red and white balustrade wrapped around it. Centrally facing the street at the top was a frieze of stained glass capped with a wooden triangular pediment that bore an intricate skirting. On it were the letters C and N nestled within each other, a beacon for those with a swing in their step. The music was louder the closer they got. On one side of the building was a staircase where Goku took their leave to retire for the night. The trio headed up just as the music died down.

The sights inside were everything Shirly had ever imagined. On one side she could see the verandah that overlooked the street below and Ana's house on the opposite side of the road where she had once stood watching the dancing couples. The verandah had tables and chairs, and there was soft lighting everywhere. Shirly felt the glow seep through her, making her giddy. In front of her lay a long dance floor with a few couples standing and chatting. Some were making their way to the verandah after their last dance. The ladies looked so elegant in their fashionable dresses and high heels, while the men looked redrawn anew in their formal shirts and coats. As the threesome walked across the floor, Shirly watched the band, whose members were now relaxing with a drink in hand and chatting with those who approached them. Ana led the two into another room adjoining the floor, where Lisette was sitting on a chair along a row of seats in a peach silk dress.

'Mãe!' Ana called out to her mother, who was immersed in conversation with a woman seated across from her.

Lisette turned to the lady she was talking to, 'Here is my other son, João, my daughter, Ana, and their friend, Shirly, who is also the lead in our school musical. Children, this is Dona Monica de Mello, a friend of mine whose son Xavier attends the Liceu with Tomas.'

'Hello, children, so lovely to meet you,' Monica de Mello said amiably.

'Hello, Senhora,' the three said, a little out of unison. Just then, a boy appeared out of nowhere, gave an excited squeal and ran on. Swiftly following him was Tomas. The two boys ran snaking between and around the chairs, startling those who were entering the room from the bar area with drinks in their hands. They finally stopped when they knocked into a steward, whose tray fell to the ground with a clatter. Lisette and Monica both got up and rushed to the aid of the steward.

'Boys!' Lisette chided. 'Both of you, go take a seat, and not next to each other!' Then, turning to the steward, who was standing with his tray back in his hand, she apologized, 'I am so terribly sorry, I hope you are okay.' The steward reassured Lisette and Monica that all was okay and fell into that old refrain: boys will be boys. Lisette returned to her place, but Monica reseated her son further down her row of seats, lest the two boys, whose penchant for rascality magnetized one to the other, created another incendiary situation.

Just then, the band started up with an easy beat that spilled around the room. 'The music has really started now. It was just a warm-up song earlier,' explained João. 'The band never starts before ten o'clock.' Ten o'clock was when Shirly was about to head to bed. She hadn't ever stayed up so late in her life that she could remember. Except the one time when her father was returning from Japan close to midnight, a year ago, and her entire family ignored the grandfather clock till they could greet him on his arrival.

'Mãe, what is this dance?' asked Ana.

'This is a waltz. It's easy, let me show you.' Lisette took Ana's hand and led her daughter right there. 'Count in your head, one-two-three, one-two-three . . . that's it.' Ana fell in step and twirled in the little space she and her mother had near their chairs, watched by some of the others in the noisy room. Lisette included Tomas in the fray and showed her son and daughter how to do the cha-cha when the music changed. 'One-two-cha-cha-cha . . .' Shirly watched in fascination. With the switch in music, a gentleman in coattails came up and asked Lisette to dance. She accepted, and Shirly admired her graceful gait as she went across the room on his arm towards the dance floor. While Tomas and Ana were still busy, Shirly followed Lisette in curiosity to the main dance hall and stood at the threshold. Her singing mentor and the gentleman stopped at the centre of the room. Lisette began to move, light as air, and was hopping and popping her feet to the beat of the music. The other couples in the room were bouncing with the pulsating sound, which was making the floor itself shake, sending the rhythm into Shirly's skull and flush within the centre of her bones.

'Jason and His Jolly Good Fellas.'

Shirly turned around to see João standing near her. He too was watching the show.

'The band, they are called Jason and His Jolly Good Fellas,' he repeated. 'They really are the best.'

Shirly looked across at the musician pit from where all the lively sound emanated. The band's name was on the drum, and the lead singer, Jason, she presumed, alternated between singing and playing the trumpet. There was also a violinist, a cellist who doubled up as a Hawaiian guitarist, an accordion player with a saxophone and, of course, the drummer. Shirly's heart started to harmonize with the thumping floor under her feet. When another waltz rolled out, João turned to her. 'May I have the pleasure of this dance?' he asked politely with his hand out, a little demurely.

'Um, I don't know the steps,' said Shirly apologetically, and a little scared of the wonderful attention João was giving her.

'Don't worry, I will lead, you just need to follow,' he reassured her.

Shirly took his hand unsteadily, unsure of herself, hoping she wouldn't trip. He led her to a relatively less crowded corner of the dance floor across from the band. João turned her to face him gently and smoothly as he took her hand and placed it on his shoulder. Then he took her right hand in his left out to the side. He placed his right hand under the wing of her left shoulder blade, creating a circle with their bodies. She dared to look up into his eyes and found them again, those light-brown orbs with golden flecks in them. She felt elated and uncomfortable—this was the closest she had ever been to a boy. And she didn't mind it at all. As he led the dance, her toes crunched over his. She looked on in horror as his face winced catatonically in pain. He took a deep breath and led her to fall in tune with his rhythm. In no time, she felt like she could simply fly in her grasshopper-green dress. Who knew she would be here, dancing with João, when weeks ago she was merely peeping in from across the street. She couldn't help the upward turn at her lips that stubbornly stayed on her face, and to her relief saw that João couldn't stop his grin either.

The music picked up pace. All the couples broke their close holds and started to dance wildly. 'This is rock 'n' roll! It's really fashionable now. This one is a song by a famous singer called Elvis Presley,' João had to shout over the sound of the music. 'Don't worry about the dance, just do whatever you want.' Shirly tried to imitate João's frenzied and uncoordinated movements. She closed her eyes and felt freedom. The shape of João's dancing form dangled in front of her eidetically, as though imprinted on the parchment behind her eyes. And he was still there when she opened her lids and looked straight into his boyishly awkward and yet dazzling enthusiastic face. They bumped into each other and the dancers around them, both grinning and laughing with abandon.

When the song ended, João took Shirly's hand and led her out into the verandah. It was crowded, with most seats occupied. João headed over to a relatively free spot at the wide balcony and nodded to Shirly to join him. They were both still breathless, heaving in the night air, with pearls of perspiration on their noses and foreheads.

'That was so much fun! Where did you learn how to dance?'

'Have you seen my mother?' said João rhetorically. 'She is contagious,' he joked with renewed energy, as the song changed again, this time to Cliff Richard.

Shirly floated back on her feet to the dance floor and felt her hair bounce around in measured beats, keeping more in rhythm with João than with the music. After that they danced to some Louis Armstrong and more rock 'n' roll. She took all the names of the faraway musicians who washed her feet in movement that night and tied up the João-imprinted parchment behind her eyes into a roll which she placed in a bottle. She threw this up in the air and it spun the room round and round.

When their feet were a little worn out by the dance floor, they returned to the balcony, while Jason poured his soul out in the classic 'Blue Moon' ballad on the floor, where couples slow-danced, entwined with each other.

'Let's get something good to eat. I'm hungry after all this dancing.'

'Where?' Shirly asked, the night breeze drawing her loosened hair across her face.

'I'll show you, come on.' João took Shirly's hand and led her between the well-dressed bodies on and off the floor. She marvelled at how easily he felt comfortable holding her hand, with a friendliness that caught her off guard, even though they had elbowed closely into each other over the past hour and a half. They had reached the top of the stairs when a familiar voice caught them.

'Oi, where are you two going without me?' Ana appeared, her hair popping out in all directions from her ponytail.

'Tell Mãe I'm taking you both for a snack; we'll wait here.' While Ana ran up to her mother, still on the dance floor, João and Shirly waited as a foxtrot got underway. They could see Ana mouth words at Lisette, who stopped mid-dance, nodded at João and picked up again with her partner while Ana skipped across the floor.

'Come on,' said João, 'follow me.' The three of them landed in the street, skipping, mock-boogieing and chattering away.

'Shirly, we should come dancing in March,' said Ana.

'Yes, during Carnaval,' said João, hopping ahead of the girls.

'In the evening, after the King Momo parade, there is dancing till quite late. All the musicians are on the street. Oh, and they make a big bonfire! And you have to jump over the fire. But not alone, you have to do it together.'

'We would have to jump together?' asked Shirly, who suddenly thought of how her underwear would probably get scorched if she tried and didn't like the idea of her bottom reflecting the moonlight for all to see.

'Well, usually a boy will take a girl's hand and they jump over the fire together.'

'Oh,' said Shirly, not sure if she wanted a boy to see her after her jump with her underwear on fire.

'You have to come with us. It'll be super!' said Ana.

'Don't worry, it's safe, Shirly. I'll show you how to jump. It's like this, see . . .'

João took a running jump. 'When Carnaval comes, I will jump with you.'

Shirly was secretly glad that João uttered those last words. And she longed for Carnaval to draw nearer. Blazing underwear or not.

Fifteen minutes of walking later, 'Ah, here we are. Best meal after a dance,' promised João. They stood in front of a small, innocuous restaurant, which had the name Café Réal in front of it.

'Bhaji puri!' said Ana excitedly. They took a seat at one of the wood-backed benches.

'Three bhaji puri, please,' João ordered politely to the skinny waiter eager to take their order. Once the waiter headed into the kitchen with his order, he said, 'It's early, so we are the only ones. I mean, it's late for dinner but early for those who are dancing. It will get very crowded here a little later.'

Shirly felt a pang of admiration for João, who seemed to know things, facts and figures about this and that, like a real grown-up should. Like her father would.

'Mãe asked me if we are taking Tomas along, but I told her he was busy playing with his rowdy friend Xavier,' Ana said. 'He has become so silly these days. Ever since that police agente came to our house. He thinks he is like the police now. Going around telling people what they can and cannot do. He told me that I need a ticket to come to his room! I don't mind if he doesn't come along with us. He has to give me a ticket to come for bhaji puri with us!' Ana's outrage for her brother tickled João and Shirly, who exchanged smirks.

The plates of bhaji puri arrived in front of the trio, steam emanating from them. The deep-fried puris were thin, rounded with hot air and perfectly crisp, albeit a little oily. They poked their fingers into their puris, allowing searing wisps to escape from the hole they created. 'Ow!' squealed Shirly and Ana, since it was hotter than they anticipated. When the puris cooled a little, they tore into them and scooped the bhaji in its potato gravy, perfectly spicy and flavourful.

'Didn't I tell you?' asked João, his mouth full of steam.

'Mhhh uhmmm,' the girls responded, their mouths full of satisfaction. After licking their platters clean with their fingers, João paid escudos to the bored waiter and they headed out into the night air again.

'Let's take the long way back to the Clube,' said João, who was already ahead on the pavement and walking backwards to lead the girls in his direction. Instead of returning on the same route, they traversed the block of buildings and crossed the empty main street on the riverfront. The tide was high, and a few night fishermen were seated on the parapet to take advantage of the swelling river. One had a bucketful of catch that the trio stopped to admire.

'What is that long one?' asked João to the fisherman.

'Eel,' he responded.

'Oh. Some of them give off electric shocks. Be careful not to touch them,' said Shirly. She knew a thing or two about fish from the picnics the family took to Dona Paula. There she watched the amateurs stand with fisherfolk, baiting their lines and reeling in at the slightest tug.

'You try?' The fisherman offered the line to Shirly. To her delight, when she reeled in, with the fisherman's help, a gleaming piece of silver flapped and wiggled at the end of the line. The catch was of no consequence, the size of her forefinger; the fisherman unhooked and released it into his bucket. It was João's turn to look at her in admiration.

After they marvelled at the slimness and size of the fish in the bucket, they moved on further down the waterfront in the direction of the Palácio. Then they heard thumping. Very faintly, but distinct. It wasn't coming from the Clube, which was one street behind the waterfront, to their right. In fact, it wasn't coming from any of the streets. It was being carried in the wind across the water to them, from their left. As they focused, the sounds got louder and Shirly felt her organs calibrate to their rhythm. 'Do you hear that?' she asked finally.

'Yes, I do,' said Ana.

'It's coming from the dhows,' said João, indicating a dark cluster in the middle of the water. He pointed out the boats moored in the river. A great light seared up from one of the largest vessels, illuminating the others around it. The fire cracked and spat up skywards.

'Oh! Fire!' said Ana, worried. 'The boat is on fire!'

'No, no. Don't be afraid, it's a bonfire! My friend Hamid told me about it.'

'Hamid?' asked Shirly.

'Yes, he is a gypsy. He is usually near the shore. Unless he is with the others.'

'You should be careful of the gypsies! They can rob us and put us to work. Because that is what they do—they take children,' said Shirly, fearfully, not sure that she should be saying 'children', because maybe, certainly, today she was older than that.

'What? No, they are not like that,' reassured João. 'I'm telling you. I've met them. They are my friends. I'll show you.'

Shirly's trust needed more convincing. 'They . . . they are . . . tricky. Yes, they can be tricky and be friends with you and then when you aren't looking . . .'

'No. I don't know where you heard this but you are being scared for no reason. Let me show you.' João put two fingers in his mouth and drew a loud, sharp whistle. The girls were taken aback, more by his impressive whistling skills than its suddenness. Ana furrowed her eyebrows and tried putting her thumb and forefinger in her mouth to achieve the same result. She succeeded in simply blowing air into the night breeze. They stood there like that for half a minute and then heard another whistle in the distance.

'Since they are on boats, this is how they communicate with each other,' explained João. 'They don't have the modern systems we do to talk to each other over distances, like telephones. I think they have a Morse code but I don't really know it. I think it is something like our telegraph.' A small canoe cut through the waters, dimly reflecting the light of the bonfire from the boat. 'There!' said João. 'It's Hamid!'

Shirly nervously held on to Ana. This was the same boy they both had seen a few days ago, who had tried to scare them off. Who knows, maybe he would have just taken them away in his boat if they hadn't run for their lives. Despite her misgivings about the situation, she stuck by João. She felt like there were two streams moving in opposite directions within her—the first had João drawing her into the terrible, fearsome world of the gypsies, and the second was gratefulness for his presence. It was an awful and delightful confusion.

As Hamid came closer in his canoe, João leapt on to the parapet. Hamid wore the same sandy-looking shirt over a vest and rolled-up trousers as the last time Shirly saw him. He was barefoot and his face looked as crusty and unwashed as before. The streetlights played with the rolling dark of the river, causing the whites of the boy's eyes to shine against the brown of his face. As he drew near the parapet, the canoe created small waves against the stone wall. When Shirly saw Hamid's eyes, she gave a small scream and stepped back on to Ana's foot, who screamed too. The boys ignored them.

'Hello!'

'Hello. I saw you calling, João. You are outside very late tonight?' Hamid got straight to the point. Shirly continued to nurse her mistrust and didn't say anything.

'Yes, we have been dancing at the Clube. We were just going back. What is going on there? You have a big fire tonight,' João asked.

'Yes, we are also dancing. It is the new moon, so we celebrate with a bonfire.'

'How is . . . how is . . . how can you have a bonfire on a boat? I mean, isn't it made of wood? Won't the fire burn it down?' Shirly thought Ana brave for asking.

'Haha, no. Nothing to worry. We have the fire in a large metal bowl, how do you say it in English? Cal . . . Caold . . .'

A large metal bucket sounded suspicious. Something in which to cook other humans, Shirly panicked. 'Is that how you cook people?' she blurted out in a high-pitched voice, unable to control the pathway her thoughts took.

'Cook people?' Hamid frowned, perplexed.

'My sister and her friend think that gypsies like to steal children when no one's looking, take them away from their families to make them slaves and also cook them when they are hungry,' João said, unable to control the smirk on his face.

'It's not funny! Sister Olga said so!' asserted Ana.

'We Romani never steal people or make them slaves or cook them.' Hamid remained matter-of-fact and kept a straight face. 'But if you want to see what we are doing, you can come with me on my boat. I can take you there.' Hamid put his hand out. Too eagerly, remarked Shirly. Without flinching, João took the boy's support to jump off the parapet and nimbly land into the vessel. Next, he held his hand out to Shirly. She and Ana looked at each other before slowly clambering on to the parapet and allowing themselves to be led down into the canoe. When they were seated, Hamid pushed his oar into the riverbed. He directed the canoe with the current towards the bonfire in the large central dhow.

The further they drew away from the riverbank, the jungle-like drumbeat grew stronger. When the drifting troupe approached the big dhow, they felt the heat from the fire warming the air.

A couple of men with earrings greeted them and helped them up into its bark. In fact, all the men on board had earrings. Ana and Shirly stuck close to João. The dhow was quite spacious compared to the other smaller dhows parked in the river around it. The double-mast triangular sails that reached upwards billowed gently in the wind, creating delicate blapping sounds. Under it, at the centre of the deck, was a wide iron cauldron from which the flames of the bonfire spewed. Around it were the dhowmen of the boats.

They were seated or standing, some with country liquor in their hands, others dancing, clapping and whooping in ecstatic intoxication. Ana screamed a little when one of the men accidentally bumped into her, and clung closer to João and Shirly. Two of the sailors were seated with bongos, which explained the rhythm they had heard on the waterfront. Only now, the beats penetrated every bone in their bodies. One man had a tambourine, and another seemed to be singing in a language that the three didn't understand. All the boatmen were muscularly lean, yet appeared unwashed and salt-encrusted. Their skin was sun-drenched, and their hands and feet were coarse, indicating the laboriousness of their days. The dhow had a huge barrel on one side covered in bamboo matting, from which the sailors were drawing a liquid into bowls and cups, and from which the sharp smell of country liquor emanated.

An imposing-looking man who was quieter than the rest and seated near the stern motioned to Hamid. 'Follow me,' Hamid said to the three. The four weaved through the revelry and were presented to the older-looking dhowman. He had piercing light green eyes that stood in startling contrast to his darkened skin.

'This is my papa,' said Hamid.

'Come, come, sit,' Hamid's father said with thick geniality in his voice, inviting them to share the wooden bench that was a part of the stern. Shirly was intimidated by his earring and the snake-and-anchor tattoo on his forearm. His worn-out cotton pants were loose and cut off mid-calf, and he sported his oiled hair in a small ponytail at the back. He was a vision from Shirly's nightmares. Once the three sat, he spoke in a thick accent, 'Whalecome to our boat. My name, Agope. And who arrrrr you?'

'I'm João de Araujo, this is my sister Ana and this is Shirly Quarachim,' said João bravely.

'Oho . . . Quarachim, I know,' Agope said, tapping his very red protruding nose with his index finger.

'How . . . how do you know?' asked Shirly in consternation. Was she on their kidnap list? Were they keeping track of her? The agitated hairs of thought flipped around her mind.

'I gif him gold.'

She didn't understand.

He continued, 'You know Calouste Gulbenkian? He is honourable man. He live in Londown or Parees, I don't know where. He is everywhere. But the Pasha of Arabeea give him the oil. So he is rich, verrry verrry rich. Gulbenkian come Armenia, he give me job and money for my family. He tell me to take in a boat ze things, ze merchandise, to Eendeea. So I bring sometimes oil, sometimes gold, sometimes mermaid.' Agope guffawed loudly and slapped the wood of the stern. 'That is a joke. No mermaids. Mermaids we keep for oursef, is not it, Hamid? And the sea monstars!' Hamid chuckled at his father's joke. 'Anyhow, I give gold sometime to this Quarachim, your papa. We bring from Bai-root. He like. He make business. Together we make the real Goa Dourada.'

I hope he won't make business with little people. Shirly shook that thought out of her head. He was a friend of her father's, after all. Who'd have thought that the bangles and other gifts for her mother, or the things her father sold in his shop, came from this riverine boat a few furlongs from their front gate? She fingered the gold chain with the emerald locket around her neck, the gift from her mother. They were more interconnected than she could have realized. Shirly felt more and more comfortable with this exotic man who did business with her father. His seafaring way of life overwhelmed her, but somehow he seemed at home. Where was Armenia? A faraway place to explore for a future time when the current would take her on exotic, thrilling journeys, she earmarked. And as the vessel rolled gently on a wave, she felt her fictional Zulekha inhabit her a little more.

Shirly turned to look at the crowd near the bonfire. There were more musicians on deck now. The sweet strains of the reed-like duduk, the fast-moving bow of the quamacha and the plucking of an oud joined the bongos. A couple of the men got on the shoulders of other men who hopped to the rhythm. One of the bongo players gestured to João to join him. João held himself in place until Agope tapped him encouragingly on his shoulder and said, 'Make the music.'

As soon as João went across and started beating on the bongos, the tambourine player gestured to Shirly. Half-shy and half-keen, she got up and took over the tambourine. In a surreal twist of time, fate and planetary motion itself, Shirly found herself playing the tambourine to a bunch of dancing Romani, of whom she had been petrified only an hour before. Next to her, João thumped on bongos while Ana skipped around with Hamid and the others in circle formations. The music was heady, their feet were feverish, and their spirits were in raptures. Shirly was sure that with all the noise they made, they had summoned all the fish from the far seas to swish around them in curiosity while the stars were ready to swirl downwards from the onyx sky and join them all.

Later, as Agope and Hamid personally dropped the three to the waterfront, Shirly felt more at ease than she had in the last several days. Sister Olga couldn't dangle 'gypsies' as a sword before her anymore. And she had the inexplicable urge to sing, so she hummed under her breath, 'Water droplets on leaves, dance like diamonds for me/ the light on the river, valuable as silver . . .' Ana was skipping slightly ahead with newly learned Armenian Kertsy footwork. João, who was walking deliberately right next to Shirly, heard her and turned to face her. She mimicked his movement and turned to him. She stopped humming. His smile rivalled the glow of the streetlight, and she had to look down to avert her shyness. 'You play the tambourine very well,' he said to her.

'Thank you. You play the drums well,' she responded, looking up again into his hazel eyes full of openness.

'I really enjoyed dancing . . . with you,' he added, facing her with that sincere, surrendering smile of his that sent her heartbeat off-tempo.

'As did I,' she replied, her words sounding more awkward when outside her body than in her head. 'The Clube . . . and then the boats . . . it has all been like a fairytale,' she confessed in a narcotic fog of euphoria. Shirly's blood was pulsing through her veins faster than all the bongo-thumping that had surrounded her ears earlier.

Ana was already at Shirly's front gate and ringing the gate bell. She turned back to look at her brother and her best friend, where some magnetism was definitely brewing.

A sleepy Goku, who was bidden to spend the night at the Quarachims for this very event, opened the gate a minute later in her nightie. Her black and grey hair, matted and loose around her face and back, stuck out in places, making her look like a straw figure used in crop fields to scare away birds. Ana raised her little finger, a request to use the toilet, and Goku led her in. Shirly and João reached the gate and found themselves both awkwardly and deliciously alone. Shirly had to use the toilet too but wanted to hold on to the moments of this ripe night. Sukkoo and Bukkoo squeezed through the open gate and went to rub themselves against their ankles.

Shirly caught João gazing at her and panicked from feeling too much joy. Say something clever, she urged herself. 'Do you know these cats can talk?'

'Huh? Is that so?' asked João.

'Yes,' said Shirly, hastily bending down to pet the overfed cats and averting João's eyes. 'I ask them, "Sukkoo, Bukkoo, what month comes after April?" And they say . . .'

'Maiao,' mewled the cats loudly, almost in unison.

'Ha!' said João. Shirly immediately wanted to kick herself for such an awkward attempt at a joke. He added, 'Ana and I will go back to the Clube for Mãe. She will be waiting for us.'

'Won't it be too late?'

'No. They are all probably still dancing. So many of them go straight to Sunday mass right after,' chuckled João. 'They will sleep in church during the sermon.' Shirly relaxed and giggled. Then without warning, João took Shirly's hand in his and squeezed it.

'You mean like you?' asked Ana as she stepped out of the gate, straightening her dress. Shirly's cheeks felt flushed from God-all-does-knows-what. João still held her hand. He simply made a funny face at Ana, who reciprocated with her own simian impression.

'Shirly, come,' said Goku, her voice gummed with grogginess. Shirly turned to face João. The long fingers of the Mandovi's breeze ruffled their hair and danced around their limbs lovingly. The stars lay in a glittery scatter overhead. João brought his face close to hers. For a moment no one else existed as Shirly swam in the flecks of his eyes. He kissed her on the cheek, a quick and forever brush. 'Goodnight,' he whispered giving her hand another squeeze while pulling back.

'Goodnight,' she whispered back. 'Goodnight, Ana,' the two friends waved at each other.

18

The smoke in the room filled the air like feathery fumes emitted from a ferry just leaving the dock. Shirly and her mother were back at Advocate Freddy Baptista's office in his Fontainhas residence-cum-bureau. Mamtu's knuckles appeared taut and bony from gripping her daughter's hand. Shirly coughed from the dense air, but Mamtu didn't notice. The words of the advocate had crashed over her like a large wave and in the aftermath she felt a huge metal anchor drop into her gut.

'Why doesn't he want to accept it?' she asked, perplexed.

The advocate let silence slip into the conversation, deliberating on what to say to Mamtu.

'There is no reason for the agente's actions. He is known to be capricious in his decisions. He is driven by greed, no doubt. This amount would have pleased him in exchange for your husband's freedom. I have seen it happen with previous clients. However, his cruelty has overtaken his senses these days. I'm afraid this route is closed.' The advocate's words hung thicker than the smoke in the room.

Shirly coughed quietly. Mamtu sighed. 'Is there anything else we can do?'

'The only other option, Senhora, is to see what the courts will have to say.'

Mamtu panicked. 'The courts? You mean he has to be tried? Like a criminal?'

'I'm afraid so.'

'And he has to be in prison till the trial? When will the trial be? Can't we do anything?'

The advocate's maid, who had let them into the house earlier, stuck her head in through the doorway. 'Senhor, you rang bell?' she asked.

'Yes, Natalie,' replied Freddy. 'Please bring tea and biscuits for myself and Senhora, and a soda for Baby.' Shirly knew she was 'baby', a term for her that the maid would understand meant a young girl. Part of her wanted to object in light of what she had learnt about herself this morning. As she had prepared to disrobe for her bath, her mind was preoccupied with a light cloud of bonfire dancing and the diaphanous texture of João's kiss on her cheek from the previous evening. And then she saw, clear as a slick bathroom tile, that she was about to die.

Her underwear had crimson splotches and there was a trickle of blood running down her thigh. She had shouted for her mother at the top of her lungs, fearing her imminent end at any minute. Soon, there was a crowd collected in the bathroom—Goku, Mamtu and Devika. Shirly had never felt so naked, and she cowered on the floor of the bathroom with her arms wrapped around herself in shame. Everyone would know that she had held a boy's hand because this was the punishment.

Mamtu shooed Goku and Devika out and gently helped Shirly up. While straining over her very pregnant abdomen to ladle water on her daughter's limbs, the way she had done for a five-year-old Shirly, she explained to her bewildered, sobbing daughter that she had crossed the threshold to becoming a woman.

Then, when Shirly was dried and calmed, Mamtu demonstrated to her daughter how to position a homemade cloth napkin in her panty. In that circle of fecundity, so close to her daughter's promises of womanhood—the outline of a hipbone, an arch in her neck, a dip in the waist—she found a gentle protrusion at her chest. Lovingly admiring the infinite miracles of atavistic nature and biology in her daughter's form, Mamtu's heart overflowed with a mother's milk of tenderness. 'I will have to stitch you a brassiere, Puttha,' she said, cupping her daughter's delicate chin, and explained that for the next five days she should simply rest. However, now that Shirly was a woman, she still most definitely wanted to accompany her mother to the lawyer that morning. So, on her way out, she dipped her finger into the pouch on the dresser, given to her on a long-ago trip to the mines, brought it to her tongue and ingested the grains of the blood-red earth that clung to her fingertip. A metallic taste, a sandy texture. As Shirly swallowed, she imagined becoming one with its powers. Latent in the pouch but animating her veins with lightning bolts once it passed through her mouth. And so there she was, in the advocate's office chair, slightly uncomfortable with the homemade cloth pad, wearing her new body as though for the first time. Her blood and bone bonded with the ground beneath.

Once Natalie disappeared, Freddy turned to Mamtu.

'It is a difficult situation. The government is very, very, very, very . . .' Freddy paused dramatically, '. . . very nervous.' He explained further, 'They are arresting people on the slightest suspicion, because frankly they want to prevent any insurgencies. There are too many questionable activities occurring outside our border, so they are arresting first and asking questions later.'

'But then this is not a civilized government!' said Mamtu haplessly.

The advocate silently agreed with Mamtu. He knew that in British India, political prisoners were tried by civil courts. But in Portuguese India, they were tried by the military court. Salazar's government considered Goa, Daman and Diu as 'integral parts of the Portuguese nation', so unlike India there was no principle of self-rule as an option to consider, where those with charges of acts against the State could defend themselves in court. Here it was simply called treason. This meant there was no real chance of any defence for her husband. But how could he explain all this to the pregnant woman and her daughter in front of him?

Shirly squirmed in her seat, half-listening. She hoped that her body wouldn't betray her and release a copious amount of her lifeblood on to the advocate's seat, staining it and shaming her permanently.

Freddy tried to explain, 'It will work like this, Senhora. There are three categories of prisoners nowadays. Well, actually, there are two, and the second one is split further. One type is just your regular criminal, people who are arrested for robbery or tax evasion. These are criminal prisoners, and their trials happen in the high court. The second type are political prisoners. They are arrested on suspicions or overt threats to the government . . .'

They were interrupted as Natalie opened the door with a tray in her hand. She set teacups on saucers in front of Mamtu and the advocate, and placed soda and biscuits in front of Shirly. There was a sense of relief as the refreshments arrived, offering a break in the intensity of the situation. The fizz of the soda reminded Shirly of the guddi-soda she'd have with her father on their drives to the mines, and she was temporarily distracted from the imagined red tide between her legs. After taking a few noisy slurps of his hot tea, the advocate continued.

'As I was saying, erm . . . ah . . . yes . . . political prisoners . . .' The advocate quickly debated in his head about mentioning that Mamtu's husband was very lucky not to have been placed in the Panjim prison where prisoners were usually subjected to third-degree treatment at the hands of the cruel Agente Monteiro. Then he swiftly thought against it and stayed on track. 'They are presented before a military tribunal. This is a panel of three judges, one from the civil court, and the other two are military officers.' The good advocate avoided mentioning that a squad of soldiers with bayonet rifles were usually present in the military courtroom and that the judge who had native roots disliked satyagrahis—freedom fighters. 'Freedom from what?' he was once said to have quoted in the privacy of his chambers. 'Sophistication and culture?'

'Doutor, have you ever managed to save a political prisoner from the tribunal?'

'Senhora, look, any individual brought before the Portuguese military tribunal is basically defending themselves against treason. Most of the prisoners who are arrested are actually "guilty" of their actions. They are usually, by default, defended by the military tribunal pleader. A few of these cases have come to me as a private lawyer. However, I can't honestly say that I've had a hundred per cent victory rate because the irony is that some prisoners usually don't deny their "treason". In fact, they are very proud of it and openly admit it in court. There are indeed several Goans who want Goa for Goa, not for Portugal, not for India, not for bloody Timbuktu. And they are vociferous about it if they can be. For this reason, I rarely enter the military court so often. Occasionally, I have had some cases come to me, some quite like your husband's situation, where there is a chance that the person is innocent. When I say innocent, I mean that we don't know really. The person may be guilty or may be innocent. So my tactic is not a usual one.' The advocate stopped to slurp on his tea some more.

'Yes, Doutor,' prompted Mamtu.

'Yes, my tactic . . . Usually, it is impossible to avoid the claim made by the tribunal. So we go ahead and say that your husband is guilty . . .'

'But, no, Senhor Freddy!' Mamtu protested. She couldn't bring herself to believe that her husband was culpable of anything remotely like this, and she wouldn't bear it if this incident, as she still considered it, would smear his good name. This was Deepak she was talking about. He was a husband, a father and a businessman. He wasn't one of those great satyagrahis like Ram Manohar Lohia or Juliao Menezes or even the Ranes and Pintos, all of whom raised rebellions against the Portuguese governing rule.

'Wait, my dear, hear me out.' Freddy's voice was now cushioned in patience and gentleness. 'The last case, this is what I did. The prisoner admits to the guilt. However, my tactic, as I was mentioning, is to attack the law itself. The rigid nature of the law deems anyone who is fighting for a sense of freedom a mercenary. We just have to shift the entire blame on the injustice of the government's legislation.' Met with acquiescing silence from Mamtu, Freddy continued, 'Believe me, Senhora, this is the only way. Most prisoners can languish their lives away for years in prison.'

Mamtu didn't want to say yes or no to the advocate. She didn't want to say yes since she obviously didn't believe that Deepak should admit to being guilty. But she didn't say no because she had no one else to turn to.

'Anyway, we can only act once the chargesheet is created and a court date is set. I will be in touch with you when I hear more about this. At the moment it seems that nothing will happen till after Christmas since the courts are fully booked at least till then.' The smoke in the room had dissipated, their beverages had been drained, but Mamtu couldn't breathe any easier.

Once they left the advocate's house, Shirly walked back hand-in-hand with her mother, who lumbered laboriously, more from a weighty heart than her cumbersome belly, towards their house. Porous as their palms were to each other's, Shirly could feel all the emotions running through her mother. Even dancing with João now felt like a faraway dream from another world, and all Shirly could sense was their helplessness as a family in this grand universe that had an ebb tide of its own design.

When they reached their front gate, Shirly's glance fell on Abbé Faria's statue in his garden. Her garden. Their garden. Mamtu, sensitive to Shirly even through her despair, understood. 'Go, Shirly, go spend some time in the fresh air, you were coughing too much in the smoky room.' She patted her daughter's back and pointed in the direction of the garden. 'Come back in half an hour for a bath and then dinner, okay?' And Mamtu disappeared into the vestibule beyond the gate.

Shirly went over to the garden and sat astride the old cannon there. She moved around, checking to see if José the statue's eyes were following hers. But they weren't. They hadn't for years. She rocked side to side on the cannon, trying to dissipate the dull ache that had filled her abdomen since the morning, but nothing shook it off. No, Abbé Faria's gaze was definitely fixed on the lady in front of him, who stayed under his spell.

She remembered the time his eyes had moved as she played in the garden. She was five years old, and it had drizzled lightly that evening. She was balance-walking on the stone boundary skirting the garden and skidded on its slippery moss growth. Her legs went over her head before she fell with a thud in the drain. The water in the drain was clean from the rain showers, but all Shirly could feel was a searing pain in her back and shoulders. As she lay crumpled in the drain, about to scrunch her face up and let the tears fall, she felt strong, swift hands pick her up. 'No, no, nothing, nothing . . .' she heard soothing words through the blur. To her surprise, it was José. She knew he could move and watch her, but she didn't realize he could even pick her up.

'José!' she exclaimed. Shirly felt safe, and the tears that wanted to spill were dammed in place. She almost wished that she would tear up, so she could get even more attention from the movable man in stone who had made her way as a friend into her heart. She didn't remember him as having rocky solidity but as being fleshly in his robes. She wondered how her five-year-old mind had had the depth perception to experience that. Now that she thought about it, was it someone else and she had projected the action on to José? Or had it really been him?

'Don't worry, querida, nothing has happened. You are in one piece.' José had set her down so that she sat astride one of the cannons, a heavy iron one, slightly rusty from disuse and now serving as decoration in the garden. 'Let me see.' There was a scrape on her left calf and another on the side of her left knee, which had been at the receiving end of friction against the inner side of the drain as she went down. The wound was raw, and some of her tender skin had peeled away from the burn. 'It is on the surface, but you must be feeling a little pain, no?'

Shirly pouted, equally for the searing gash as for the kind attention she was receiving from José. 'Yes,' she said with pathos. 'I can't walk anymore,' she added dramatically.

'You know, when I was young, this was many years before I became a hypnotist . . .'

'Hi . . . hi . . . hip . . . nost . . . iz,' said Shirly in her five-year-old voice.

'Yes, hypnotist,' José continued. 'Anyway, before I became one, I was training to be a priest. My father was a very good priest, and so I was training to be like him. We were invited by the queen of Portugal, and she told me to give a holy speech in her chapel.' Shirly was riveted and impressed that José had met a queen in a faraway land. 'It was my first show, and the first time I had to perform. I was so nervous. Really, I was shaking and scared. But my father told me something that made all my fear go away. He said . . .' José paused dramatically, 'Do you know what he said?' Shirly's eyes widened as she shook her head no. 'He said, "Hee sogli, bhaji; cator re bhaji."' From the way her eyes narrowed blankly, he realized that Shirly had definitely missed the big message, so José had to translate. 'All the people in front of you, they are all vegetables; cut down the vegetables!' José's laugh was so deep that Shirly felt it through her shoulder, where his palm was resting, which made it contagious. The thought of all the people with vegetable heads made Shirly laugh too. As Shirly sat chuckling on the cannon, José added, 'I also laughed like this. And then, abracadabra. I lost my fear and spoke, and made my holy speech so well.' José added soberly, 'I understood, with my thoughts and my words, what it is that I can do. I could change the situation for myself. I was able to stay and not run away. There is great merit in just staying and continuing.' Then he touched Shirly on the side of her scraped knee. 'Does it hurt?' Shirly tried to bring her thoughts back to her pain but she didn't feel its waves radiating from her scraped leg. In fact, it felt perfectly normal and peaceful, even though her skin was blood-encrusted and lacerated. She shook her head no.

'See, you are fine,' said José enigmatically.

Shirly felt light in her chest and deliberated a little before blurting out, 'I was named after a Shirley Temple.'

'Aha, you have found out. And what is a Shirley Temple?'

'My daddy says that she is a . . . she is a . . . actress,' Shirly said in her little voice after she found almost the exact words she remembered her father telling her.

'Oh ho. An actress. Beautiful. So you too are destined to make a performance, and when you do, what do you have to remember?'

'Cator re bhaji!' Shirly and José shouted out the line together, each making a slicing movement with their hands as though they were chopping off heads, or vegetables. And then they cackled like conspirators.

Shirly remembered her five-year-old self sitting astride the iron cannon now. She looked over at her leg and saw that there were no lesions, no traces of the scrape she had endured. It was magical how the body had created brand new skin to replace the old mess that was once there. Her recollection of José was still clear, and Shirly realized that she hadn't understood then what her statue friend had meant. She wasn't entirely sure now either. But the impression of his words made more sense . . . somehow.

19

Capitão Carlos Alexandre Morais stood on a rock encrusted with tisrya, local clams. He welcomed the ocean breeze grazing his sweaty neck but kept his stern face on, not wanting to let his guard down in front of the army men. He was upset. Not about the several bottles of liquor he had found in the quarters of the agrupamento, the small detachment of troops in the Portuguese-Goan military, to whom he was paying a surprise visit that day. Not even for the fact that some weren't in proper uniform during work hours but were slovenly lounging around their posts wearing unbuttoned shirts, vests and slippers. He was most unhappy about having to report all that he had learnt to the Governor-General of Goa in a few hours.

The island of Anjediv, just under two square kilometres in area, rather like a long, misshapen hammer, wasn't unusual or grand in itself. It was simply a piece of land that found itself divided from the southwestern coastal mainland of Goa—quite close to the fishing village of Karwar in Karnataka—by an expanse of water. However, it wore the palimpsest of history. When it was part of the Vijayanagar Empire, the famous Moroccan traveller Ibn Batuta had set foot here in 1342. Thereafter, it was taken over by Muslim and Arab traders who had destroyed the temple dedicated to Goddess Aryadurga, after whom the island was presumably named. That is, if it wasn't named after the Konkani term for 'fifth island', referring to it being a part of an archipelago of surrounding islets. Other wayfarers passed through, such as trader-navigator-and-Malabar-coast-discoverer Vasco da Gama, who made it a base of operations in the standoff between the Portuguese and the Zamorin of Calicut. The remains of the fort that could be seen hemming the island was the first that the Portuguese ever built, where Afonso de Albuquerque himself took shelter right before conquering Goa and establishing the start of Portuguese rule in 1510. Recounted history says that a local Hindu named Timoji, a privateer or a pirate, depending on whom he served or fought against, wanted to oust the Muslims from Goa. At the time, Mughal ruler Yusuf Adil Shah, who ruled the sultanate of Bijapur, had his palatial residence sitting sentinel on the Mandovi, where the Palácio do Idalcão is located. The ruler was also referred to as Adil Khan. In fact, the name 'Idalcão' is a bastardization of the Portuguese pronunciation of Adil Khan—the Portuguese accent wrapped its tongue around his name to reproduce it as 'Hidalcao'.

It may be innocuous enough now, thought the captain, but he marvelled at the island as being a defining piece of Portuguese history. Timoji had used Anjediv as his base and had enlisted the support of Afonso de Albuquerque to wrest Goa from Adil Shah. Armed with enough forces, Albuquerque is said to have delivered Goa in less than a day, and those who lived within it were stoically butchered. The conquest of land in twenty-four hours. A grand military coup, no doubt. Changing the map as well as the course of mankind in a day. The captain stood in awe at the recollection of those first great adventurers. Afonso established Goa as a Portuguese territory in the East and instated Timoji as a representative of the native population. However, in a twist of fate and soured relations, Timoji was replaced. He returned to piracy, was captured and made prisoner, and eventually died of opium poisoning. The midwife of the Estado, a kingmaker of the new regime, was crushed under its very wheels.

Currently, noted Capitão Morais, the population of the island consisted of two old women, a retired Goan soldier and a teenager. Sometimes there were visitors who came to pay their respects at Our Lady of Springs, a church rebuilt over the temple ruins. There was also an agrupamento whose recent dealings he had come to investigate under the orders of the Governor-General himself.

The captain had boarded the warship *Afonso de Albuquerque* at Mormugao harbour and reached the island that morning. When he walked into one of the six makeshift posts, he found the men in a dishevelled state and promptly marched out before he lost his temper at them. They were a ridiculous desecration to this corner of the world where history had altered its course through the ages. However, he wasn't here to help these desultory men pull up their socks, quite literally, but to glean some information about disturbing recent events. He stood facing the Arabian Sea for a long while before the sentries made their way out of the barracks. In the not-too-far distance, he could see a couple of ships that didn't belong to the Portuguese naval defence plying the horizon. What he had heard was definitely real. And worrisome.

'According to my sources, they are calling it Operation Chutney,' Capitão Morais explained later that evening to the Governor-General in a meeting with him and Lieutenant Colonel Andrade, who was Chief of General Staff. They were in an office quarter at the Palácio do Cabo or Cabo Palace, the residence and seat of the Governor-General, the highest command in Goa, answerable only to the head of state in Portugal. The men rolled the words 'operation' and 'chutney' inquiringly in their mouths like it was something tart and distasteful. The captain explained, 'This is the term the Indians are using to describe their activity. I saw it with my own eyes when I was on the island. Two of their ships are patrolling the waters approximately thirteen to fifteen kilometres from the coastline. My guess is that they are monitoring our activities there and are capable of retaliation, or attack, if necessary.'

'How did this happen, Capitão?' asked the lieutenant colonel.

'Well, Senhor . . .' Capitão Morais cleared his throat. 'Basically, the men on the island say they noticed unusual activity. As you know, the Indian passenger ship SS *Sabarmati* was navigating past our shores and somehow came between the island and the mainland. On the seventeenth of November, our men fired a warning in their direction. But later, around twenty-fourth November, there were roundabout twenty tonas, fishermen's boats, in the waters. Our men fired at them, and this time there were casualties. So my sources say that the Indian frigates we are seeing offshore are part of an operation to safeguard these Indian fishermen, who appear to be from the Karwar area.'

The representative of Portugal in Estado da Índia, the Governor-General—selected by the Presidente do Conselho himself, Prime Minister António de Oliveira Salazar—looked pensive. Morais knew that this fresh news coincided with the information he had received the previous week from reliable sources abroad that the Indians were preparing for an attack. But then, these threats had been constant ever since they had overthrown the British. But we Portuguese, he mused as he awaited a reaction from the Governor-General, are not like the British. They were different, not to be clubbed with other European nations. Our identity is entwined with Goa, he said to himself, which is not merely an overseas colony. It is actually an overseas province, ultramar Português, Portugal abroad, and part of a pluri continental country. This is how he had received his training, and now that he was here serving his countrymen, this was the world view from which he operated. Even Salazar had backed it up by emphasizing that the residents of Goa were Portuguese citizens conforming to the religious, cultural and social spirit of Western Europe despite being geographically based in Indian territory.

'We must get ready,' the Governor-General said to the two men in the room. Both of them knew exactly what he was thinking. Plano Sentinela—the military operation that would be put in action before and during an attack from outside forces in order to defend the territory. However, from what he had seen of the troops today, full of sloth and sloppiness, the captain was doubtful if the Portuguese forces could even put up a decent defence. He wanted to suggest to the Governor-General that it was perhaps time to concede to reason. Even though he was grateful for Salazar's policy, which allowed him to stay a descendente in Goa, the land of his birth, most of the world's political systems were changing over to democracy. And all the NATO nations looked down on Portugal for still holding on to their title of colonial ruler within Africa, in places like Angola and Mozambique, or India and Macau on the Asian continent. Yet, he couldn't dare suggest the one thing he wanted to. The word that kept flashing like monsoon lightning across his mind: surrender. It would be dignified. It would save the lives of his precious fellow men. Even if the Indians took over, ultimately, everyone who had a piece of this land forged in their hearts and their identity would be capable of self-rule. And how glorious the next chapter could be. However, he didn't want to appear a coward in his uniform. So he saluted his leader and commander.

20

Rosie kissed the cross on her neck after thanking the Lord and the Mother for a good month of sales. Her husband was the one who caught fish, prawn, crab and other fruit of the sea, but it was she who spent the day going door-to-door with the fresh catch, selling to her now-regular patrons before settling in her spot at the Panjim market with the other fishwives. For the past four weeks she had sold all the catch and saved the bundle of money she made in a knot in her sari. If things kept going this way, she could finally save up enough to make their hutment brick-solid and register it in her name so she'd have security for life.

Dinner was ready, the same as every meal. Sorak, or curry, accompanied by dried fish and a mound of local red rice grown in her brother's paddy fields. She was hungry and her husband, Cajetan, wasn't home. It was his usual practice to head to the taverna in the evening and come home late, usually singing loudly and waking her up from her sleep. He would snore boorishly in his drunken sleep, and she would have to shake him awake a few times at sunrise so that he could head out in the boat at Dona Paula for the day's haul. The thought itself angered her, so she sat down in front of her thali and ate her dinner.

After her meal, Rosie was overcome with weariness and prepared to go to sleep. She left Cajetan's dinner covered in the back room of the hut, which served as the kitchen and storeroom. She changed into her nightie and loosened her hair from the tight bun she had worn it in from the morning. She was just about to dive into her mattress when she felt an urge to indulge in a small moment of joy. She went to the corner of the room, where she stored her clothes in a metal trunk. She wanted a quick look at her earnings for the week, something to add a little gleam to her dreams. Her real dream was to own a proper house, not this ramshackle wooden structure where the monsoon torrents would stream through the earthen tile roof. She wanted to touch the possibility of that future tonight in the form of coins and notes. The possibility of a life of dignity. Who knew, maybe she too would have a fish lady come sell her some fresh catch in the mornings, right at her doorstep. She'd haggle over the price while her morning chai developed a layer of cream from getting cold.

Rosie fished out her green sari, the one she usually wore on special occasions like marriages, feasts or to the local tiatr. Its brightness reached out to her quick fingers and she gently yanked it out of the pile of petticoats and sari yardage. She found the corner that she had knotted into the size of a large fist. Her heart sank. It looked considerably smaller, shrimp-like. First a wave of disbelief shook her entire body, which cell by cell turned into such a rage that all she could see in front of her for a second was a brilliant blackness. Without bothering to change her clothes, she got her slippers on her feet and stormed out in her nightie into the night.

Fifteen minutes later, Rosie reached a road that wasn't far from the empty Dona Paula jetty where her husband's boat was tethered. Most of the shops on the street were shuttered at that hour. But sounds of chatter spilled out from a closed door bearing the sign 'Romeo' above it. She followed the noise; whoever was inside sounded broad and raucous, albeit muffled, and was stumbling about drunkenly. She stood on the threshold and, with anger, pushed open the door of the taverna so strongly that it slammed with a thud against the wall.

The patrons of the low-lit bar, sitting at the tables, looked up with startled eyes, as though this was a raid. They were met with a sight to behold—a woman with wild streaks of frizzy hair streaming past her shoulders wearing nothing but a flapping nightdress. Women didn't usually come into the taverna so all the Goan men there—European, indigenous, descendente and mestiço—looked as curious as they were amused. Some were in uniform, some were dressed like fidalgos, and the rest were a medley of less affluent vendors or fisherfolk. All classes of men seated in one room and united in spirit.

Rosie wound her way to the corner at the back of the room where the bar was located, her slippers slapping noisily against her heels, a mean scowl on her face.

'Augusto! Tell me where he is. I know he is here,' Rosie hissed at the barman.

Augusto looked around inquiringly. 'He was here.' He looked over at a trio in the corner, 'Ei, Pinto. Where is Caji, Patrão?'

'I think so toilet,' Pinto responded casually and turned back.

Rosie left the bar just as suddenly as she had burst in and went to the side of the building where the toilet was located.

Just in time. She heard the creak of the toilet door, along with familiar whistling.

'You stupid!' Rosie shouted in the narrow space between roofs.

'Yagh!' Cajetan responded clutching his heart. It was more the spectre his wife presented in her nightie, her hair falling rawly around her, suddenly standing there in the tiny space that surprised him. He believed in ghosts and ghouls, and she could easily have been one that came across from the nearby cemetery, lying in wait to inhabit the life of a poor, defenceless drunken soul. His worst fears on these nocturnal outhouse visits had come true to haunt the life out of him.

'Where is the money?' she demanded straight off.

'Money?'

'Bebdo!' Drunkard, shouted Rosie as she slapped her husband on the back. He cried out a little and stumbled forward to the empty road, nearly tripping over himself.

'All the savings of the month, which I had tied in my sari. Gone! I know you took it, you thief . . . you . . . you scoundrel!' Rosie whacked Cajetan on his head. 'We will never-ever ever-ever be able to make something of our lives, you drunkard!'

Cajetan caught hold of Rosie's flailing hands. 'Wait, wait, Rosie darling.'

'Don't darling me,' she cried.

'See, yes, I took the money.' Rosie started to wail upon Cajetan's admission. 'Shh, but see, some went for Augusto, your brother. But some I . . . didn't drink. I gave to someone important.'

'Who is so important?' Rosie wailed again.

'Shhh . . . Rosie. There two boys inside, white-face ones. They are playing cards. They are making bets. I talked to them. One boy—he was quiet boy—was saying that he work in big man's office. In Cabo Palace. He is important, he say. You know, his job, he make telegraph for the Guvna General.

'He say, when prime minster sitting far away wanting to send message, he send from telegraph in Portugal to telegraph in Cabo. One person writing this note. Then second person typing on paper. Third person takes paper and sticks on big paper to make letter. This boy, he is first person, writing from telegraph. He is big man, this boy. He say he pays me Monday.'

'You stupid! Stupid! Stupid!' Rosie was livid and started smacking her husband wherever she could. The fool, giving her money—*her money*—to another fool at the bar. To a silly drunkard pacló gambler. He didn't even think to charge interest on it. Did she have to think of everything! That night, Rosie shepherded Cajetan home, to their hovel, with curses and smacks.

21

Shirly sat at the dining table, her hair neatly braided into two pigtails, with a ribbon at each end, drinking fresh orchata. She could overhear Goku's idle chatter with the customary morning vendors. She was sure that there was something fishy brewing between Goku and the poder. Between sips, she caught fragments of the conversation between the housemaid and the fish seller, who sounded loud and upset this morning.

'Can you believe it? He gave away all the money, pisso! To a drunken pacló. Gambling! Only Jesus can help me now . . .' The fish seller proceeded to narrate the events of the previous evening, from the horror of her missing money to finding her husband in the taverna toilet, to his pathetic explanation, to her assessment of her poor luck in life—all to Goku's sympathetic ear, who cluck-clucked while selecting the choice bits of fish and prawn she required to make the meals of the day, while Sukkoo and Bukkoo, mewling and purring in intoxication with the piscine aromas, rubbed their rumps lovingly against the two.

In the other room, Shirly could hear the rumble of the sewing machine. Mamtu was already at work on her costume for the musical.

Shirly followed the sound to her mother's bedroom and stopped to watch from the threshold. Mamtu sat at a wooden table that had a cast iron base and a Singer sewing machine on top, pumping the treadle with her foot. The machine was black with a flourishing gold design and a hand pump on the right, which could be substituted for the treadle to operate the needle. A wedding gift from her grandmother right before their move across borders. With every pump of the treadle, Mamtu imagined that it was a step closer to home. From the lessons she had gained from the old matriarch, Mamtu was adept at making her own sari blouses and even her daughters' clothes. As soon as each piece was finished, Mamtu would turn it over in her hands and imagine her or her family wearing their new clothes as they crossed the threshold of her childhood home in Karachi. The anticipation animated her treadling foot further and the machine roared with gusto. All Shirly heard was a Singer at work. But she was used to the noise by now and was invited by her mother to participate by turning the hand crank on occasion. On noticing her at the doorway, Mamtu beckoned her.

'Look! Do you like it? It is velvet. Like a kitten against your skin.' Shirly ran her fingertips over the cloth. She had never touched velvet before. It was indeed unusual and plush as a rose petal. 'Your father brought this for me on the last trip he took to the Far East. I thought it would be perfect for your costume.'

Shirly noticed the catch in her mother's voice at the mention of her father. She looked over at the altar where an incense stick released a snaky wisp into the sunlight in front of a photo of a turbaned saint Jhulelal. Seated on a huge pallo, river fish, he gazed peacefully at her, bearing a halo, like Jesus. But today, for the first time, she caught herself wondering why he wore a turban. She had never seen a man wear one in her small world here, and in fact, none of the gods in any of the chapels or temples she had come across had turbaned saints. She couldn't say why, but she knew in her gut that this perhaps made her family different from the other city folk who had crosses or tulsi plants in their doorways. If there was any implication in their very singular turbaned saint, Shirly didn't know it because her family was considered as Portuguese as any other Panjim neighbour could be. Their passports said so. Her mother had narrated stories of the saint, spooned into her along with her meals. Faraway stories from across a border where he usually saved hapless victims, showing them the miracle of their faith. Shirly couldn't understand the power this man in the photo had over her mother. How could he help her unless he stepped out of his frame and released her father from prison.

'This maroon will look beautiful against your silky brown hair.' Mamtu lovingly brushed a stray lock behind her daughter's ear. Then she turned back to make the Singer machine roar as she fed it more maroon velvet, grateful to have the task at hand to distract her from drowning in her whirlpooling emotions. Shirly was confident about her mother's seamstress skills and knew that she would look exactly the part of Zulekha in the musical. But even the best costume in the world couldn't erase the woolly unease she still harboured about going on stage in front of an audience.

22

Familiar hymns chorused throughout the school. Sister Olga was prepping the hapless students selected for the Christmas choir all day these days. Now, when she saw Shirly and Ana passing through the corridor, she didn't get so red under her wimple and instead looked softly at them. Just the fact that they were in a musical together made her feel like they were finally in the Almighty's hands and all would be well with the world.

It was nearing afternoon, and the girls in Shirly and Ana's class were restless. It was a science lesson with Sister Epifania, a tall, lanky nun who bored the class with her droning intonation. When she wasn't monotonous, she could get high-pitched, especially now, in her frustration at the girls' incorrect answers. Rowdiness tended to be contagious in a class of disentranced girls, much to the teacher's exasperation. The class finally descended into anarchy when she turned around to write a correct answer on the blackboard and a crude drawing of a monkey on a piece of paper was found stuck to her cloak.

'Look here, be quiet!' she attempted bravely in her falsetto, but then turned back to the board. The girls went into an uproar of laughter again. Poor Sister Epifania just couldn't figure it out. She tried to silence the lot but her voice was unable to rise above their collective rabble and she started to wheeze from the effort.

Even Shirly, who had fallen silent these days, couldn't hold back a chuckle that bubbled up involuntarily. Ana, strategically seated that afternoon in the front row, looked across at her friend with a naughty and satisfied grin. 'I'm going to ask Sister Olga to call the gypsies now! I'm going to hand you to them,' Sister Epifania wheezed out her threat. Unfortunately for her, Shirly and Ana shared a delicious disparaging laugh.

While Sister Epifania was going hoarse, the familiar shape of the headmistress appeared outside the class. She wafted in unexpectedly, causing the laughter to die down. Sister Epifania smoothed her cloak and habit while her words retreated to the back bench of her throat. 'Er . . . they were . . . I was just . . .' she began, but the Mother Superior raised one hand silently to interrupt her.

The girls stood up to greet the headmistress, and she raised both her arms to indicate that they be seated. 'Girls, there is an important and very momentous event coming up this week. We will be taking a school trip to visit the Basilica do Bom Jesus in Velha Goa. Most of you know it. It is a beautiful church and very special. It carries the sacred remains of our revered Saint Francis Xavier. There will be an exposition of the venerable body at the Sé Cathedral, which by miracle is perfectly preserved.' The science teacher Sister Epifania made the sign of the cross at the word 'miracle'. 'Before leaving for the cathedral, we will assemble together on the rua and go by caminhão. For this day, we require a letter signed by your parents that you be allowed to join the school trip. Please do bring it by tomorrow as we are planning to go by the end of the week.' The Mother Superior turned to Sister Epifania, 'That's all, Sister, carry on.' She peeled off the offending paper from Epifania's back, handed it to the teacher and headed out.

Sister Epifania's face elongated into a tight line. Holding the paper in her hand, she grunted a squeak of displeasure at the class but was drowned out by the school bell.

23

'An artist never reveals their secret,' said José to five-year-old Shirly.

'I promise I won't tell anyone,' Shirly entreated, fully ready to absorb all the secrets of the universe in her eager ears from this magical, paternal statue man.

'First of all, my dear, do you know what an artist is?' Faria quizzed.

Shirly wobbled her head no.

'An artist, my dear Shirly, is a hypnotist.'

'Hip . . . hip nost?' asked Shirly.

'Yes. All painters, poets, musicians and dancers, they are hypnotists.' said Faria. 'But only very few can be true artists. Do you know what makes one truly an artist?'

'No,' said Shirly, her feathery lashes framing her wide-eyed intrigue. 'What is hip nost?'

'A true artist, one who can really be a hypnotist—and *this is the secret*—is someone who can change nature.'

Shirly took a deep breath, and her little chest rose and lowered itself with the magnanimity of the shared secret.

'A true artist can make it rain, or make a rainbow appear in the sky, or . . .'

'Or make shapes in the clouds!' Shirly hopped on to the bandwagon in excitement.

'Make wood catch fire!'

'Make froggies dance!'

'. . . and sing!'

'Make the wind blow!'

'. . . and sing!'

The two unusual friends tried to outshout each other in their enthusiasm and comradeship when suddenly Shirly had to snap back to the present.

'Shirrrrrrrly,' João's voice reached out across the road. She had walked back from her afternoon singing session with Lisette and, instead of directly heading home, now sat on the garden parapet. She was staring at the cannons and wondering why they were there. Could the garden have been a battleground? If she had to battle for the garden, *her* garden, would she fire the cannons? Or like the ladyfish in her father's breakfast-time story, would she surrender, so the babyfish, in this case the garden, could stay intact and whole?

And yet, she had heard that her father had been caught with dynamite. Would he be okay hurting her garden, her land, her world?

Why couldn't José tell her something? Anything! That everything would be okay with her father, that she would be okay in front of the audience singing for the first time. How easy the Christmas show would be for him; he was a hypnotist, after all. He could simply sway the audience to love him. She remembered his advice about picturing them as vegetables to be chopped and made a mental note about trying that trick when the time came.

She looked in the direction of the sound brought to her by the breeze and saw João over by the waterfront several yards down, opposite the Araujo house, waving in excitement at her. Hamid was with him. Shirly jumped up, crossed the empty street and reached their spot.

'Shirly! Hamid says that Agope will be going to the Aguada prison.'

'Why?'

'Do you want to go?'

As though he could read her mind, Hamid explained, 'He has to deliver something. It could be possible to meet your father.'

'Are you coming?' Shirly asked João.

'Yes.'

'Okay,' she said bravely. After her first visit to meet Deepak in prison, her family was denied papers to revisit him. So she would take her chance today.

'Let us go.'

'Now?'

'Yes, now,' said Hamid. 'The water is calm, we go now according to the tide. You are coming?'

'Yes.' Shirly remembered that Mamtu was waiting at home for her. Luckily, more and more, her adolescence relieved her of the weight of such niggling responsibilities as informing her mother that she was sneaking out on to the river with dhowmen.

The Mandovi fluttered like a ribbon in the gentle wind as the trio made their way downriver. They caught up with a mid-sized dhow, over which Agope was presiding, supervising the filling of supplies.

'Put there. Ah, Quarachim! Good you come. We try to see Papa Quarachim.'

The young adults boarded the large dhow and settled on the wooden seats as Agope adjusted sacks around them. The hull had some water in it which sloshed at their feet as the dhow bobbed up and down. João and Shirly were distracted from their purpose by all the activity around them.

'See, it is good now. We go.' Agope and an oarsman adjusted the sails, cupping the river breeze in them. The fuller sails pulled the boat and its cargo towards the other bank, the one beyond Betim, which was closer to the lighthouse. 'This water is our mother,' said Agope poetically. 'She feeds us, she shows us the way, she gives us what we need, what we want. What you want . . .' Agope gently touched Shirly with a barnacled finger under her left shoulder, close to where her gold chain sat near her heart. 'She give you. You only ask.'

Shirly didn't know how to ask for everything to be normal again. To want her biggest fear to be facing an audience with her voice, instead of imagining the worst happening to her father in a prison. She wasn't sure if she nodded or if the dhow bobbed in a surface current. But she went with the flow.

'There is secret under the prison. Aguada is water. There is passage of water underneath. We try to see, hah.' Shirly couldn't imagine a secret water passage under the Aguada prison. She perished the thought that an escaping convict could drown under there. Or that she might too, in an airless pool swallowed by darkness where no one could know. Not even her mother, whom she hadn't warned about this adventure. Why couldn't she just try to go across by road with Mamtu, as she had done earlier? What exactly was the point of this trip? Her mind played tricks on her, but Shirly didn't keel over. Not yet.

The cannon-lined shore drew closer, with the low, rectangular blocks that held her father somewhere within, topped with a lighthouse. As she got nearer to the reality of a looming prison for a second time, her feelings were mixed. What if the man whom she had had on a pedestal all her life was really on the wrong side of the law? Did her father harbour a facet that his family didn't know about? The next wave that bobbed the dhow helped her shake the thought out of her head. A stone-and-tar concrete jetty rolled out into the water from a side of the prison that she hadn't noticed on her first visit. The prison commandant's office looked down directly to the landing where the dhow could dock.

'They can see us,' said João, reading her thoughts.

'Don't worry,' Agope said enigmatically, sounding a little too unencumbered. Shirly wanted to believe him. Two officers in shorts came into view at the mouth of the dock, and one of them came forward as the underside of the dhow scraped the surface of the quay. The oarsman lowered the central sail halfway.

'Hello, Agope, happy to see you,' said the officer, to the surprise of Shirly and João. Both men seemed very relaxed in the other's presence.

'You are getting stuck over here. You come, become one of us. I give you pirate ship,' Agope said with back-slapping cheer to the officer, who grinned back. 'Hamid, give him.' Agope motioned to the three heavy jute sacks sitting in the hull. João stood up to help Hamid lift the sacks off the boat on to the dock. After the first sack made it to land, Agope added, 'We can meet one of the rats in the cage?'

The officer who had opened the sack to peer in said nonchalantly, 'Which one?'

'Quarachim,' Agope said without hesitating.

For a few moments, only the sound of water flapping on the dock surrounded them. When the second bag was hauled on to land, the officer said, 'It is not a problem. You know where to go.'

'Good man, ah, good man, my friend.' This time Agope helped the two boys with the third haul. 'Everything is there. Very good, very good.'

The officer touched his nose as though it was a sign, one that Shirly only understood by context, if she did at all. Hamid hopped out to help the officer and was joined by João. While the boat waited, the three lugged the bags to the other end of the jetty, where the second officer stood. After the two officers exchanged words, the second handed Hamid a small brown envelope. The two boys clambered back into the boat and Hamid handed Agope the envelope, who promptly checked its contents. Then it was Agope's turn to do the finger-to-nose sign back at the officer. Hamid used one foot to push off the dock, and once more the oarsman lifted the central sail to harness the wind while he employed the long pole to steer.

They weren't heading back. The dhow pushed on downriver to the west, towards the ocean where the vermilion orb still burnt brightly above the horizon.

'What was in those sacks?' asked Shirly with trepidation.

'Hahaha, you don't know?' Agope's bronze tooth caught the sun at the back of his smile. 'We are "gypsy", we sell the small children to Portugay,' said Agope with an edge of self-deprecating humour. 'Tell her, Hamid.'

Shirly's lips were upturned—she had outgrown her fear of 'gypsies' that she knew were mostly concocted in the imagination.

'I making the joke, little one. The Portugay like the fancy things—tobacco, spirit, nice cologne. They not allowed to take from main gate, so I bring for them.'

Once they reached the mouth of the river, the Gaspar Dias beach stretched out further on the left. 'You know that one?' Agope asked.

'The Cabo, right?' replied João.

Beyond Gaspar Dias was a rocky outcrop above which stood a large white building roofed with terracotta tiles. Shirly had never seen the seat of the Governor-General of Goa from the ocean before. She had only heard stories of how her mother and father used to be invited to important parties there. In the photos that appeared in the *Diario de Noite* papers, her mother was usually the only woman in a sari surrounded by frocked Luso ladies.

Agope signalled to the oarsman to head right towards the land beyond the Aguada prison. There were no docks or guards standing sentinel here.

'Is here,' said Agope as he pulled the pointy stern of the dhow towards the rocks that had a dark, V-shaped opening licked by waves. 'Tide is rising, we go quick,' the boat's captain declared. Shirly's fears rose too. How could the boat survive the rocks they were driving into? Nearing them, a huge salmon-coloured crab with one large pincer thumb appeared out of the fissures and scurried higher above the spray of the ocean. Shirly shrieked and João held the sides of the dhow as it rocked its way towards the cliff of boulders. Agope wore a peculiar smiling grimace, displaying his rotten teeth, while Hamid wiped away saltwater spray from his face.

The opening seemed wider up close, except that the sail wouldn't fit through. In answer to her thoughts, the oarsman dipped the sails halfway and slanted the central mast forward so that it bowed down as the boat proceeded to the entrance.

They left the light behind them, the slickness of the wall of boulders on either side glimmered less and less. Shirly looked up and immediately covered her head with her arms, letting out another shriek. Overhead, using the ceiling of rock as their living room floor, were multitudes of fiddler crabs, vying for space one over the other. These were not the small harmless ghost crabs she would chase on the beach at Gaspar Dias; these were muscular crustaceans that could inflict powerful pain with their pincer grip. Shirly often scared herself with the thought of the three-bladed fan disengaging from the ceiling of her room while rotating at high speed. Now she imagined what would happen if this sea of orange-brown overhead suddenly lost their grip and saw the same splash of colour behind her eyes.

João heard her gasp at her own thoughts and put his arm around her protectively. The boat jostled them and they smacked heads together. 'It's okay, don't worry,' still serious, he whispered to her and she was mildly reassured as his bony weight wrapped around her shoulders. The water became calmer, and with each wave, they floated further down the cave. Plopping sounds echoed around their ears in the darkness. After an eternity of five minutes of pushing through, there was a clearing of light up ahead, almost drawing them magnetically.

'He is coming, I hope,' said Agope.

'Who is?' asked João and Shirly in unison.

'Why we are here,' Agope replied just as enigmatically.

And then a voice, beautiful in its familiarity to Shirly, echoed, 'Agope? Shirly?'

'Daddy!' Shirly felt a surge of excitement. She heard a piece of herself that was outside her own body.

The canal opened up to a shallow cavern where the dhow ran partially aground. There stood Deepak, thinner than in her memory of him, face stubbled and lined with roughness. Shirly felt a wince of sorrow at the sight of her father, more deflated than ever, looking a little ghastly in the play of shadows within the cavern.

'Shirly,' Deepak said tenderly as she hopped on to the stony ground where her father stood. He didn't fail to notice the attentive way João gave her a hand and his daughter blushing mildly at the gesture. Steps were coarsely hewn into the stone wall which led up to the light, where the officer whom the passengers had just met at the quay stood, presiding over this covert meeting. He peered down and tapped his nose.

'What is up here, Daddy?' Shirly asked.

'This seems to be a secret seawater canal. In the past this was used to bring in supplies to the fort, it seems. Now only pirates and gypsy girls use it.' Deepak pushed a wind-worn strand of his daughter's hair behind her ear. 'Hello, João, Hamid,' he acknowledged the boys and Agope with a nod of his head. Then he looked at Shirly. 'You have to take care of your mother and sister for me, all right?'

Shirly didn't feel like this was the time to correct her father about the Romanis not being dangerous like pirates, or at least how she had realized this truth. She had so much to ask and gave vent, 'Even Goku doesn't feel like eating anymore.' Both of them chuckled at the tragicomic picture Goku cut in their imagination, sitting before her mountain of curried rice, unable to plunge her fingers into it. Then Shirly grew serious. 'What happened? I don't understand why you are here. Why can't the lawyer get you out? You are innocent, no?' Shirly wondered why the answers to these questions couldn't be simple like black was black and white was white and maroon was maroon.

'I am innocent. I have done everything I can to make this world right.' Shirly wasn't sure what that meant. Deepak looked into the sensitive, open-hearted eyes of his daughter and detected the umbra of uncertainty darkening over her sense of trust. She was no longer the little girl who created imaginary worlds, replete with conversations with friends invented from the stories he told her or the books he showed her in the library. She was learning to question things, using her own judgement. He wouldn't have her unconditional confidence in his every word now, and it was natural. He had to appeal to her rational mind, give her his explanations with tangible shape and form. But how could he do it from here, in this place of shadows? 'Shirly, listen to me. I am going to arrange a meeting for you. You will understand everything. But I want you to be very, very careful, do you understand? You are not to tell anyone about this.'

For the first time in her life, something in Shirly didn't latch on to the false hope that Deepak was suggesting she enter. How could he arrange anything from here as a prisoner? He didn't seem to realize that he was not as omniscient as she had once believed him to be. Didn't he know that even Freddy the advocate wasn't sure about his case? This cause seemed frustratingly lost. She was the free one, and maybe she just had to save him, right here, right now. 'Come with me, Daddy. Let's go. We'll hide you in the house.'

Maddeningly, Deepak just laughed off her words. 'They will catch us before we reach the other side of the river, Puttha.' Despite the echoes that took their whispers and bounced them off the stone walls, Shirly knew that the officer hadn't heard them. She wasn't sure if she should feel mildly reassured at her father's avowal of innocence and his ease in this situation. However, their meeting was cut short by the rise in tide. Agope motioned that it was time to leave, and she had to wrench her eyes away from the frame of her father who was led back by the officer.

As they pushed off once more through the eye of the needle into the tormented ocean on the outside, despite herself, Shirly had an unmistakable ripple in her gut that she didn't have to seek adventure; here it was, spelunking face-to-face with her. But she had a new feeling that she didn't require it anymore. At least, not elsewhere. Not away from this river that open-mouthedly kissed the ocean, this land, these people. She felt the spirit of Zulekha, the one she had to give voice and life to, enter her.

24

Capitão Carlos Alexandre Morais watched the rise of Glory's naked form under the sheet. The moon was a hungry crescent eyeing them from its dusky-skinned perch outside the window. He pulled up his pyjamas and walked barefoot on the cool tiles to the salon. They had barely had a glass each from the bottle of port that Glory had gifted him earlier in the evening before they fell upon each other with the passion of all the seas that had separated them.

The capitão poured the night-red drink from the carafe into his wine goblet and stepped on to the balcão. The officer's barracks on the Altinho Hill was a luxurious vantage point to survey the cidade's streetlights that meandered along the bank of the Mandovi. In the distance, the Aguada's searchlight occasionally swept the far horizon. He sipped from the glass and tasted the Duoro Valley aged in oak. Its sweetness was different, of another world, a little alien to him. Glory had tried to convince him to take a posting back in Lisbon, now that she had graduated from the Escola Médico-Cirúrgica in Panjim and received her employment letter from the Clínica Lusíadas in Lisbon. But he wasn't sure about leaving the soil of his birth. His parents—of European stock, from Portugal—were retired to their villa in Damão, where his father was last posted. He, their only living son, naturally took up work with the government as his father had done, but the difference was that he was from this water, a son of Goa.

He took another sip of the port and marvelled at its warmth. Capitão Morais remembered the same sensation filling his veins when he had first met Glory at Sunday mass. She was in her last year of medical college, and he had caught her brazenly looking in his direction during the sermon. Her earthen skin shone with the lighting, soft and diffused from the ornate stained glass on either side of the high ceiling, and her dark eyes swallowed him whole. Right after the sermon, they simply gravitated towards each other and had been engrossed so ever since.

Carlos's mind flitted from the luscious port to the meeting with his higher officer, Lieutenant Colonel Andrade, and the Governor-General. Would India be prioritizing its agenda to integrate Goa into its territory or would it focus on repelling the Chinese aggression up north near the Himalayan border? Even the Indian politicians were debating this. Perhaps there was some hope then that his men wouldn't have to pick up arms and show what they weren't made of. Not that any of this would make his decision to marry Glory any easier. Her heart was already in Portugal, it was just that her body happened to be born in Goa, like his. For Carlos, the thrills of Lisboa weren't tempting enough to entice him away. Would the long distance rupture Glory's love for him?

He took another sip of port. In case the Indians took over, what would he really do, even if Glory weren't in the picture? Should he stay? He remembered that even Portugal had taken the rumblings across the border seriously enough to warrant sending a note of accord to India, stating that despite the territorial violations in Goa, Portugal was extending a hand of truce and a suggestion for the world itself to evaluate their legitimate right over Estado da Índia. So Carlos had to authorize clearances for the international press officers sent by the UN to gauge the state of affairs, while they officially documented the land and its people in order to show the world that Goa was indeed peaceful, with an identity of its own. But then some bloody fool had set off a bomb at a police station to screw it all up. No one was killed or injured, but it was enough to invite global criticism at this highly sensitive time.

And then, in the last meeting with the Governor-General, he was made privy to the written response by the Indian government, which essentially stated that Portugal's time was up, and it should exit the estado peacefully, or else. And for good measure the promise was dangled that Goa would retain its individual character with regard to language and tradition.

Carlos desperately wanted to believe that Goa's culture and individuality would be fully preserved when it became part of the Indian Union, like the former French settlements had. Or had they? If that was indeed the likely situation to follow, there wouldn't be any need to abandon ship here, so to speak. He had learnt from Glory that her parents—who were also local doctors—were fiercely supportive of their daughter's achievements and her impending move to Lisbon, where the pay was better. For this reason, they hadn't forced her to look at suitors, all from long-standing indigenous families, from their church. Glory hadn't told them about him yet, and the only way forward, if he wanted it, was to ask for her hand in marriage after seeking blessings from her parents.

Carlos drained his glass and headed back to bed. He slipped his body against her shape and put his nose against her hair with its familiar smell of coconuts. He would have to talk to her about it in the morning but secretly hoped that he wouldn't be confronted with the hardest choice of his life.

25

'In the much hypothetical case that Goa ever becomes a part of India, you can be sure that her culture will be lost, just ell o ess tee, lost to the aggressive and . . . and . . . and unaesthetic ways of the rest of the country.' Maria Menezes didn't realize she was spraying spit all over the tea cosy in her vehemence. 'The peace will be replaced with a frenzy stemming from a new economy that is growing rampant, without any planning or control. Not only will the old caste system find new life, but new forms of caste will be cast. I shudder to think of living here, say, fifty years from now. That Senhor Nehru should just leave our Goa alone.'

Maria was quite adamant on the issue. Every cell of her body was filled with the desire that things should remain just as they were. Why would anyone rock the boat at all? Goa was progressive, women had equal rights to property, and for those who chose to embrace it, the Hindu caste system was completely escapable. Praise God. 'We are all of us Portuguese, no?' Maria was a native of Goa whose passport and heart bore the stamp of Portugal all over it. It didn't matter that she was located so far away from the country, her identity was as continental as the pastéis de nata she served with tea. She poured out the hot brew into fine blue-and-white porcelain teacups on an ornate silver tray. She brought out the good crockery on pleasant afternoons like this, spent with dear friends. 'Anyhow, why are we talking about this? We would surely know about any threats to the borders. For years there has been talk of a "liberation", and nothing. I tell you, it wouldn't be a liberation, it would be a damnation!'

Two other women in the room, Irma da Costa and Clara Lopes, chuckled light-heartedly at Maria's deliberately summed-up rhyme on her stance of Goa delivered from Portugal and into the hands of an Indian nation. Lisette, who was also present, sipped quietly on her tea.

'How did we come up with such a topic?' Irma asked, looking around the room.

'Lisette was telling us about her Man Friday, Mosha . . .'

'Mushu,' said Lisette. 'He is always worried about us leaving to go back to Lisboa. He's made us promise to take him with us, if ever there is reason for us to return.'

'Well, Mushu should just rest his poor head. There is no reason at all,' said Clara. Her husband, Anibal Lopes, who was a ground officer at Transportes Aéreos da Índia Portuguesa, the State airline, was privy to information from the army and navy, and so far there wasn't any news that could stir a Goan cat from its siesta. 'Any news of your husband?' Clara asked in Lisette's direction.

'No, nothing yet,' said Lisette. Her husband, and the father of their three children, Eugenio, was the head of accounts at the fazenda. A few times a year, his job took him to Lisbon, a period usually filled with meetings and number-crunching for an entire week. This time he had been gone nearly a whole month, and Lisette was really feeling the pangs of separation in all the fado she had ever sung. Luckily, she had the school musical to occupy her. Yet she longed for the weekly calls she received from him, and her heart would lift just hearing the sound of the operator's familiar Lisbon accent on the phone, right before their lines were connected. Each week he would say that he would be home the following week, but it was always deferred.

Her answer was followed by a melancholic lull, so Maria changed the subject. 'Let's all make a trip to Cine-Teatro Nacional next week. *Roman Holiday* is playing. I shall tell Christian to purchase the tickets for us. Lisette, hopefully you can spare some time from the musical rehearsals? Audrey Hepburn is in it. I just adore her.'

Lisette had already seen the fine, porcelain-boned actress she loved so much starring as Ann, the princess who throws off her royal mantle to see the sights of Rome incognito. Lisette had felt the rush from the screen as the delicate-waisted Audrey Hepburn zoomed about town on the front of a scooter, with square-jawed Gregory Peck's solid arms around her, and she didn't mind watching the screen romance play out again. She wasn't sure if her husband would return in time to accompany her and the other couples, and once more she felt the blunt stab of his absence but nodded in Maria's direction that she would join them.

26

Aphonso Kamat switched off the transistor. There was nothing noteworthy on the radio that evening, so he proceeded to boil the red rice he had received from his neighbour's land. He'd have it with the leftover sukhi bangda—dried mackerel—purchased from the widow in the next village who sometimes sold her preserved pre-monsoon catch by the roadside. He would have preferred river fish, which he found more flavourful, not just as a taste that lingered from his childhood memories, but for its juicy piquancy. To make up for the lack, he resorted to what was on hand, with generous dollops of radish pickle, steeped in toddy vinegar and coarse sea salt. Sitting cross-legged on the stone floor, he filled his belly. When done, he licked his fingers, poured water on them from the beak of a clay rooster pot, and then closed his eyes for a siesta.

Nothing much happened that day, as ever. Till later that evening, when the house echoed with the crescendo of crickets thrumming in the surrounding bushes. There was a sharp rap on the door. Not expecting any visitors, a cautious Aphonso pulled his pants over his trunks and opened the door a mere crack to see who it was.

'Ulfanzo Kamat?' A man with a thick moustache, in a soldier's uniform, stood at his doorway.

'Aphonso,' corrected Kamat, opening the door fully.

'Sir!' The thick-moustachioed man gave way to a second tall man in an olive-green turban, who also had a moustache and a beard. His eyes were big and bright, and his olive-green uniform was more decorated than the junior officer's, who had stepped aside.

'At ease,' said the turbaned man, more for the sake of the officer than Aphonso. Turning to Kamat, he said, 'Major Diljeet Singh Kapoor from the Sikh Regiment.'

'Namaste, welcome, Sir,' said Aphonso, staring at the tall, strapping, turbaned man, a sight alien to Estado da Índia. 'What is this about?'

'We thank you for your good work and intelligence. We have received orders to launch an ambush and we will require your assistance,' said Major Kapoor, ignoring the fact that Aphonso was staring north of his eye level at his turban the whole time.

'Ambush? Just say when and where, Sir!' said Aphonso, not lowering his eyes from turban level. After almost four years of being camped out in this no-man's zone, could the adventure he was seeking finally have knocked at his door?

'This is all I can tell you now. We are proceeding to an assembly area east of Dodamarg. We have the coordinates, and you can accompany the regiment.'

Aphonso stood at attention in his vest and raised a sharp salute to the major. 'Ready, Sir!' The major did an about-face and headed out the door.

Aphonso, acting quickly, shoved spare clothing and his watch into a shoulder bag. Deciding not to take the transistor with him, he shut and bolted any open windows in the ramshackle brick hut. Before heading for the door, he looked across at an altar in the corner with incense sticks and ash droppings before a small stone Shiva lingam and a calendar image of Mother Mary. Along with this, there was a photo of a family of four, steeped in tea stains and sepia tones. He pulled this from the altar and gazed at it silently. Aphonso Kamat tucked the picture in his bag as well and made his way out, padlocking the door before setting off to change history.

27

The footsteps on the flagstones grew louder in their approach. The prisoners who could hear them strained their ears to gauge where they stopped. A visit from outside could mean anything. A surprise inquisition, or a new inmate. It was very unlikely that it would mean someone's release, but the fact didn't stop the tiny glimmer of hope that lay buried in their ribs. Deepak was lying indolently on his side, rereading one of the newspapers that Mamtu had given him during her first and last visit. His newspaper had been passed around by the other inmates in his cell a few times over, an attempt to defuse the longevity and drag of time. The paper showed an old world that he once knew. It was full of news from the outside, advertisements, editorials and obituaries.

The officer belonging to the footsteps stopped outside Deepak's cell and turned the key with the rasping sound of iron scraping iron. He entered the cell and after scanning the room rested his eyes on Deepak. 'You, Deepak Kur. . . kur . . . kora . . .'

'Yes, Quarachim.' Deepak sat up.

'Come this way, please,' the officer said to him.

The inmates stiffened. Clinton looked over at him, offering him invisible ripple tides of courage and perseverance should the worst befall him—torture. Deepak acknowledged this in the pupils of his brown eyes. He followed the officer out.

'Visitor,' the officer said enigmatically as he led him down the grassy, cannon-lined walkway from the men's prison towards the bridge of office blocks over the arched tunnel underneath.

'Oh . . . thank you,' Deepak said with relief—it wouldn't be a torture session today. Light-heartedness started to bubble within him at the thought of seeing his wife. The hardness of the cell made him think often of swimming in the gentle, glistening features of her face and breathing her in, filling himself with her scent that was a mix of her Panjim kitchen, talcum powder and jaggery-flavoured perspiration. She would be in his arms once more, and all this would be his, even if momentarily, but it would be enough to go on. As they neared the arches of the wide tunnel, Deepak saw a figure that didn't belong to his wife.

'Thank you, officer. Senhor Quarachim, hello.' Freddy Baptista's voice echoed out as he stood there in his black advocate gown with a white collar and bands and a briefcase. The officer escorted Deepak to a stone seat carved into the base of one of the arches, then stepped away to stand at ease, resting one leg atop a stray cannonball and gazing out at the aqua view.

'Hello, Doutor, some good news, I hope?' Deepak asked, addressing his advocate with a respectful appellation mingled with good-natured trust that all would be well.

Freddy remained silent, which was very unusual, Deepak knew. The doutor was a quick-thinking gladiatorial man who usually shot his words out from rapid, well-angled legal assessments of a situation.

'Deepak, I want to tell you a little story.' Freddy ignored his question. He inhaled heavily and launched into a small tale, pursing his lips ever so often. 'There was once a tiger cub who made friends with a sparrow.

Every day, the sparrow and the tiger cub played together. Until the tiger cub grew up and stopped drinking his mother's milk and started to eat the flesh she hunted for them. Soon, although he loved his sparrow friend, he pushed him away because he knew one day he would bite down a little too hard during their play and the sparrow would not survive it. He hated to think that he would be the cause of the sparrow's death.'

'I don't understand, Doutor,' said Deepak, confused.

Freddy continued patiently, 'There is an old Konkani saying my grandmother used to tell me—dhant-ui mhojé ani vontt-ui mhojé. Do you know what it means?'

'The teeth are mine, and so are the lips?' Deepak translated quizzically.

'Yes, but what does it mean?'

'I really don't know, Freddy,' said Deepak more seriously.

'It alludes to avoiding hurting someone close to you.'

Deepak was surprised at all the dialectical small talk the usually direct attorney was making. Clearly, something was wrong, but Freddy was cha-cha-ing around the facts. Deepak needed to know before their time was up for this visit.

'If there is some bad news you need to share with me, Freddy, please feel free to express yourself. Once we know the problem, only then can we work on the solution.'

'I am unable to represent you, my dear Senhor Quarachim,' said Freddy heavily.

Deepak was silent for a while. 'I see. Why? What has happened?'

'There are some on the tribunal—I don't want to name names since I don't have evidence—but there is, I think, a judge on the tribunal who doesn't want to unbalance the status quo. Yesterday I was served a notice that I am defending enemies of the flag wilfully. My powers of immunity as an advocate are looking dim these days. And I'm afraid that simply by association with your case, I will be jeopardizing your chance of any freedom. Therefore, without going into too much detail, I wish to let you know that I cannot take your case any further.'

Deepak thought that Freddy's story didn't fit quite so well with the situation, but he understood. Freddy was the tiger cub and the teeth that could harm him though he didn't intend to.

'I understand your disappointment.'

'I don't know what will happen next.' Deepak felt trapped, with his options imprisoned by the situation.

'Things will go as usual. You will be given a trial and there will be a court-appointed advocate to defend you. However, it is best that I stay away since I don't know if I will be arrested anytime soon. And with me, your name will be dragged through the mud.'

A gust of wind blew through the airy tunnel, shifting the dirt in swirls around their feet. There was little left to say. With all the dignity he could muster, Deepak stood up and held out his hand, 'Thank you, Doutor, for telling me in person.' Then he added, 'I hope what you say isn't true and I wish you luck.'

Freddy and Deepak stood grimly shaking hands for a few seconds, then the advocate gripped his client's hand in both of his. 'I don't have any doubt that you will leave here. I leave it in His hands.'

28

Shirly and Ana walked up the steps of the Araujo house with ice fruit in their hands. They stood outside catching the melting drips off the lolly sticks before ringing the doorbell. Ana stuck her tongue out at Shirly, which had gone a deep orange. Shirly reciprocated with her own tongue, stained green. The door opened and Lisette found the two girls standing there with neon tongues. She chuckled indulgently at their chameleon-like palates and led them into the house on that idyllic afternoon.

Once Lisette was at the piano, Shirly and Ana went through the rehearsal for the musical. They usually picked different songs to work on and sometimes worked with Lisette in independent sessions. However, that day, Lisette wanted to blend their performances so that they could get used to their cues. The next session would be rehearsals with the rest of the student actors, who had more minor roles than Shirly and Ana. Shirly noted that the singing on Agope's boat was freer, fuller with thumping energy, while the music of the dramatic narrative they were working on featured classical ballads, completely lacking true 'gypsy' spirit. The recent midnight musical on the Mandovi had felt easier. Shirly also noted that she felt more comfortable with the speaking parts, and her memory of the script surprised her. Having Lisette as a mentor was completely unexpected. She was definitely not like their matronly music teacher Sister Olga. Lisette was gentle, with a sense of humour which greatly put Shirly at ease, and very encouraging. She inspired Shirly to want to do better. However, it was still the singing bits that Shirly was uncomfortable with. She felt that when god was handing out musical body parts to Goans—since every household seemed to have an artist—somehow she was passed over.

'Let's take the forest song. Shirly . . . and one, two, three, four . . .' Lisette prepped the cue for Shirly, but Shirly missed the time. 'Don't worry, and one, two, three, four . . .' Lisette's soothing voice relaxed Shirly and she caught the right entrance in the opening bar for the song.

'Water droplets on leaves, dance like diamonds for me/ the light on the river, valuable as silver . . .' Shirly sang. She realized that having ice fruit right before singing stiffened her voice and she made a mental note only to have it once the musical had concluded. Okay, too far off—maybe simply after a session and not minutes before it.

As the session wore on, its reality seeped into her. She not only had to remember her part and get fluent technically, now she also had to emote her lines and strike up a real pretence with Ana's character for authenticity.

'We will keep practising projection,' said Lisette gently.

But Shirly didn't know where she could mine the emotion from. And even if she did find it, she was no actress. Lisette's instructions foxed her and she didn't know if she had the right psychological muscles to pull them off. 'Articulate every word', 'make eye contact, but don't stare', 'be poised, yet relaxed', 'don't be monotonous, yet don't make a sing-song out of it'. The more contrary the instructions, the more Shirly was inclined to recede into herself to avoid facing each paradox. Ana seemed to find it much easier to 'project', like a natural. Shirly just wanted to curl up in her father's lap and have him stroke her hair, telling her another story about his travels to the Far East. She was glad when the sessions terminated for the day, mostly because João and Tomas entered the house, back from school.

João caught Shirly's eye, and she was grateful that he wasn't there minutes earlier to see her wilt under musical pressure.

Lisette noticed her elder son gravitate towards her protegée but didn't let on that she did. Shirly was grateful for that too. She was sure her parents would have cast a knowing glance at her and made her feel awkward with her new emotions for this boy. They were definitely more conservative than Dona Lisette. To imagine she and João were right under her father's nose in the Aguada cave; thankfully, he didn't suspect a thing, she thought with relief. She decided to worry about her parents learning of her first romance some other time.

Tomas was distant with her, as usual. As soon as he entered the house with his brother, he wheeled around the living room like an aeroplane, his arms out, making a high-pitched, nasal sound like an engine and ploughing quite close to his sister, who slapped him away.

'You were singing?' João asked Shirly softly, looking with heart-stopping directness into her eyes. Those eyes of his, that felt both foreign as well as like home. She didn't know that João loved the details of her eyes too. The way they were shaped perfectly, like curved almonds, her long, dark lashes that belonged to a boat sail, and the way her lush brows framed these perfect windows that bored through him.

Shirly felt contrarily nervous and relaxed in her new and complicated feelings. 'Yes,' she said, through the song-used ropes of her larynx. Lisette stepped out of the room to the kitchen. This prompted Tomas to get louder with his engine sounds and flappier with his arms. At one point, he flew between João and Shirly, breaking their spell. To get back at him, João chased him and pinned him down till he started screaming, which highly entertained the girls, at which point João let him go.

'You are just trying to make yourself look good in front of her, your girlfriend,' Tomas directly pointed at Shirly, who was discomfited. From the look on João's face, she didn't know who was more embarrassed, he or she. A bellicose Tomas continued, 'You be careful, her father is a traitor, revolutionary. He is our prisoner,' he said, oozing testosterone.

'You stop it!' Ana intervened on behalf of Shirly, who was too startled by such overt aggression to defend her father's reputation at the moment. 'Her daddy is not a revolutionary, is he, Shirly?' Ana turned to Shirly, who nodded with wide eyes. 'There, now be quiet,' she chided her brother.

'Tell me, you know he has bombs or no?' he asked Shirly. When she didn't respond he poked again. 'He has bombs or no?'

'He uses them for the mines!' Shirly said defensively.

'He set off bombs in the Betim Police Station. He is dangerous, I heard Agente Monteiro say it.' Tomas looked Shirly straight in the eye and dropped each word like a bomb, 'He . . . is . . . a . . . revolutionary.'

The room went quiet. Shirly's doubts cast an eclipse on the solid sphere of integrity and goodness she imagined sat inside her father. On closer inspection, it was pocked and wracked with deep cracks all over it, her faith in him taking the same shapes. Her gale of thoughts stopped behind her teeth and instead a piece of iron ore dripped down her gut with its hot weight. She found that she couldn't avoid taking the tone of the boy in front of her seriously. This boy-child with his brawly histrionics and Monteiro liens. 'Anyway, he won't last long.'

'Why? What do you mean?' asked João belligerently, glancing in concern at the anxiety he found in Shirly's silken lashes.

'You act so big, but you don't know anything!' Tomas's expression turned quiet and treacherous. 'There are bombs everywhere. Portugal says there are Indian troops at our borders. Goa is Portugal, it will never go to India. Even if a war is lost, then we will blow up Goa so they can't have it. Salazar himself will order it.'

The atmosphere itself could have exploded with the tension.

'You are lying! They will never blow us up,' said Ana, upset by her brother's vindictive pronouncement.

João was quiet, unsure if this was really his little brother talking. Shirly didn't know what to think.

'Not us. But the prisons for sure, where the traitor revolutionaries are,' said Tomas drawing out the word 'revolutionary'. Shirly had no control of her heart, which had slipped down to her knees. And the feeling worsened when she remembered that in his office, the advocate Freddy Baptista had mentioned that her father was branded an insurgent.

'Come, Shirly, let's leave him. He is just good at making noise,' said Ana. Taking her friend's hand, the two of them trooped out of the front door with João in tow. A few minutes later, when Lisette returned to the salon with refreshments, only Tomas was standing there, plinking at the higher end of the piano.

Outside, Shirly, Ana and João walked towards the Quarachim home. The sound of their mismatched breaths, which pulled and pushed through them heavily, dragged along with their steps on the footpath. They crossed the road and found themselves at the waterfront. Shirly stopped and perched on the parapet there while her friends ambled to join her. Their breathing stabilized as they stared out at the dhows dancing on the waves in the distance.

'Is it true?' asked Ana, articulating the question on Shirly's mind, aiming it at João. Without hearing the answer, Shirly already had goosebumps at the nearness of it all.

'Scorched earth,' said João enigmatically, staring off into the distance.

'What is that?' asked Ana. Shirly leaned in to listen.

'Scorched earth is . . . is . . . how do I say it . . .?' João paused dramatically. 'It is a thing, a government rule . . . I mean, law . . . like a . . . I don't know how to say it . . . but what Tomas has learned from the agente means that if Goa is ever invaded by India, Salazar will not be happy at all. With this he means that if Portugal is to lose, then no one can have Goa. So bombs are placed everywhere and instead of a peaceful surrender, the whole of Goa is to be . . . destroyed.'

Shirly looked at the placid river water lapping with pupp-pupp sounds against the parapet and the smooth sheet of the Mandovi glistening into the horizon where it merged into sea and sky. She didn't know which part of João's story to believe.

'The prisons are full of bandits and revolutionaries. There are already bombs in place there. Those will be one of the first places to be bombed.'

'How do you know this?' asked Ana in disbelief.

'I heard it. Agente Monteiro came by the house yesterday looking for Papa. Papa wasn't home so he began talking to his young admirer. I didn't imagine that he would understand what the agente was saying but it seems like he did. I didn't know what to think so I didn't say anything to Mãe or anyone. But . . . yes . . . his story is . . .' João allowed his sentence to trail, letting his eyes complete it. And the piece of iron ore in Shirly's gut expanded in girth, squeezing her organs.

For Shirly, Salazar was a faraway name, usually floating around at the dinner parties her parents attended, always patriotically, or at the dinner table at home, not so patriotically. But then, what was this they were hearing from the trusted João? India at war with Goa? She was sure that from where they were sitting she and Ana couldn't see an inkling of it. Behind them on the streets, life went on as usual. A stray cat followed a fisherwoman with a half-empty basket on her head, two ladies in frocks, probably from the Jardim Garcia d'Orta, walked with a stroller. A gentleman was exiting the bank, while some children accompanied by their mother and a housemaid were heading to Gaspar Dias.

Shirly drank in the calm everydayness, which seemed to attenuate João's words. Even if there were bombs, she thought, it would depend on war. And war in Goa was simply a remote, practically unfathomable possibility.

29

'Ulfanze, we are stopping here for camp,' Major Diljeet Singh Kapoor addressed Aphonso Kamat. The Sikh Regiment had just crossed from Karnataka to Maharashtra along the edge of the Goa border. They were close and would reach the assembly area east of Dodamarg within a matter of a day. Aphonso felt a little proud that he was selected by the Indian Army to lead one of their groups. He didn't mingle too much with them because they mostly spoke Punjabi to each other and his Hindi grammar was wanting. If needed he would speak or banter in a broken mishmash. Like, 'Come, we go,' or 'Eat food, abhi' or 'Cross river, swimming'. Even though it had been years since he had lived on the Goan side of the border, he noted that the roads on the Indian side were decrepit and mostly non-existent. Even the village dwellings looked smaller and more shrivelled, just like their inhabitants, who came out on occasion to sit on their gaunt haunches and stare at the passing soldiers. Aphonso looked at them but didn't really choose to see. He was on a mission.

When the dal–rice ration was served, Aphonso sat on the ground cross-legged with his shoes on, like the others. Strewn around them were tender green mangoes filled with sourness. The men picked these and bit into them to add a dash of excitement to their meal.

'You take?' One of the men of the regiment offered a smooth-skinned one to Aphonso, who accepted with a nod. Smiling as he gnawed into the pale flesh, the soldier held up his bitten raw mango, 'Ulfanze, mango.'

Aphonso had got used to everyone mispronouncing his name the way Major Kapoor did and chose not to correct their version. Aphonso wasn't sure if the soldier was asking or telling, and he shrugged his shoulders slowly and apologetically since he didn't understand. 'Ulfanze! Ulfanzo! Mango! Swaad, ummm, very tasty,' the soldier said. Aphonso understood and gave a condescending laugh. He wasn't sure if he felt good being associated with a mango but the fellow did have a point. Even though he shared the name of Afonso de Albuquerque, Aphonso usually shrugged off the fact that he shared his name with a variety of mango, bright as discovered gold dubbed after the Portuguese conqueror.

Uprooted from everything familiar, Aphonso contemplated his fruit namesake. If the Portuguese hadn't come by all those years ago, perhaps the alphonso wouldn't exist to impart its tropical, honey-kissed flavour to the Indian summer.

Like the alphonso, he too was a cross-breed. When his Christian mother and Hindu father had the unfortunate destiny to fall in love, they were not just helpless in the webs their hearts spun but also with the stumbling blocks of familial disapproval.

They'd meet covertly—on a rocky beach, under shady banyans in a jungle, after tiatr in an empty football field. They were usually careful because they both knew the story of other Hindu–Christian romances. These usually ended with the lovers walking into the ocean, hand in hand. Or else feeding each other a poisoned mankurad, mingling juices for a sweet and swift end.

His parents had found refuge for their amour under the generous benevolence of the stars. But they couldn't hide under this dark velvet blanket for long when his mother's stomach began to grow. In the face of their predicament, his father was ready to stand by his lady gallantly, but she was kept under lock and key by her family to protect her honour and theirs. Local goons—it was unknown whether they were Hindu or Christian—beat his father unconscious and left him to bleed to his death. Shortly after Aphonso's birth, his mother's life ebbed from her. It was unclear whether she succumbed to an infection from the accouchement, which took place furtively at home, or if her heart had been shattered into a constellation of teardrops. His parents didn't even have the luxury of taking their lives together.

When Aphonso learned of his tragic entrance into the world, he covered his heart with an old cloth and joined a local gang of boys, causeless rebels who wanted to stir up the stillness of the bucolic air in his village. They made torturing cats and dogs their mission.

After Aphonso got bored of this, he opted out and later was befriended by some youth who were setting up a makeshift radio station out of their communidade meeting hall. They played a mix of records they had managed to procure—from American rock-'n'-roll to Western classical and mando music. In between song segments, Radio Romeo slid in some propaganda demanding a 'Goa for Goans'. Within a few months, the police showed up to shut them down, and the leader Clinton was jailed. To hide his tracks, Aphonso fled, releasing the vestige of shame his grandparents harboured with his presence.

He started a repair shop in another village where he brought life to anything from watches and clocks to the occasional old radio. When a member of the covert Assagoa resistance group met him, he found a fresh calling. His new job, secretly funded by the Indian Army, was to station himself at Anmod and await orders. At first he hesitated. Why the Indian Army? Even though Aphonso didn't have any allegiances, he still had some of the imprisoned Clinton's ideals in his breath. That is, Goa for Goans. A separate nation, an independent territory, a deep-rooted indigenous identity. Once he was assured that the Indian Army only wanted to help Goa become this ideal of liberation, that Assagoa were merely the catalysts, the ones who had the inside wherewithal to overthrow a centuries-old colonial power, only then did he agree to cooperate fully. Plus, this would be a way to get Clinton out of prison, get back at his jailers, and restore their freedom to say and play anything they pleased on the airwaves.

At Anmod, he lay in wait, only harbouring a stray member of the cause here and there for a night or so. He debated during solitary hours whether he needed to head across further to the army headquarters in Belgaum. So he was pleased when not much more than four years later the army showed up at his hovel door.

30

'Forçan zore di re!'

The conductor put in more muscle and cranked the iron bar on the engine lever at the snout, just below the two-flap bonnet of the caminhão. As the bus jounced to life, the passengers felt their teeth and bones rattle in sympathetic vibration. 'Borem!' Okay, shouted the driver behind the double-paned windshield once more and honked twice in succession, no doubt a code between him and the conductor. Four of these coaches, filled with the nuns and students of the Our Lady of the Ocean of Providence School, stood cranked and ready to rumble forth on Rua de Ourem to ferry everyone to Velha Goa on the occasion of the exposition of Saint Francis Xavier.

The line of coaches trundled past the Ourem Creek and over its bridge along the Ponte Conde de Linhares, a causeway leading out of Panjim—just under four kilometres long—named after the Portuguese viceroy who had had it constructed. Of course, Shirly and Ana took seats next to each other, and made sure to stick their heads out the window to taste the wind, much to the consternation of Sister Boniface. To their left, the stately Mandovi flowed in the opposite direction and to their right were the salt pans, squares of fields drenched in water with piles of powdery white peaks.

Through the jostling and chatter of the girls, Sister Boniface tried in vain to point out information and instructions about their trip and landmarks along the way. 'Girls, it is our great good fortune to make this journey to view the incorrupt body of the great good Saint Francis Xavier. He came and spread the faith of Christianity in our country almost four-five hundred years ago. And he made many, many miracles. So many that he came to be known as a saint.'

Questions followed, asked by the girls. 'Where did he come from?', 'What miracles?', 'Is his body really fresh?', 'Will we be able to touch the body?'

Sister Boniface's voice competed with the sometimes gargling, sometimes thrumming engine. 'He came many, many years ago from Portugal, I think . . . no, no it was Spain, yes, Spain. He was born in Spain, and he came with a Portuguese mission. In between, he became a priest I think in Italy.' Luckily for her, the girls were no critics of Sister Boniface's history lesson. 'Anyway, he was a holy saint, really and truly. After he died his body did not rot. It is said it still smelled clean and nice for many years, and he looked rosy.' With her heart full of devoted faith and adoration Sister Boniface vouchsafed that there was a lifelike blush in the cheeks of the dead apostle of the Indies over the years.

The cavalcade wound its way through the quaint village of Ribandar, whose narrow roads wormed through close-knit, noble-looking houses. They passed the town's impressive structures, like the Hospital of the Poor and the church of Nossa Senhora da Ajuda, at the sight of which Sister Boniface made a sign of the cross before carrying on. 'I'll tell you something, my girls,' she said conspiratorially, as her students leaned their ears into the circle of her words, 'He makes miracles. Sometimes just after going to see his incorrupt body, a deaf person can hear again, or a mute person can talk again, or if someone is not well, they become okay again. He is our protector, Goencho Saib.' The good sister made the sign of the cross again in reference to the saintly 'lord of Goa'. 'Even during last time's exposition, which was almost ten years ago, I had the great-good fortune to kiss his holy feet,' she added with satisfied piety.

The babble of the girls rushed to fill in the halo of awed silence around Sister Boniface. 'Oh my god, I hope he will answer my prayers', 'I shall also ask for a miracle for my brother', 'Will he give me a boyfriend?', 'My mother makes a novena to Saint Francis every year', 'Ohmygoodness, is his body really still there?'

'Yes, it is there, you shall see,' reassured Sister Boniface. 'Only his toe is missing, though.' The nun pulled at her wimple near her ear and got a faraway look in her eyes as she put on her best pulpit voice, 'There was a lady, Dona Isabel de Carom. We don't know what it was that made her do it. But she went crazy when she saw the body of the saint, and when she went to kiss his holiest of feet, she bit his toe right off. And you know what happened after that?' She paused dramatically, then added, 'His toe started bleeding. It was bleeding and bleeding, and wherever Dona Isabel went, the trail of blood followed her.'

Shirly couldn't understand why anyone would bite someone else's body part, especially a toe, and then tried to picture the sight of a trickle of blood following the culpable chari-pishem-nutcase-louco woman everywhere she went, even to the toilet when she had to do muth.

'It is said that the blood that followed her frightened her so much that she pleaded and pleaded, and prayed to the saint to make it stop.' Sister Boniface ended, perfectly punctuated by the sound of the caminhão's blowhorn—ponkka ponkka ponkka. On the road, pilgrims walking in their Sunday best were making their way on foot. As they neared Velha Goa, the caminhão caravan competed with increasing numbers of them for space on the narrow road.

Once the buses were parked and the blue-pinafored regiments had alighted, they were shepherded by the nuns in twos and given instructions to partner up and hold hands. Lined up in pairs, they walked down the path, along a large, open square with grand old buildings and churches peppering it, navigating between and around gathered crowds. It seemed like all of humanity in Goa had come to get a glimpse of the revered saint. From the towns and villages, in frocks and suits, in saris and dhotis, some wearing hats, a few in skullcaps, some in pagdis, several ladies with black mantillas, a top layer of umbrellas over heads as sun shields. There were families, couples, old, infirm, devout, agnostic, simple, fashionable and everyone in between. Stalls bearing candles, crosses, rosaries and effigies of all sizes of Jesus Christ and Mother Mary were doing brisk business. There were also waxen body parts, like an arm or a leg, and even a whole baby, which Shirly found very mysterious. There were stalls with snacks like roasted gram, sugared dolls, jaggery-coated khaje and glistening saffron laddoos, around which the girls crowded like overeager flies to honey. Sister Olga had to herd them loudly to keep them moving.

In their two-by-twos, they filed their way to a sidewalk that led up to the Sé Cathedral, inside which the remains of Saint Francis Xavier lay for public viewing and veneration. Beyond the lawns on their right was the main thoroughfare with the imposing laterite structure of the Basilica de Bom Jesus. On their left, they passed first the Chapel of Saint Catherine. It was small, in laterite and white lime wash, and dwarfed in size by the other churches and structures in the area. Sister Boniface explained that Afonso de Albuquerque took possession of Goa from the Mughals in 1510 on a day that happened to be Saint Catherine's Day. He built a shrine in about that location as a tribute to the martyred woman of Alexandria. Effectively, she was declared Goa's patron saint.

'But we thought Francis Xavier is the patron saint,' asked Ana, a bit perplexed at the designations Sister Boniface was doling out.

'Yes, yes, my girl, he is. Because of him, Shambhaji, the son of the Maratha warrior Shivaji, could not conquer Goa. He came all set to fight with his troops and then Viceroy Tavora placed his sceptre in the hands of the incorruptible body. There was a miracle, and the Mughals invaded Shambhaji's kingdom at that time. So we were saved. We are so lucky; we have two saints who are watching over us,' Sister Boniface said hastily.

'Why did Shambhaji want to conquer Goa?' asked Ana, who didn't understand why the invader didn't prefer to spend time with his friends at a nearby waterfall or learn something enjoyable like singing and avoid fighting with his neighbours for no reason, much like her brother Tomas liked to do.

Shirly decided that she would reserve her request to restore her family to order directly in the incorruptible ear of the great-good Goencho Saib. His miracles seemed more guaranteed according to what Sister Boniface was saying, so she would save the reverence building up within her for just him.

'I don't know, my girl. We were just minding our own business and he came. Just like that. Anyway, praise to Goencho Saib, nothing happened. Otherwise, big mess.' Whether the big mess referred to the blood and gore that comes with war or else to Goa being appropriated under the Maratha flag in 1683, therefore placing it under the Indian tricolour, the good Sister didn't elucidate on her gut reaction.

'Here, my girls.' Sister Boniface led the paired troops of her assigned caminhão cortege to join the tail of a queue of people for the Sé Primacial e Patriarchal, commonly called the Sé Cathedral.

As the lengthy queue plodded ahead, the visitors to the cathedral were swallowed into its side entrance and appeared to spill out later on to its front grounds. When they entered, Shirly and Ana found themselves on the left hand of the transept. The air inside the cathedral was immediately different, filled with the melodic solemnity of Gregorian chants. Shirly wasn't sure if she shivered because of the cooler atmosphere in there or from being in the same room as Goa's most revered saint, whose body was supposed to be as fresh as the day he died. She was intrigued by now and simply had to see it.

The sight was magnificent all around. Gilded altars featured effigies and carvings of haloed saints, and frescos showed scenes from their lives in vivid detail. Paintings of Saint Francis Xavier hung on the walls, in alcoves and near pillars. Saint Ignatius of Loyola, Saint Christopher, Saint Paul and Saint Peter gazed down with beatific grace. When you looked up, the vaulted ceiling soared overhead, and sunlight streamed into the cathedral from strategic oculi all around. The nave was flanked by rows of wooden pews where the congregation kneeled or sat, praying or soaking in the space. Wooden pulpits jutted out from a couple of large pillars that met at arches and a muscular gilded organ sat above heads on an overhanging balcony. The main altar and pièce de resistance of the cathedral was ablaze in golden grandeur. The imposing gilt retable that was dedicated to Saint Catherine depicted scenes from her life and martyrdom. The sheer detail on the vast and immense scale of artistic expression was an intoxicating spiritual experience in itself. The whole scene was colossal and heady for Shirly. She loved the way it made her dizzy just to look up into the arching ceiling while the flesh on her arms prickled. A stray sparrow or two fluttered in as well and danced overhead to partake of the grand day.

Then she saw what the multitudes had come for. Lying innocuous and peaceful at the central junction of the transept and nave, under an ornately frilled glass chandelier and before the main altar, was the raised casket. Saint Francis Xavier was positioned with his head to the altar and feet facing the main entrance. As the girls shuffled perpendicularly to the casket, it came into view, despite the crowded throb around it.

Shirly was a bit disappointed. The casket was lidded with a thick glass that was being profusely kissed and caressed by the pilgrims passing it. It wasn't open so that she could touch the incorruptible body, as Sister Boniface said she had done the last time. Pilgrims were allowed to take their time offering their hearts and devotion, and weren't herded away by the priests who stood there in their white waisted-belt cloaks. One woman started wiping the glass of the casket with her handkerchief while another kissed the length of it.

Shirly was struck with guilt. She didn't feel an onslaught of profuse devotion impelling her to do some similar gesture of piety. As she brought her face close to the casket and peered into the glass, hope flattened inside her. Despite wearing ornate robes with golden threads, the body of the saint didn't look like an incorruptible miracle. It looked shrunken and sunken in. More like clay than flesh. The face was indiscernible with a hole where the ear should be. The fingers look gnarled and claw-like, and the toes were missing. Did miracles wear out? If so, would it even work if she asked Goencho Saib to help free her father? Thoughts swirled around her like the smoke off a swinging censer. And so the prayer she had been holding inside her to bring to the feet of the saint lost its tensility. Aware of the line training behind her, in a demonstration of reverence, more as an outward gesture than to express her soul, Shirly kissed her fingers and touched them to the glass.

'What are these?' Ana asked, looking at the ground beneath their feet.

'Shh, my girl, keep going,' responded Sister Boniface. And answered as an afterthought, 'They are graves.'

Shirly looked down too and saw marble slabs wedged flush in the stone floor. Many were carved with coats of arms and an ancient inscription that looked like Latin.

'They are too small to be graves. Shirly, see . . .' Ana lay down on a grave, which she filled up vertically end to end. Of course, and but naturally, Shirly followed. When Sister Boniface turned around she was horrified to see the two girls lying side by side on two graves and cackling at each other.

'Get up, now!' she thundered in a loud whisper, and the priests at the casket turned to look, to her mortification. She flushed crimson as she pulled the girls up by their shoulders and personally marched them past the pews. 'Do you want to see the Cross of Miracles, or no?'

'We want, yes,' said Ana politely, trying to appease Sister Boniface, one of the few nuns she liked in school, who took the phrase 'forgiving trespasses' to heart.

'Come, girls,' called out Sister Boniface, easily appeased, leading her flock past an arch to the entrance of a small chapel featuring a large wooden cross.

'Why is it called the Cross of Miracles?' asked Shirly, perplexed at the plain-looking cross, echoing the sentiments of her classmates.

'It is said,' responded Sister Boniface, 'that this cross keeps growing.'

The girls all stared hard at the cross in silence, just in case it gained a few inches before their eyes. When nothing much happened, they turned away one by one to the exit. As they spilled out into the sunlight, and into the Terreiro do Sabaio, the grand and ancient Adil Shah Square, Shirly didn't feel earthshakingly different. There was no light beam that descended from heaven or a rainbow made of butterflies that appeared. Things were as they had been before she entered the church. The incorruptible body of the saint and the growing cross left an underwhelming sensation inside her.

Sister Boniface clapped her hands for attention and said loudly, 'Girls, stay in your line. Make sure to hold your partner's hand. We will go to the next church.'

In its human chain, by twos, Shirly's caminhão troupe made its way past the throngs on the wide pedestrian road of Saint Francis Xavier Square. 'Ah, the great poet.' In the central island of the square, surrounded by churches in that olden bosom of religiosity, oddly, was a statue of sixteenth-century poet Luís Vaz de Camões, standing in Shakespearean dress with an unfurled scroll in his hand. Sister Boniface couldn't help proselytizing as they passed him. 'His words, my girls, have made Portugal great. And you know, he was sitting somewhere in Goa only, and writing his *Os Lusíadas*.' God-all-does-know what *Os Lusíadas* is, thought Shirly as she looked at him, wondering why a poet would get a statue. Did he change the world? Could he perform miracles? If he came to Goa and all he did was write a poem, he wasn't much of an adventurer. She wondered what the conversation between Faria and Camões would have been if they were to bump into each other in a garden. And Goencho Saib too. The hypnotist, the poet and the saint. All of them statues of the imagination, the originals of trance and soul.

The Our Lady of the Ocean of Providence School group crossed the broad avenue and entered into the open space in front of the Casa Professa e Basilica do Bom Jesus, the terraio. A three-storeyed structure facing west, with buttressing arches on one side. It stood in stark contrast to the white lime-washed buildings in the area, its weathered laterite stone façade looking sunburnt. As they stood in the courtyard, waiting for the rest of the schoolgirls and their accompanying nuns to join them, Shirly absently contemplated the letters 'IHS' that stood above the archway in pink Bassein stone.

'What's IHS?' Shirly asked about the Latin acronym reflecting the ancient emblem of Jesuits dedicated to Jesus, *Iesus Hominum Salvator.*

'In his shop,' said Ana.

'I'm here, silly,' reparteed Nancy, who was within earshot.

Shirly knit her brows with exaggerated suspicion. As the three entered the threshold into the interior coolness of the basilica, she joined in with her own, 'I hope so.' The three giggled aloud.

'Shhhhhh,' reprimanded Sister Boniface, looking in Nancy, Ana and Shirly's direction. Though the unwashed façade looked austere, there was a wealth of embellishment within. Shirly was faced with rows and rows of wooden pews, surrounding which were altars, cenotaphs, chapels, a richly carved wooden pulpit with a canopy, wooden boxes for donations, statues, a tiled floor and ornate oil paintings, the grandeur making her dizzy again.

As the group moved down the central nave, Sister Boniface began narrating some more miracles by the saint to whoever would listen. Nancy indicated to Ana and Shirly to follow her and slipped away.

They went past a small door that opened into an al fresco garden courtyard, wrapped on all four sides by pillared corridors with geometric tiles in ochre and sienna. Their eyes, now filled with sunlight, had to adjust after the darkness of the church. At one corner, a padre sprinkled holy water on a couple kneeling in front of him and chanted under his breath. The woman held a waxen baby, probably bought from one of the stalls outside.

'They want a child. That is why the wax baby,' Ana explained to Shirly, reading her friend's quizzical look. Shirly began to entertain thoughts of blessings on a waxen doll of her father, but she was too exhausted now.

'Come!' Nancy entered the courtyard and bent down, waving her hand over a host of touch-me-not. Soon, Nancy and Ana were bounding on all fours, engaged in their delight of closing the leaves of the shy plants into their purple sleep.

Shirly, however, was drawn to another corner of the square courtyard. There a metal table stood, set afire with a surface full of burning wax candles. As the flames licked the daylight, their prayer enveloped the reverberations of her mind. This candle here was a failed legal system. That candle there was a current not fast enough for an attempted escape. Another candle was the threat of weapons and violence looming over her world. However, each flame perched with an intense persistence on its wick, scorching the canvas of her thoughts. And she found that surrender could smoothly take her right through the eye of the needle, into the sweet void of acceptance.

31

'Well, when are they arriving? Hmm, I see. Thank you. I will keep you posted once they arrive, Lieutenant Colonel.' Capitão Morais replaced the receiver of the telephone. He had just briefed his senior officer on the strategy he would employ for the execution of Plano Sentinela, a direct order given to the army from the Governor-General himself. The captain didn't allow himself the luxury to stop and think about the dismal numbers in their ranks at the moment. If there was a war, they didn't have a fighting chance. The only action they could take at this point was a delaying tactic: to stave off the Indian Army from taking over Goa for as long as they possibly could. He just prayed that the new troops he had asked for would arrive within the next day or two. He stepped outside his office at the barracks and walked through the corridor towards the entrance, facing the grounds. The officers around him looked relaxed and at ease. Some were joking, some were mock-fighting on the grounds. Probably a few were in their quarters over a game of cards. Several would visit the local tavernas and get drunk again, and then, god forbid, land up at the brothel in town. They looked like a vision of the gift that peace could offer.

The captain imagined the sight in case the Indian Army attacked on that night itself. His men red-faced, slurring, unable to walk straight, a bottle of Madeira in their hands, a song on their lips and their pants around their ankles. He took a sharp breath in. This would not do. He had to have a talk with the men at the morning assembly and put certain procedures in place.

Back at his desk, he looked once more at the defence plan. Three agrupamentos—groups—with infantry and artillery were chalked out. One to cover the north, one to cover the centre and the south, and one to cover the Mormugao peninsula. He read through the aims of his defence strategy once more. To concentrate forces on the peninsula and the city of Goa. Delay control by the enemy, using armed resistance. And, of course, in this case, he added stoically, there would be the inevitable Plano de Barragem.

32

Sukkoo and Bukkoo were inordinately loud by the evening. Their fervent mewling rose above the sound of the evening crickets and wafted in through the heavy main door. The hefty cats lounging on the top of the stairs had stirred to the aromas that had caught hold of them from the wide crack between the door and the floor. Goku noisily unlatched the bolt from inside, flung open the doors and made her way down the stairs, her slippers slapping between heel and tile. The felines wended through her feet all the way down to the front courtyard, raising their pitch to hormonal levels.

Goku set down a tin bowl full of fish parts, and soon enough, the cats were crouched there and chewing their dinner. Then Goku proceeded to polish the glasses and cooking pots with feni, sneaking a sip here and there; good for immunity, was her reasoning to herself. Mamtu was so washed out in her own hormonal turmoil that she didn't question Goku. However, when she raised a banana to her nose, she asked her maidservant why the skin had got a feni massage too.

'Mosquito not coming, Bai,' was Goku's inspired reply.

Once Shirly, Devika and Mamtu were served their dinner, sleep started to blow its mist into Shirly's eyes. After all the lights were put out, Shirly and Devika were ensconced in their pillow forts under the small, safe, gauzy universe of their mosquito nets.

Thupp. Shirly stirred, her eyes forced open. She dismissed the sound as a rowdy gust of wind and began to relax her eyelids once more. Thupp. There it was again, an unmistakable sound against the window. It was something too hard and small to be a fruit bat that had lost its sonar. Shirly gingerly stepped barefoot on to the cool tiles and made her way to the window. The moonlight on the river didn't offer enough of its reflection to the street, but she could make out the shadowy form of a man beneath her window, standing at the edge of the Abbé Faria garden. The figure beckoned to her.

'What a funny fellow, I wonder if he has the right window,' thought Shirly.

The man kept motioning. Shirly shook her head, hoping he'd realize he was at the wrong address. Or maybe it was Budhu, the tongueless man. Mamtu used to take pity on him and ask him to do an odd job in exchange for a few coins when he came around begging. But this person here wasn't standing with his head cocked to one side, drooling, so perhaps not.

'Shirly baby, can you come down?' This was most definitely not Budhu. The man looked up, and a sliver of light that slipped through the shadows fell on his face, which looked vaguely familiar. Her curiosity warmed. The thought that she had never left the house this late without her parents' knowledge passed through her mind only fleetingly. Then she picked up her rubber slippers and padded her way on quiet feet past her mother's bedroom. Shirly was sure that all of Goku's feni smells had knocked her mother out cold.

She gently unhinged the large lock on the front door and slipped outside. She wasn't being irresponsible. It was safe enough in Panjim to keep the main door unlocked. No one would know in this darkness, and anyway she was probably returning soon. Sukkoo and Bukkoo raised their ears but not their heads as one of the daughters of the house they had adopted made her way down the stairs and out of the main gate. Here, she dropped her slippers to the floor and slid her feet into them. As Shirly turned the corner to the side of her building under her window, she saw the man waiting for her.

'Shirly baby, it's too late for you? You must have been sleeping, no?' he said, stating the obvious. 'Don't be worried, it is me, Sushant.'

Recognition was slow to click into place.

'Remember you met me when your papa took you to the mines?'

The visual came back to her, Sushant on his bicycle, a narrow path through a field, and an aluminium tin.

'You gave us cashewnuts,' Shirly confirmed, nodding.

'Yes, you remember.' Sushant kneeled down to her level. 'Now, Shirly, your papa told me you met him at Aguada, and he told you he would arrange for you to understand something. This is why I'm here.' Shirly didn't nod, but Sushant saw acknowledgement framed in her delicate eyes that had brushed sleep off its lids. 'Come with me, baby. I want to take you somewhere, but it is a secret. Promise you won't tell anyone?'

'I promise,' said Shirly, more curious than concerned at this interesting after-dark adventure, sanctioned somehow by her father from the faraway walls of his prison cell.

Sushant held out his hand, and Shirly slipped hers into his. They quietly threaded their way through the needle-narrow roads of Fontainhas, the tempo of chirruping crickets following their gait and their own breath filling their ears.

At last, they came to the steps of a house that Shirly recognized well. The lights inside were off, she noticed, and she wondered if this was a mistake. Sushant turned to her and held his forefinger to his lips. He then placed his fingertips against the door and pushed slowly. The door swung open quietly on its oiled hinges, leading to a dark living room that Shirly was all too familiar with. Shirly held on to the back of Sushant's loose shirt as they made their way into the depths of the hall. She was about to retreat and bolt out of the door, away from the mysteriousness of this late-evening tryst, when another door opened and a woman in a nightie came forward with a dimly lit kerosene lamp. Shirly recognized her immediately and was compelled to stay.

'Come this way,' Natalie said. Shirly followed her into the room. Natalie walked up to a bookcase and appeared to search for something. She pushed the bookcase aside like a sliding door and, to Shirly's astonishment, revealed a space beyond its hardbound bounty. A secret trapdoor from a thickening Hercule Poirot plot.

The light of the kerosene lamp started to bob as it descended and Shirly followed it downstairs. After a short flight, they found themselves in a room, well lit with kerosene lamps. A large teak table bounced table-tennis-sized balls of light off its well-polished surface. The vermilion walls featured a cross at one end with a motherly Mary looking down at her child, and a framed oil pastoral of a brook in a forest. Plumes of smoke filled this underground living room, and shadows sat around the eyes of the several faces that were seated at the table.

'Ah, you found the girl. Well done, Sushant,' Shirly heard Freddy Baptista's familiar voice. Freddy turned to Shirly. 'Don't worry, Dona Shirly, everything is okay. Sushant met your daddy at Aguada, who told him that it is okay to bring you here. He knows. Come, come, my girl, here, sit.' Freddy motioned for Shirly to sit at a chair that was to his right, a little away from the table. Sushant took her over to it and remained standing beside her, while Natalie went upstairs again and disappeared with her lamp.

Freddy turned to the others. 'Quarachim's daughter.' Most of the faces around the table were unknown to Shirly. 'As I was saying, we need to emphasize our goal to them . . .'

Freddy was interrupted by one of the men around the table. 'But look, when there is an ally, why don't we take their assistance? They only mean to help—and then we take over.'

Freddy responded, 'My dear fellow, it will be like the situation of a Trojan horse. They will appear to come in peace and then do just as they please once they are in. Don't forget what happened to French India. It was also a territoire d'outre-mer and then when India swooped in, they called it "liberation". Let us remember the coup of Yanaon and how Pondichéry was quick to have an Indian flag on top of it, like a conquered territory.'

My Dear Fellow responded equally vehemently, 'Pondichéry is now granted union territory status. What are you saying then, Freddy? That Goa should be its own country? Is it large enough?'

'I am saying yes. It should be its own country. Look at the Pandit's own state. Kashmir is separate from both the countries. We can show the world that our Goan identity is a unique one, deserving of its own flag colours. If we allow India to help us, then it will stake its claim, they will simply take us as a debt owed. The Pandit's agenda is all too clear. We have to stay strong on this matter, and any resistance should ideally come from within Goa itself.'

'Freddy, this is not realistic. We have reports that the Indian Army is at our borders. Don't you think that it is a little late for a resistance from within?'

There was a pause before the advocate said, 'Look at us.' Everyone turned their heads to look at everyone else.

'I mean, really, look at us!' Everyone was bewildered by the advocate's disquiet. 'It is as though each of us is a different version of Goa. Me over here, my dear fellow over there, some of those in prison elsewhere, the soldiers on this side, the soldiers on that side, the chaps running the show from the Cabo, the fellows calling the shots from Delhi . . . the . . . the . . . the . . . who knows? Even . . . your wives muhrey . . . the . . . the fisherman in the market . . .'

Goencho Saib, Abbé Faria—Shirly was tempted to pipe in.

Freddy continued his argument in front of his nocturnal court, 'Every one of us has a notion of how they want to save our Goa. Some want the Mandovi to stop going to the ocean, some want her to go faster to the ocean, some want her to change course and flow side-by-side with the ocean. And you know, unless we are able to agree on a common idea of this estado, then we may as well, each of us separately, be rescuing a river breeze from each other!'

Shirly granted herself a small sense of achievement for understanding the advocate's metaphorical delivery style. She kept her eye on Freddy's upper lip as his chest rose and fell dramatically. Even when he was agitated and breathing heavily, it stayed firm, unlike Sister Olga's. No one around the table said a word during his outburst. When he had calmed down a few notches, he turned to My Dear Fellow, 'To answer your question, whether they come or not, we will have to save amchea Goem from being lost in the continent of India, by hook or by crook.' Freddy looked at Shirly. 'We cannot let the hard work of some good men go in vain.'

It was as though My Dear Fellow hadn't heard a word that Freddy had just communicated, confirming all the advocate voiced in concern, and went back to the refrain of his peeve, seasoned with a dash of sarcasm, 'Well, let's not forget how he tried to gain favour with the agente. There are some who err on the side of perceived strength.'

'If you are saying something, my dear fellow, you should say it, instead of catching your nose from behind your head,' Freddy shot back.

'I heard that Quarachim gave Agente Monteiro his spanking new Pontiac. It cannot be denied because I saw him with my own eyes. Who knows how else he must have gained favour?'

'Oh, is that so?' asked Freddy, crossing his arms and leaning back in his chair. 'If the agente was in his pocket, then how is it that he landed in a jail cell at his very hands?'

'That is precisely the reason the agente has not subjected him to any torture. Besides, he was careless and was caught breaking the law, was he not?'

'My dear fellow, you go too far. Especially as you know his young daughter is in the room.' My Dear Fellow avoided Shirly's eyes, who was slightly disbelieving of this strange dream that she had landed in. She also wondered why the lawyer would call that man a dear fellow as he certainly didn't seem to be acting the part. 'Ridiculous fellow' should be his appellation. 'Sushant bab, would you like to explain to Quarachim's daughter?'

Sushant reached into his pocket, extracted a photo and held it up to Shirly. It was an image of Sushant along with a few women sitting casually under a tree alive with abolim flowers. 'That is my sister Sunita,' Sushant pointed out one of the women. The name was familiar and rang through Shirly's mind. 'In 1955, there was a lot of trouble in our village because many were doing satyagraha. Portuguese army soldiers came and tortured . . .' Sushant's voice broke, '. . . and killed her husband . . .' Shirly saw that the woman in the image had a brown birthmark and dots tattooed near her wrist. The Jeep ride to the mines with her father flashed in front of her. She was the tamarind seller to whom her father had given a lift. Sushant wiped his tears, then, folding away the photograph into his pocket again, he continued, 'After that, the pacló . . . er . . . soldiers would harass her two daughters. We were all scared because these army boys can take the girls and dance with them in the bushes. Then what are we to do?' 'Dancing in the bushes' almost went over Shirly's head but she was old enough to know what had caused her own mother's stomach to bulge. Shirly's thoughts strayed further to Nancy, her football-loving classmate. Shirly had never heard her speak about her parents; all she knew was that Nancy had come from the orphanage on the Altinho Hill, and the Mother Superior had arranged for her lodging at the school. Was Nancy the result of a 'bad' army pacló and a helpless girl, from any one of the several unseen villages outside the cidade who hadn't wanted her? The story of Sunita's daughters, however, seemed to end better than Nancy's mother's. 'After my sister told her story to your father, those soldier boys stopped troubling her daughters.' As Sushant concluded, his eyes were wet with tears and his voice brimmed with deference. 'Your father is a good man, Shirly baby.'

Freddy had to clear a lump in his throat before he directed his gaze to My Dear Fellow and said, 'Allow me to set the record straight with regard to Quarachim. He is a Goan who is committed to the land. He believes in peace, yes, and he has profited from the present system of governance. He is liked by all our societies. When he saw the agente had his eye on his new car, Quarachim used it as an opportunity, é claro, sim. Not to gain personal credit with the cruel and dangerous fellow, but to send his driver to accompany the agente—in this way he learnt of his whereabouts. He then informed me. We used the information that Quarachim gave us to carry out our operations.' My Dear Fellow remained silent. The advocate addressed the gathering as though he was making his case in court. 'Furthermore, Quarachim was not careless. He is being punished for *our* carelessness. We should have ensured greater security for him than a tin of cashews.' The lawyer looked straight at Shirly, 'Yes, my dear Shirly. Your father is a true-hearted Goan who could not stand by and do nothing for the spirit of the land that is a part of him.'

'Um, but . . .' The question mark that was nagging at Shirly all this time, the one Tomas had inflamed when he called her father a revolutionary, reared up and she couldn't stop it. 'Is he a revolutionary? Did he kill people with bombs? They said that's why he was arrested.'

'Oh no no, my dear girl,' Freddy responded. 'We are the ones who asked him to ferry the bombs for us. We thought he would get away with it since he could use the excuse that he needed them for mining activity. We were careful not to be found out. But when he heard our plan, he made us promise that not one of his precious countrypeople would be harmed by the bombs—they were very small, just something to make a big noise. Our plan was only to set them off near a police station so that we could get the attention of a delegation of international media in Goa sanctioned by The Hague. Your father is not a mercenary and he would never take a life, no matter the cause. He is a good, good man.' There were several of the advocate's words that Shirly didn't comprehend: delegation, mercenary, The Hague. Freddy looked over at My Dear Fellow, 'And we are all deeply grateful for his act of courage. If we call ourselves true Goans, we are indebted to him.' This Shirly understood.

Shirly's doubts about her father vanished. The globe of him wobbling in its orbit around her sun was set right on its axis once again. The advocate's words confirmed what one part of her had known all along but couldn't prove. The barbs in the words that Tomas had thrown at her disintegrated now, along with the snag wounds they left. But there was one more thing Tomas had told her that washed through her guts like a chilli burn. 'What about the other bombs?'

'Other bombs?' asked Freddy.

'What other bombs?' asked My Dear Fellow.

Shirly had two words that she remembered from João's lips, 'Scorched earth.'

Foreboding dropped into the room like a fallen coconut branch.

'How did you hear about this, my dear girl?' asked Freddy.

'My friend's brother. He looks up to the agente and spends a lot of time with him. He must have heard something, and so he told me,' Shirly responded without a breath.

'Like father, like daughter. Both of you are like Sherlock Holmes with the agente,' said one of the gentlemen at the table.

'What is this, what does it mean? How can they burn the earth?' asked one of the men at the table.

Another man answered. With his pale skin and epaulettes, he appeared to be an officer within the higher echelons of the military, and an unlikely guest at this secret table conference. To Shirly he was very familiar, as by now she realized were most faces in the room. 'It is an abominable military strategy. Tell me, have you never heard of it?'

In the pregnant pause, Shirly remembered him as Teodoro da Costa from the Araujo dinner party. He was the one who had said that her home had once housed slaves. 'Well, it refers to leaving nothing that is of any use for the enemy. It can be done as an army advances or even as one retreats, as is suggested in this case. It has been practised since ancient times by the Persians, Romans and Greeks. Just over a century ago, Napoleon attacked Portugal. The people of Portugal were so fed up with being plundered yet another time by the French general and his army that they decided to destroy all their food supplies. As the French army moved through their lands, the soldiers didn't have any food to sustain themselves.'

'They didn't have any supplies with them?' asked My Dear Fellow.

'No,' replied the officer. 'There were no canned or packaged foods at that time, remember. The soldiers would loot locals as they passed through the land.'

'So what happened to the locals, would they not die without food?' asked My Dear Fellow.

'Yes, they did,' the officer responded. 'But they preferred it to allowing the French to succeed over their dead bodies.'

'Is it possible, Freddy?' asked My Dear Fellow. There were murmurings full of question marks among the men at the table.

Suddenly, footsteps rattled above them. The group fell silent as the trapdoor opened and the steps got louder. They all let out a breath of relief as Natalie shuffled in holding a generous-sized tray. On it was a large steel pot of tea and several cups and saucers. There was also a large, round dish with a cake that had sweet, sticky, brown layers.

'Ah, chai. And bebinca. Please, everyone, take. My dear fellows, I hope you will have some. Please pass it around.' Slipping into host mode, Feddy easily swung the conversation from bombs and armies to beverages and dessert. The cups and saucers shivered and clattered noisily as Natalie set down the heavy load on the table between two men who each promptly took charge of the service. Natalie lifted her lantern off the tray and set off back upstairs. The sounds of the renegade revolutionaries pouring, stirring sugar, slurping hot tea, munching bebinca slices, smacking their lips in satisfaction and protesting or accepting second helpings filled the room. Even secret revolutionaries need late-night snacks to keep up their energy.

The two words uttered by Shirly were held suspended and paused in the air, like a caminhão engine that shuts off while waiting for a passenger. She too was encouraged to have a slice of bebinca. She spooned into each of the thin layers carefully before rolling the pudding consistency on her palate, savouring the taste of coconut trees, idyllic fields and a sweet ocean breeze.

'Is it possible, Freddy?' As their drinks were drained, a dab of gumminess was the only trace left on their dessert plates. My Dear Fellow repeated his question after a particularly hot last gulp which made him scrunch up his face tightly, 'Scorched earth, is it possible?'

Freddy smacked his lips grimly. 'I'm afraid it is.'

'The Governor-General would never do such a thing. We have all had tea parties and dinners with him. How could he . . .?' asked one of the men at the table.

'My dear fellow, you are right, right you are. By himself, he would not think of such a thing. He is one of us. But it would be possible if he received instruction from Salazar in Portugal. However, we have not heard anything yet, so no reason to panic. Just the word of a young lad who may have overheard something.'

After this discussion, the conversation around the table broke into several parts that segued into polite personal inquiries—'And how is your wife?', 'Oh is that so?', 'Please give your parents my regards . . .'—indicating that the meeting had come to a close. Shirly left as quietly as she had arrived with Sushant, and once she reached her bed, she fell into a dreaming sleep that seemed as real as her last few waking hours.

33

The Governor-General reread the message that had been handed to him. His eyes lingered on the signature with its imposing and decisive flourish—Oliveira Salazar—before delving into the letter's contents. After reading it, he rose from his desk and walked over to the window, where he could see the waves futilely attempt to clamber up over the wall separating the Palácio do Cabo grounds from the rocks below. He had mixed feelings about it all.

On the one hand, he was grateful that the Presidente do Conselho had such faith in him to carry out the onerous task of maintaining the traditions of honour, such as holding fort in the face of an advancing enemy army of freedom fighters. Of course, he referred to them as terrorists. However, resisting the Indian Army for eight days—Salazar's request in order to mobilize an international political parley—would be like preventing a ripe cashew apple from its downward gravitational summons by simply ordering it to do so. He wasn't so sure he could keep this promise if he made it. Could it be possible that he would be the last Governor-General of Estado da Índia? However, more than this thought were the words that alternately haunted him and steeled him in case any defence were to be futile—total sacrifice.

34

Aphonso was bored and tired of swatting flies. The Sikh Regiment had been camped out east of Dodamarg for a few days and was growing restless. Each morning, D-Day would shift. It was first scheduled for the fourteenth, then the sixteenth, and now the following day, the eighteenth of December. Aphonso felt like the Indians had their own concept of punctuality and operated within a time zone of their own. At first they were awaiting a unit from here. Once the said unit arrived, he was told they were awaiting the arrival of another fleet from elsewhere. His frustration mounted with the stench of the accumulating forces. They slept, shat, did mock drills and played cards out in the open. Their stubbles grew and their bodies took on the hot, spiced scent of unwashed armpits.

But as the great orange eye was being sucked into the horizon that evening, casting a net of coolness into the air along with the hungry buzz of mosquitos from their lair, things took a turn.

An important-looking general with a bigger turban than Major Kapoor, who had arrived that morning and had spent the day in a makeshift tent discussing strategy with a fleet of majors and colonels, called for an assembly. The troops gathered to attention for the announcement.

Once it was silent enough to hear the general clearing his voice, he began. His speech was a series of bullet points. 'Firstly, the people of Goa have caused the collapse of colonial rule' and 'Secondly, the people of Goa are Indians . . .' The points weren't how Aphonso would phrase them. After all, here was a Sikh army man presuming to know Goans as a Goan would. Did the people of Goa cause the collapse? What collapse? As far as he knew, things were ticking as usual within its boundaries. Due to the wireless silence over the past few days, civilians weren't likely to know that there was a gathering of troops at the borders. In his musings that begged to differ with the general's points, Aphonso entirely missed seventhly and eighthly. All would be fine once he managed to get Clinton out of the Aguada jail. He made a mental note to remind Major Kapoor that he wanted to lead the troops there first. He was sure he could convince him that freeing prisoners of the cause would only strengthen their advance.

And then the general said something that made him attentive. 'H-Hour will be at first light tomorrow.' Finally, the action that Aphonso had been waiting for all these years would bear fruit. He hadn't thought far enough ahead of what he would do with himself after Goa began ruling herself since he was so used to having a cause to side with. But for now, he believed that his life was in perfect alignment with the forces of right action.

As the general read out the names of regiments and battalions, all colour-coded, he drew up plans for 'an eastern and a northern thrust and a decoy entry from the south'. The army was so confident of winning that it had been decided that there was no need for the navy or the air force to intervene. 'In three to five days, Goa will be free of colonial rule,' the general prognosticated.

That night, Aphonso couldn't sleep. It wasn't so much adrenaline or fear. He was looking forward to seeing Clinton's familiar face again. He imagined all the ways he could play saviour and be reunited with his old friend, who was as dear as family could be to him.

That night, Shirly dreamt that she was on stage, and even though she was singing, no sound emerged from her. The ominous-looking audience sat before her, expectant, impatient, as mute as she was. She rolled over in her sleep, her body trying to turn the page of her slow nightmare.

While she slept, a tide of candles moved outside the house. As the lights bobbed, they bounced off the dark, yielding skin of the Mandovi, and their quick, bright flashes silently knocked on the small window near the foyer, catching Mamtu's eye from where she was curled up in the living room. She rose, a protective hand on her full belly, and padded to the window in step with the night crickets. She gazed out serenely. Just the faithful making their way in the dark to the church where their Goencho Saib lay. And Mamtu said a prayer, hoping the lights would ferry her wish into his ear.

35

The next day, Shirly was woken by a frantic Goku in the corridor outside her bedchamber. 'Bai, Baby, what is happening? All dizord in the streets outside. I not knowing what is happening. Something bad, Bai. Just you see . . .'

Disorder was a rare animal in Panjim. Shirly didn't even have time to stretch her limbs. She searched Goku's face and saw anxiety written around her eyes and lips. Devika sat up, unmoving and wide-eyed. She had absorbed Goku's fear, and Shirly felt the need to be her big sister at the moment. She went to her little sister's bed and placed a protective arm around her fragile shoulders. In the adjoining master bedroom, Mamtu was awake and came to the threshold in her nightie. She reached out to Goku and put an arm around her. 'Kai nai gho,' Don't worry, it is nothing, Mamtu tried to placate her.

'Bai, please look outside on the street before you say it is nothing,' entreated Goku. The four of them went to the window in Shirly's room and opened the inner wooden flap of the window. Under the flag floating aloft, rows and rows of marching men filled the road outside the Palácio do Idalcão. Except for the parade during Carnaval, Shirly had never seen so many people on the street in front of her home. And it was just as surreal now, like a scene out of a war movie. Mamtu's eyes dilated with alarm.

'You are right, Goku,' she said, this time clutching her shoulder, white-knuckled, no longer consoling her. 'How did you even make it here?'

'Don't ask, Bai. Poor me,' said Goku, 'I really had to pushing way. They telling me go home, stay inside. But I telling them, "Look here, you don't let me go, then my Senhora Bai, she kill me. So you shooting to me if you wanting, otherwise anyway I'm dying!"' Goku looked vulnerable and fiery at the same time, and Mamtu smiled wryly at the stubborn faithfulness of her maidservant whom she was grateful to have and loved like family. 'What they'll say, so they let me coming here.'

'Oh, well done, Goku. That was very dangerous what you did. You should have stayed at home, we all would have managed somehow.'

'No no, Bai. I not afraid of them and their guns. I am having stomach for proper hot-hot chillies.'

Mamtu left her to it with a raised eyebrow, her mind flitting as always to concern for her husband, locked away in a dreadful prison, far from his bed, his girls and the nourishment of her cooking. 'Okay, Goku. Girls, come, let's have breakfast.'

The others departed from the room, but Shirly stood at the window. More than ever now she was sure that this meant trouble. Like the army of ants that thrummed blackly on the landing outside the door when the poder dropped some breadcrumbs, the soldiers on the street marched thickly and endlessly in four rows. Shirly felt an enormous sadness well up inside her. She had to tell her mother.

'Mummy, there are bombs everywhere.' Shirly realized too late the tactless delivery of the news as they were seated at the table in the kitchen.

'What, Puttha?' Mamtu looked at her daughter quizzically.

'You know how Tomas is . . .'

'Tomas, the Araujos' second son?' Mamtu confirmed.

'Yes, Mummy, him. He licks the boots of the agente . . .'

'Shirly!'

'What, Mummy, it's true, everyone says so. Anyway, he gave us the news that there are bombs everywhere in Goa. And the Governor-General has been given the order from Portugal to make them go boom, boom, boom, wherever they are. And Tomas, he said . . .' Mamtu narrowed her eyes, trying to keep up with her daughter's wild narrative. 'He said that they will make them blast at Daddy's prison, because they want . . .' Shirly noted that Mamtu was emotionless, disbelieving, not allowing anything to approach her sore wounds. 'They want . . . he said they want to kill the . . . Tomas called him a traitor, a revolutionary. He said they want to kill such people first.' Shirly didn't know which was harder to say: 'kill', 'revolutionary' or 'traitor'. Her mother remained unmoved.

'Saiba! Shirly Baby . . . Bai . . . Baba is good man. Nothing happening . . . ai gho. Take breakfast, Baby,' Goku said patronizingly. Clearly, she didn't believe her either. 'The Portuguese, what they are doing? I not understand. Someone should tell Govner-Geral . . . That Rosie told me she knows somebody . . .' Goku continued distractedly as she served a sunny-side-up on Shirly's plate. Not hungry, Shirly passed on the plate to Devika and instead nursed a glass of milk with a side of unndo. And when she chewed the last of Goku's sentences in her head, she frowned with the weight of her thoughts.

Could it be possible? But she'd need help. Shirly drank her milk, forgetting to dunk her unndo into it at all, and excused herself, saying she was going to Ana's for a practice session. She rushed into her room to put on her slippers. On the way out, her eye fell on a small cloth bundle on her dresser. She deliberated and then grabbed it. The heavy front door banged shut in her hurry, over the loud protests of Mamtu and Goku. 'Mostem! Always naughty, that girl,' Goku exclaimed with a harassed pout.

Shirly zipped carefully along the sidewalk like a wind gust and rapped at the Araujos' door, panting. As usual, Mushu opened it. 'Ah, Shirly Baby . . .'

'I'm in a hurry, Mushu, I cannot stay, can you call Ana or João out here please?'

'One minute, Baby,' Mushu said in his sagely voice. Shirly rocked on her foot, back and forth on the tiles, in anticipation. When the heads of the two Araujos popped through the door, Shirly placed her finger on her lips. They closed the door slightly behind them and sat for a meeting on the front steps, presided over by Mika, who benevolently offered his furred body for rubs.

'We need to tell the Governor-General what is happening. We have to stop him,' said Shirly to the siblings fiercely. She watched herself, as some grown-up version of her seemed to take charge and control the rowing oars of her selfdom.

'If he has orders, Shirly, it is not like he will just listen to us,' said Ana in her voice of reason.

'Why won't he listen to us, he may just . . .' reasoned João.

'I think . . .' Shirly's words interrupted them. The words of her old friend José Faria made more sense. 'Cator re bhaji, cut the vegetables!' Softly, she said, 'I think we don't need to tell him. I have an idea. We change the message.'

'Message?' asked the siblings in unison. Shirly had to slow down her thoughts and communicate them properly to her friends. She took a deep breath before launching into an explanation.

'I heard Rosie tell Goku, so it must be true. They have a system in the Palácio do Cabo with the telegraph. It arrives by a code.'

'Morse code!' João said.

'Yes, and then that paper is sent to a typist who types it, and a third person pastes strips of the typed message on a letter, and then it is sent to the Governor-General. There is one person who gets the message, another person who types the message and yet another who pastes the message before it is delivered to the Governor-General.'

'Even if we do change the message, how do we enter in the first place?' asked Ana, thinking it all sounded very complicated and out of their grasp.

Shirly was silent. 'Yes, whenever my parents go to the Cabo, they take the car. And there are guards at the gate who check their invitation.'

More silence. And then João spoke up, 'Hamid can take us.'

Of course, why not. This was one of the reasons João made her heart surge with life. 'Yes, Hamid and Agope, they will know!' Was she sure of what she was doing? Of what she was asking her friends to do? Of course not. But they'd be doing it together, wouldn't they? She and her dear, dear Araujos. Shirly couldn't find a reason not to go, so she clapped her hands in excitement. Ana didn't seem too thrilled but she wasn't going to be left out.

'Come on,' said João, leading the pack. 'Let's go find him.'

36

'Excuse me, Major Kapoor. You said that we are not going to harm civilians. Why are there bombs going off?' asked Aphonso, who had turned back from the head of the troop to the slow-moving Jeep at the rear where the regiment head was seated. The Sikh Regiment was marching on its route towards Panjim when explosions could be heard going off in the far and near distance.

'Not Indian Army bombs, Ulfanze. These are your Portuguese bombs,' said Major Kapoor gravely.

'You remember the deal, Major? Once we reach Betim, I will accompany the next group to the Aguada prison. You will have to proceed without me from there.'

'Agreed, Ulfanze.'

The pulse on Aphonso's neck raced as he ran to the front line again. The sound of ammunition made the day suddenly real. Then, once they reached the creek at Assonora village, he stood in front of the stream, perplexed. Just a few broken and blackened timbers remained on either end, where a bridge had once stood.

'The Portuguese have blown up the bridge!' yelled someone.

Aphonso had to talk to some locals, and the group spent a precious hour building an overpass strong enough to carry its weight across to the other side. The regiment advanced till it reached Tivim and found the bridge there demolished too. To mark yet another delay, the sun rose higher in the sky before the party could move ahead. Closer to Mapuçá, the group encountered anti-tank mines, which had to be cleared painstakingly, as well as roadblocks like felled trees. The troops were also informed that all bridges and culverts had been blasted away. But the Sikh Regiment pushed on, sometimes taking a longer route, with their goal to reach the banks of the Mandovi at Betim before nightfall. Directly opposite their critical endzone: Panjim.

37

The lieutenant colonel was operating on adrenaline. The news at the borders was grim. In the southern zones, the Indian troops had tricked them by simulating a concentration of a large force. Scattered cookhouse fires and empty vehicles without lights were sent approximately ten kilometres behind their own positions in the night and then brought back into new positions. Misleading wireless messages had been sent in the previous days, which the Indians deliberately wanted the Portuguese Army to intercept. In this false anticipation, the majority of the Portuguese troops were deployed south of Panjim, which left the remaining barracks in the north with a trickle of soldiers, who had promptly left their posts once the bulk of the Indian Army came marching through those areas.

'IAF Canberras have partially bombed Dabolim, and the TAIP air services are disrupted. Evacuation plans are being put into place by ship now. The Emmisora de Goa, the wireless station within that location, is out of commission so there is no way for us to communicate with Portugal or anyone in the outside world from there.' As the lieutenant colonel listed reasons to convince the Governor-General to surrender and cut their losses, his leader's responses were delayed and a little too off-target for the army man's liking.

'Hmmmm. Yes . . . what about the plans that you have effected?' the Governor-General asked distractedly.

'Plano Sentinela for the defence of Goa is running out of steam at the moment. With the concentration of forces in Mormugao, the north has been left defenceless to attack. Our efforts now are tactics to delay the advance of the enemy. We have troops set up along the Mandovi, Candeapar and Sanvordem Rivers.'

'Yes, the rivers . . . good . . . good . . .' the Governor-General nodded absently.

The lieutenant colonel continued, 'The destacamento de engenharia . . .'

'Hmmm, what is that . . .?'

'The destaca . . . well, the engineering detachment has been divided subsequently for the execution of Plano de Barragem—the demolition of bridges and obstructions on roads. This is again a delay tactic to prevent the control of the cidade de Goa as far as possible.'

'India isn't as peace-loving a nation as the Mahatma has made it out to be. This Nehru fellow is a tricky eel with a shock up his scales,' was the leader's response. Then, like a balloon renewed with air, the intention came back into his eyes as he directed his chief of command, 'We have been given orders from Portugal,' said the Índia Portuguesa leader, slowly and deliberately, 'and we will honour them.'

'This is a beco sem saída,' thought the lieutenant colonel. A staggered retreat without any escape. Basically, painting oneself in a corner. Outnumbered and outmatched, a disaster was waiting to happen. Only God could save them now.

38

'Where are you going? Hey you, you all, go home now!'

Shirly, Ana and João were idling near the Customs House but were waylaid by some local troops of the Portuguese Army, one of whom shouted out to them. The once-familiar boulevard was bereft of citizens, now occasional flanks of soldiers were making their way in several directions. Some of them indicated to the trio to turn around and return home. The three nodded in agreement but didn't move.

A loud whistle swiped the air.

Shirly turned around excitedly. 'Hamid! Agope! Here!' Shirly jumped up on the parapet separating the river from the road and exerted all the power in her lungs. A lone dhow that had broken off from the murmuration of sails on the water was headed directly to where they stood. The water level was high this morning, and as the dhow neared, wavelets slapped against the parapet, wetting their slippered feet.

While Agope steered with a giant oar, Hamid extended his hand to pull the trio on board one at a time, each in a swift balletic movement. They found their perch on the planks, and Shirly stared at Hamid's worn trousers, rolled and cuffed to his calves. His hair, sun-bleached and matted, was longer than when she had last seen him, flicking into his eyes. His fingernails were lined with dirt, but Shirly didn't flinch from his presence this time. She felt a strange kinship with this boy—so far away from his birthplace, but equally at home with this river as she was.

As the dhow steered into the centre of the watercourse in the direction of the sea at Gaspar Dias, Shirly glanced back at the banks they had left. To her surprise, they weren't being followed. Instead, in the distance, a familiar figure was alighting from a Jeep while army troops surrounded him to pay him obeisance.

'What is the agente doing near the fazenda?' asked João, echoing Shirly's thoughts. Shirly couldn't be sure whether Monteiro had looked directly at the three of them, across the road from where he stood amidst a thicket of his soldiers.

'Oh ho! What is here? We 'ave got some sea monstars! Hamid, make a fire, we will cook them and eat them.' Agope's green eyes crinkled as he laughed at his own joke. Shirly had left her childhood fear of this fairytale man who joked about stealing her away to make a meal out of her far, far behind her. Beyond their crustacean-like exterior, he and his people were no less human and as kind as nuns. Perhaps more so. In fact, the irony wasn't lost on her that the real fear she experienced was towards a land creature who wore the garb of protection and mixed in regular society but bore a wolfishness beneath his veneer.

'Agope, we have to get to the Cabo. Can you take us?'

'The Cabo?

'Yes, please, the Palácio do Cabo . . . the Cabo, where the Governor-General stays.'

'Yes, I know the Govna he stay there. What work you have there?'

So Shirly explained her plan to the barnacled man birthed by the ocean gods and watched the expression on his face change dramatically.

'Quarachim! You have the blood of your papa in your boday. Hamid, put the second sail up. Op-op-op, we go now.'

Quietly, full of mission in their bones, this dhowful of unlikely friends came around the bend past the Gaspar Dias beach. They were confronted by a cliff on which the majestic, russet-tiled, whitewashed Palácio do Cabo lay loftily like a crown. It looked so peaceful from the distance, with white rushes of surf below the steep cliff face as the wind blew waves over the rocky waters. Agope's intensely minty eyes scanned the coastline to find an appropriate dock.

Agope's reference to blood reminded Shirly of the cloth pouch that she had swiped from the dresser on her way out this morning. While the others looked away, she pulled it out of her skirt pocket and, opening it, took a pinch of its carmine grains and placed them on her tongue. Just a dash of the ferrous dust for luck, to conjoin her with the body and blood of this about-to-be-scorched earth. And her father. And God-all-does-knows what else. The sea breeze wrapped around her thoughts, carrying them into the flashing horizon.

'No, no, Hamid, not here, we go on west,' said Agope to his son. Although there was a natural stone jetty as they approached the Cabo, Agope was suspicious. 'There are guards watching us.'

'If they are watching us then won't they catch us as we pass the landing place?' asked Ana.

'They think nothing, they think we are "gypsies" only. We no problemo for them.'

For the first time in her life, Shirly was relieved to be mistaken for one of these kindly and honour-driven dhowfolk. Her heart secreted warm affection and an airy gratefulness for Zulekha, wherever the princess-turned-peasant girl was—etheric sisters, between this world and another.

The dhow passed the jetty, and the two sentries guarding it followed its trajectory with their eyes.

Fearlessly, Agope caught their attention from a distance as he waved out. Just like he'd predicted, the sentries dropped their guard, smiled and waved out to the wayfarers as though acknowledging it was just another good day to go for a sail.

The dhow circled the fringe of rocks at the base of the cliff around ninety metres above which sat the Palácio do Cabo. The wayfarers could see the Zuari River much ahead, spilling into the Arabian Sea where she mingled with her sister the Mandovi, which now lay behind them. Further westward, they could spot the Mormugao harbour, where a large Portuguese cruiser was being stealthily surrounded by smaller Indian frigates.

Shirly, however, remained focused on the palace she wanted to enter. She hadn't imagined the enormous breadth and scale of its three levels and several windows. And she realized that she wouldn't know which room she would have to look into for her quest to be successful. Oh, maybe it was all a bad idea. Oh, and what had she done? Oh, and why did she leave her kitchen at all?

'Maybe we should go back?' Ana voiced her thoughts aloud.

'When the wind is going one way, the boat cannot go another,' said Agope enigmatically.

'Over there.' Hamid pointed to a small ingress in the cape's reef.

As father and son steered the dhow into the narrow opening of land surrounded by boulders on the westerly side, Agope made a small announcement in his matter-of-fact way, 'Quarachim, Araujo—we are going home.'

The others stared at him. 'What do you mean?' asked Ana. Wasn't home the Mandovi for them?

'To the village of my mamma and papa in Armenia,' said Agope. Then he explained to the frowning young things in his boat, 'This India is another world. Now they come to Goa, and they make politics here. No good when army comes like this. Too much trouble. Now we make quiet life in Armenia and we find nice wife for this Hamid, ey.' Agope winked at Hamid to lighten the mood but the three remained silent and sombre.

Agope's premonition was lost on Shirly. How much could anything change from this day forward? Nothing had changed here over the course of their *entire* lives and for possibly over hundreds of years before that. The sun would rise and sink as per usual. The crabs would still scuttle on the beaches, leaving sand balls around their sand-holes. And Goku would argue with the egg-seller in the morning and then have a mountainful of rice for lunch in the afternoon. Things would surely be back to normal. The dhowman was being a little too dramatic in her opinion. That is, if you didn't count the mention of bombs in the recent past.

Then Agope shouted, 'Now go! Finish it! The guards, they will come find this boat otherwise.'

João rose from his plank seating, went up to Agope and shook his hand silently. Then he shook the hand of his dear friend Hamid but quickly appeared overwhelmed with a sense of impending loss. He didn't know when he would see him again. Sensing this, Hamid let his hand go and instead pulled João into an embrace.

Ana and Shirly shook the hands of the father–son duo. 'Thank you, bye,' they said in unison. Then they reached out to take João's outstretched hand and hop on to the sandy strip between the rocks.

39

As Cajetan lifted his line at the parapet along the estuary of the Mandovi River and Gaspar Dias sea, he heard the thunder of wheels behind him. He turned and saw three armoured trucks swish past him on the road. 'More noise, fish will be scared. Shey!' Today was an unusually unproductive day. There was no chance to attempt a catch this morning because the streets had gone berserk with marching soldiers. Bombs had exploded in the distance, and when earlier he had positioned himself at his spot at the Dona Paula jetty, he was herded away by the local army men. It was a strange morning in Panjim. And on top of this, all the shops were shut, including the taverna. So he couldn't even enjoy a few drops of his favourite pastime while he had time to pass.

The sun was overhead now. He had to bring home something for lunch and dinner or else Rosie would singe him worse than the sand baked by the afternoon heat. She was so much meaner when she was hungry. She always complained to him that their house was not big enough, that she was doing all the work by maintaining it and adding to it. What was she complaining about? Cooking the meals? Maybe she should try *catching* the meals. Yes, she had never had to fish for her dinner. Never waited endlessly, not knowing what would bite at the end of the line. Or on some mornings—this was happening more and more often—when he went out in his boat and returned with human-made trash, like an old shoe or an empty tin of pomade, in the net. How could she shout at him for what the ocean decided to offer him? Maybe she should take the boat out! He punctuated his vehement thoughts by forcefully yanking the line backwards over his head.

Just then, another armoured car slowed a little past his position and halted on the road. The driver's door opened, and a man in uniform stepped out. He leaned by the rear end of the vehicle, looking out at the moving waters sparkling in the warm December sun. Then he fumbled in his pocket, lit a cigarette and took a deep drag, releasing a summery cloud of smoke.

'Ey, Francis?' Cajetan asked. He was sitting a bit farther away, but within earshot.

'Caji? It's you, Caji?' The van driver responded with his own question, squinting in Cajetan's direction now.

'Ya, Patrão. It's me. Whad'chu doing here?' asked Cajetan, continuing the questioning repartee.

'Orders, Patrão. I can't say, government secret,' said Francis cryptically.

'What secret, Patrão? And what all these soldiers are doing here? No fish only today, Patrão.'

'Yes, all hell and mess. India is attacking us.'

'Attacking us? India? Where, Patrão?'

'You heard bombs in the morning?'

'Can't hear bombs, my wife shouting too loud, Patrão,' Cajetan said morosely. 'Serious, you are? India is attacking?'

'Yes, Patrão, all our soldiers are outside, defending us.'

The two men stared into the glistening river in silence before Cajetan spoke again.

'So, who winning? We winning, is it?'

Francis took another deep drag with a sigh and exhaled more smoke, shaking his head. 'No, Patrão. Don't know. Not yet. That's why we are . . .' And then he stopped himself.

But Cajetan caught him on his half-sentence. 'What?'

'Secret, okay?'

Cajetan nodded yes.

'We are burning the money.'

'You are burning the money?'

'We burning the escudos. On Gaspar Dias beach. Secret orders.'

'Why, Patrão? The bank not wanting the money or what?' asked Cajetan in alarm, thinking he should help to unload some of it from Francis's care. It would help out his friend's work in any case.

'God alone knows, Patrão. Order from Araujo boss in fazenda.'

'Oh . . .'

The whir of approaching car wheels was twinned with the sound of Cajetan's name being yelled in the distance.

'Ayyy! Rosie! She always find me!'

'Ayyy, the agente! He coming to see we are burning all the escudo! I'm going, Caji . . .' Francis said in alarm, looking at the car heading towards them. He stubbed his cigarette, hopped into the driver's seat and drove off in the direction of the Gaspar Dias beach, from where a livid Rosie was making her way to her husband.

40

Shirly had somehow found herself in a Tom Sawyer adventure.

'Through here,' said Ana, whose little body easily slipped into an opening between the rocks. As they shifted through the stony tunnel, their breath echoed in the dank darkness. Behind them, the sound of the waves crashing on the small, pebbled shore rebounded on the rocks, filling their ears.

'What is this?' asked Shirly. The tunnel had widened, and in a grotto in the wall was an altar with an idol of a woman lying horizontally, decked in cloth and flowers.

'That is Santa Paula,' said Ana.

'Santa Paula? Like Dona Paula?' asked Shirly.

'No. I don't know, actually. But this one is a goddess, locals worship her with a feast and everything.'

Shirly was mesmerized by the peaceful visage of the goddess and also impressed with her friend's knowledge. 'How do you know about her?' she asked Ana.

'I overheard it. The Governor-General regularly has tea parties on the lawns of the Cabo. When my parents were invited they took us along. We've seen your mother and father there too,' Ana recounted. 'Anyway, some of the guests were talking about how once a year the local fishermen come to the grotto to pray to the goddess since she protects them when they are fishing in the water. Often, we and the other younger ones brought here would run away from the adults and play a game of hide and seek. This is a really good hiding place. When

I came in here none of the others found me. But I had to come out when I was hungry to get some sandwiches before they all got over.'

'Come on, let's go,' said João. They trickled through the laterite-floor tunnel, following the light at the other end. Once they reached it, they paused on spotting a guard at the side entrance to the Palácio do Cabo, which was across an open driveway. 'We cannot sneak in directly, I think.'

'What do we do?' asked Shirly.

'Oh, of course. Over there. Follow me . . .' whispered Ana decisively.

While the guard had his back to them, Ana, Shirly and João sprinted diagonally towards a small chapel. They opened the heavy door and slipped inside.

It was small, with a gilded altar at one end. 'Usually, the Governor-General comes for the mass from up there.' Ana seemed knowledgeable and comfortable on this turf so unfamiliar to Shirly. She pointed upwards to a mezzanine balcony at the rear of the room above the pews for the clergy. 'There is a staircase . . . ah, here!' They wound up the narrow staircase off to one side and looked down at the altar below.

'So beautiful,' said João, echoing the girls' thoughts.

'Through here,' said Ana, not losing focus, and led them to a small wooden door at the end, which had been left open in good trust.

'Wow . . . ohmygoodness!' Shirly was spellbound. The chapel mezzanine led them into a lavish suite. The room was high-ceilinged, with large windows facing the southwest that let in the airy light. The ocean lay buoyant and bright outside, and as the sun bounced off its surface a sheen danced in delicate patterns on the walls and floor tiles. The furnishings were regal, with richly embossed golden-yellow curtains and intricately carved teak furniture. Off to one side was a large four-poster bed with a diaphanous mosquito net draped over it.

Shirly and Ana clutched each other in alarm. They could see a sleeping form through the white net. They immediately guessed that they were confronted by the Governor-General's wife during her siesta. Quickly casting an eye around for the room's door, they inched over to it. They opened it with a heart-stopping click but realized with relief that the ocean breeze muffled the sound—the sleeper lay undisturbed in a gauzy cloud of dreams.

Their feet padded on ornate calçada mosaic through a long, empty verandah which wrapped itself around the building structure. They looked down and realized that they were on the second storey.

'Now what?' asked Shirly, feeling hunger churn her stomach and a curious breeze play in her hair. She should have eaten a proper breakfast. But a real adult wouldn't complain. Plus, she didn't mind so much. She was here with João, her future husband, even though he didn't know it yet. And, equally importantly, with Ana, this girl who had earned her trust and with whom she felt she could conquer any nun or nightmare involving bombs. 'We need to find the telegraph room,' she said to the Araujos.

'There.' On cue, Ana pointed to a wooden banister at the end of the corridor. 'On the ground floor near the staircase is the telegraph room, if I remember correctly.' The staircase zigged to a landing and then zagged to the first storey. They heard loud clattering in the kitchen and snuck into the wide dining hall to avoid any of the stewards spotting them. Except for the frenzied sound of dishes being washed and stored, there was a post-lunchtime siesta lull that gripped the air. Ana and João seemed accustomed to the dining room, but Shirly's eyes went wide as she looked around. It had the longest dinner table she had ever seen in her life at the centre of the quarters, flanked by richly embroidered chairs on both sides. There were rows of glass-fronted cabinetry with silverware of every size and shape. Framed oil canvases hung on the walls, and a sculpture stood in every corner. The pièce de resistance was a grand delft ceramic bowl covered with scenes from Portugal mounted on a teak base at the centre of the table.

'Okay,' said Ana, as she led the trio towards the staircase once more. 'The room where the telegraph comes is directly underneath us. Shirly, how do you even know that the telegraph is going to come?'

'I overheard.' Shirly now realized that her answer to quell Ana's afterthought might be a bit flimsy. It was too late anyway. They were already here.

'You are sure?'

She meant to say 'maybe', but Shirly heard herself say 'yes'. 'I overheard the fish seller telling Goku that her husband overheard someone at a taverna talking about his job as a telegraph boy here at the palace.' She definitely sounded ridiculous even to herself. Very chari, amply pishem, profoundly nutty and exceedingly louco. But somehow her thoughts and ideas had turned into fate and she was riding its breeze without any brakes.

João frowned but Ana couldn't resist giggling. 'This could be Chinese whispers,' she said.

'Yes,' agreed Shirly with genuine innocence. But her father wasn't here to comfort her, so she decided to avoid looking doubt in the face and dig for belief from her depths. She continued, 'After it is received in a code . . .'

'Morse . . . Morse code,' piped in João enthusiastically, earning a glance of admiration from Shirly.

'Yes, once it is received and noted by one person on a piece of paper, it is then typed up by a typist on paper strips. A third person pastes the typed strips together on a letter, and that person finally takes it to the Governor-General.'

There was a deep-thinking pause before Shirly added, 'Tomas said that there would be a message from Salazar in case of war. How do we know if it has already come?'

A pause.

'I have an idea. I will have to go down there and make friends with the telegraph fellow. You girls wait here.'

The girls realized that it was a good idea. Amiable João with his charming face and gentle ways won the hearts of most people. He would find it easy to do so with the telegraph operator. He could then make the change before the typist put it in ink. But what would he say if asked what he was doing in the Cabo?

Just as a resident cat passed by, João concentrated his gaze on it and said, 'Leave that to me.' He bent down, pretending to offer the cat a crumb of food. It mewled and, turning away from its tracks to the kitchen, padded over to João, who picked it up, stroked it as he tucked it under his arm and headed down the stairs. João turned to look at Shirly, and in that moment she wished she could trade places with the cat.

For once, Ana felt a surge of pride at her brother's charms. So far so good, she thought. The two girls peeked through the polished wooden balusters of the staircase, watching João descend, cat in arm. At the bottom of it, he reached a wide verandah at the front façade of the Palácio do Cabo. Before it lay manicured lawns with hedgerows, flower bushes and coconut palms, with a grand driveway leading out of the main gate.

Off to one end of the verandah was the guard who now sat watchful at the postern they had evaded earlier. Luckily, his back was to João. But then João's heart stopped when a couple of other guards pushed through the doors of an office. The sign in front of it said 'Governo-Geral do Estado da Índia'. When the men stepped out completely, they turned. Looking directly at João, they began walking towards him.

João froze, and the girls hiding at the top of the stairs watched in horror. The officers stopped in front of him, and the tension was palpable. They reached out. Then, to João's great relief, they started fawning over the cat, petting and miaowing at it, melting into big softies. The cat mewled back in pleasure. Chuckling, the two officers proceeded to walk out through the driveway, without a question raised at João.

Saved by the cat, João heaved a sigh of relief, turned to his right and found the room he was looking for. The sign outside said 'Telégrafo' and it was located a few metres before the Governor-General's office. He pushed on the door and allowed the cat to slip in.

The box radio burped on the Governor-General's table. 'Ah, we have it,' said Lieutenant Colonel Andrade. The two of them, along with Capitão Carlos Alexandre Morais, Comandante Luis Manoel de Cabral and Major Paulo Fonseca, the director of economic services, were all huddled over the wooden box with knobs, and they had to close their ears once the static burst forth before channelling a station. 'The Bambolim wireless station was blown up but luckily there is another channel that makes it possible in case we need to give the surrender message,' said Capitão Morais. 'The army is advancing and is quite close to the cidade. I have word that northward from Betim and Piligao and eastward from Banastarim and Ponda are completely secured by the enemy.'

Without looking upwards at the captain, the Governor-General sat fiddling the knobs and once the static died down he said, 'At least something works.'

'Governo-Geral, the capitão is right,' said Lieutenant Colonel Andrade, who received a grave look of support from Major Fonseca. 'Even if we want to spread a message to the outposts, there are reports that several of the troops are abandoning positions after setting fire to them . . . and . . .'

There was defeat in his words, but the Governor-General prodded, 'And?'

'They are breaking into wine shops on their retreat. They are just not capable anymore,' reprised Capitão Morais.

'What about at the Fortaleza da Aguada, the prisons, the bank and all the others?' asked the Governor-General.

'Our men are awaiting orders, Governo-Geral,' responded Capitão Morais.

There was a longish lull again. 'It is not yet time to surrender. The mission is to resist. Let God protect,' said the Governor-General cryptically, much to the despair of the men assembled there, turning the knob to muzzle the sounds of the box radio.

'In good sending form, the wrist is parallel to the table,' said the uniformed lad in the telegraph room. He placed a coin on his wrist and showed it to João. 'Look, if I place my hand on the transmission key, the coin should just sit there, like a mosquito that won't let go.' When João had entered with the cat, the lad was taken aback, but when he told him he was hired to feed this Cabo pet, the telegrafista's anxiety dissolved. 'I've been told to stand by in case some messages come in today,' he had said.

Then, while petting the purring feline, he explained to João, who was intending to stall for time in the room, the finer points of the telegraph machine. 'The contacts have to be just right, not too far apart or too close . . . the tension spring too has to be adjusted . . . the dits and dahs tell you whether it is a letter or a word . . .' João was so fascinated and genuinely intrigued by the machine on the desk in front of him—the size of a bread loaf—that he almost forgot why he had come. He wanted to try out this method of conveying messages to his classmates instead of passing notes. 'When you key it in, it sounds rather like a mosquito . . . Oh, here's something . . .'

It was happening, the event was taking place just as Shirly had said. João had to admit that he hadn't quite believed it as much as she did, though he couldn't express that to her. But she was right and it was true, after all. The operator smoothly grasped a pen and a leaf of paper near him and began concentrating on the sound that came through, quite like a cicada in the night.

'Who is it from?' asked João, anxious and hopeful.

'From the top boss in Lisboa,' the operator said without missing a beat. João watched him listen intently as he penned down words on to the paper, making sense of the nonsense electronic woodpecking emanating from the machine.

Just as he was done, the cat jumped up on the desk and began purring, looking for attention. The distracted operator, unable to resist the four-legged visitor, put his ink pen down and began petting the cat. The gratified creature proceeded to plop on to his lap, and the operator looked up at João with helpless happiness. 'Looks like the kitty doesn't want me to move.'

It was all faring too well for not having a proper plan in place, and João saw chance itself purring at him. 'Yes, why don't you let it stay? I can easily deliver the note.'

The telegrafista didn't respond, leaving João's last sentence echoing in the lacuna between them. The uniformed fellow looked up, and in a moment of panic, João wasn't sure if he would sound the alarm on him. Then he said, slowly, 'That is very fine of you. You wouldn't mind? Will you please take the note and pass it along to the office next door? That is where the secretary sits. He will type it up—the message, that is—which will be passed on.'

João couldn't believe his luck but hid any trace of relief on his face. Nodding coolly, he took the page with the inked word-scrawls on it. The operator was absorbed in delivering a very satisfying behind-the-ear scratch to the kitty, and he didn't notice that his pen went missing.

João slipped out the door and looked at the note in the raw sunlight that filled the open verandah. It was plain to see: 'Resist till death. Enforce Scorched Earth. If we cannot have Goa, they cannot have Goa.' It was signed 'Oliveira Salazar, Presidente do Conselho'. João folded the top half of the paper and wrote south of the ridge line, 'Save Goa. No Scorched Earth.—Oliveira Salazar.'

João knew that Shirly would approve because he was allowing himself to be guided by her intelligent spirit and pluck. How he had changed from a year ago, keeping his distance from the girls at school. Some of his friends had recently caught him daydreaming in class and teased him relentlessly. Of course, he had had to deny these new feelings of his. But somehow he was growing used to the idea of having a girlfriend. That sounded nice to him. Shirly, his girlfriend. If he chose to introduce her like that to his friends, would she mind?

João didn't have any time to appreciate his handiwork. He tore the top part of the paper off, crushed it into a ball and jammed it into his pocket. He looked behind him to see if the girls were there, for a sign of encouragement from Shirly's face. But their elfin faces weren't peeking from the top of the stairs. Good, he thought, they are hiding quietly. He then paused before entering by the side door into the office of the Governor-General of the Estado da Índia.

Inside, João found himself in a room that was separated from another room with a partition. He sensed that the Governor-General was seated across it. So near . . . so far. So close to . . . whatever it was they were doing here. But they were not finished yet. His mind lurched forward in time to how the trio would escape once the task of switching letters was done. But that should be easy. He may need to consider the use of the cat again. João's thoughts whirled as he handed the letter to the secretary behind the desk, who looked up inquiringly at him from his work. 'Message from the telegraph room, Senhor,' said João, his voice barely above a whisper.

The secretary looked suspiciously at João but was assuaged on seeing his erect posture and well-tailored clothes and turned to look at the message. He stared at it for a while—too long, thought João. To his relief, the secretary began to type up the words on his typewriter. Clack! Clack! Shatack! Shatack! Pah-ting! The typewriter filled the room with noises João felt grateful for.

When the typing stopped, the secretary cut the strips of paper with a file, then glued them on to another sheet. João could see his words become official in type. In the next room, it sounded like the Governor-General had visitors. The secretary officiously nodded to João, a cue for him to leave, and rose from his seat to deliver the typed letter to the Governor-General. A triumphant João placed his hand on the side door, waiting to exit. He heard the letter changing hands and the silence that ensued.

Satisfied, João slipped out the side door.

On stepping out, he saw the cat he had left earlier rubbing its rump against a pillar in the verandah. But then, a few yards away, horror! Agente Monteiro was in conversation with the lad from the telegraph room, with a couple of his henchmen prowling around. How had it all gone so wrong so fast? And then it got worse—Monteiro and the telegrafista both turned to look in João's direction.

'Well, well, well. Look what the cat dragged in,' said Monteiro in a voice that sounded grimy and despicable to João. The telegraph operator stared on, dumbfounded, unsure about his role in all the drama and whether he was in real trouble or not, while Monteiro grabbed João by his shoulders. 'Come, let's meet an important person,' the agente said and led him through the main door of the Governor-General's office.

João's dread doubled as he entered the main office. He had been on the other side of its partition just a minute ago. The Governor-General was seated behind his desk with Lieutenant Colonel Andrade standing to one side. Next to him were Ana and Shirly. What were they doing here! All three exchanged despondent glances with each other.

The Governor-General looked straight at João as Monteiro roughly pushed him towards the girls and sat down on a chair opposite the head of Goa-Portuguesa. João felt a protective surge for the girls run through him. Ana was worried about what her parents would say. Shirly's mind was blank, for once.

'You see, Governo-Geral, my speciality is finding the rats on the ship. The letter this boy has created is different from what was received.' Monteiro waved the original sheet of dits and dahs of the telegraph received from Portugal. Just their luck. He could read Morse code.

'What is that, I wonder?' Monteiro pointed in João's direction. All eyes came to rest on something white sticking out of his pocket.

João shoved it deeper into his pocket with a rustle. But it was too late. The agente walked over to him. Excruciatingly slowly, he pulled the piece of paper out, uncrumpled it and summoned an air of dead calm. 'The real translation is here, you can see for yourself.' Monteiro handed the crinkled paper with still-legible writing on it to the head of state.

The Governor-General accepted the offering and read it. The clock on the wall ticked so loudly that Shirly thought her head would explode from its vibration. After the longest minute of her life, the Governor-General spoke, 'You are mistaken, Monteiro.' Monteiro's brows narrowed as he continued, 'Your job is not to find rats and torture them. Your job is to maintain peace. Paz e calma. You have failed miserably. I have heard several accounts of your deeds. I don't know what the future holds for Goa, but as long as I am in this chair, you are relieved of your duties.'

Monteiro's face darkened as the stunned trio heaved a breath in relief, not sure why the Governor-General was sidestepping the situation at hand. But with the next tick of the clock, Shirly found that she understood. Her father would have done the same thing. It was simple. He wanted a better Goa for everyone. Without waiting to hear any further from the agente, the Governor-General indicated to Andrade to escort Monteiro out.

The agente stood up, yelling, 'I will see to it that you regret this! You are making a grave mistake. Vai p'ra merda! Salazar will imprison you! Cabrão! You have no idea . . . All of them they are idiota, paneleiro!' He was wrested out of the room, but his loud, crude words weren't blunted by the sound of the ceiling fan whirring overhead.

When the agente's words had died away, the Governor-General steepled his fingers and looked at the trio, still standing, albeit less stiffly, on one side of his office. Finally, he spoke, but not to them. 'These young women and the young man should be escorted back home to their parents.' His secretary came around from his side of the partition and beckoned the trio to follow him out of the front door of the office.

All three of them turned to go. But something felt incomplete for Shirly. She wasn't ready to leave yet. This kind, broad-minded man with the intelligence to see through Monteiro's thuggery, who didn't say a word to them for their trespass, might not detain her in case she blurted out what was uppermost on her mind. Just maybe not. Shirly whirled around. 'Is it true that you have bombs everywhere in Goa?'

The Governor-General was taken aback. 'That is classified information.'

'It's not anymore,' said Ana, quick to her friend's defence. 'We do know what is on that paper.'

'You don't have to follow the instructions,' said Shirly, a little too hopefully.

The Governor-General surveyed all of them. He responded in a grave but kind tone, 'We are not going to surrender till the end. And that means not giving the enemy our homeland. We must be good soldiers, must we not?'

Shirly's thoughts went to her father and her mother. What if she couldn't see either of them again? She believed the bombs would take them from her, just like when she had believed she would lose them forever when Sister Olga had threatened to send her off to the 'gypsies'.

In the middle of her fearful contemplation, the image of José Faria, the Abbé, loomed in her head. What was it that he had said? 'A true artist, one who can really be a hypnotist—and this is the secret—is someone who can change nature.' Was she a true artist? She didn't have the answer to that. When she sang, she still believed that even the frogs of Fonte Fenix were inclined to hop away. She may never have the chance to sing in her Christmas play. That thought hadn't crossed her mind till now. While she was standing in the most officious office in Goa. And now that she did think it, was she sad or was she glad? Or was that feeling a combination of two emotions, a wistful relief? She wouldn't have to stretch her voice in front of a large audience, which Dona Lisette had done her best to prepare her for. But she also wouldn't have the chance to be Zulekha, whose soul she had begun to inhabit. No, it was the other way around. Zulekha had begun to inhabit her.

She now summoned Shirly's attention to her presence in the mysterious depths of Shirly's own throat. Shirly felt her need to break the barrier of falsity and gush with the stream of desperate truth. She ached for the presence of her dear, dear father and the good, kind sweetness of her mother. They were so proud that she was in the musical. And Devika, the way her little sister imitated her words and manner defined her ever more clearly as a big sister. Yes, she had come a long way. But there was still a lot of distance to cover. What did it matter now? They'd all be scorched into oblivion forever. But Zulekha was there, and she was pulleying her way out. Shirly postured in the singing stance she had become accustomed to during Lisette's training. Her fingers interlocked in front of her.

Shirly was transported into the body of Zulekha in the forest so that the boy-turned-prince who was listening to her behind the trees would not help but forget time and feel one with his sincerest nature, swiftly falling in love with the singer, changing their destiny.

The lyrics . . . well, the words were all there, as she had rehearsed over and over . . .

Water droplets on leaves
dance like diamonds for me,
the light on the river
valuable as silver.

I've got golden anklets
picked from marigold blankets
and the breeze through the trees
worth more than pearls from seven seas.

I'd rather be where foliage
glitters like an emerald stage
where freedom is bliss
and the forest is my palace.

This where the days are long
where we have our song
where the sun loves to roam
my heart, my joy, my home.

As each word, each line floated out of her in its tune and eddied around the room, she was no longer Shirly. She was a girl who was given the gift of love and of finding her way to her true home.

At the end of her song, Shirly opened her eyes. The tick-tock of the clock pulled her back from her forest idyll into the rhythm of the real world. She looked at Ana and João first. She wasn't unsure of herself anymore. But she was glad to see their faces shining with pride for her. It was more important than battling the frogs in her throat. Zulekha's song was as clear to all of them as the Mandovi that ran free, twinkling under the sun.

The Governor-General looked directly at her and acknowledged esoterically, 'Goa is indeed beautiful.'

Turning to his secretary once again, he said, 'Please escort them out and make sure they reach home to their parents in safety.' The secretary nodded and hustled the three out of the office. Shirly felt spent. They hadn't been able to stop the telegraph successfully. And there wasn't any certainty that the Governor-General would, or wouldn't, follow the orders in the message to him. Shirly left the Cabo with João and Ana, feeling at odds with herself.

As they pulled out of the grounds of the Palácio do Cabo in the Governor-General's private car, a recognizable figure in holy robes was wafting up the garden pathway towards the palace.

41

Earlier that day, Mushu had thought his heart would leap upwards into his skull in his immense joy. There was all that commotion on the streets, and his master had returned from Lisbon suddenly and instructed the senhora to start packing immediately. Mushu was grateful for this absurd war. Oh, what a happy day, his life would be changing for the better.

Mushu had pulled out their steel trunks from the storage room and dusted them off, humming a fado he had heard Lisette play on the piano. As he helped her organize the packing of their essentials into the trunks, his mind wandered. His desire, which was tightly balled up and lodged in his body, was being set free; his dream of going to paradise was coming true. Lisbon, the very centre of the civilized world. He had heard stories from Lisette and her friends of how the great city was so modern and had its long arms stretching all around its territories overseas in Africa and Asia. There would be more people like his beloved Araujo family, with the best of culture and civilization inextricably harboured in their skin, and all their fairness, a word he chose to understand in its every sense.

When the senhor and senhora discovered that João and Ana were missing, they started to panic.

'There is a war outside—where are they?' Mushu heard the normally genial Eugenio thunder his frustration for the first time.

'They have probably gone with that girl Shirly,' he said, with distaste in his mouth. He had never been too keen on the friendship of that girl with his beloved family's children. Whenever she was around, Ana would become a rowdy rogue, and João, he didn't know what, but something dangerous was brewing between João and that girl. Of course, he couldn't let his opinion be known; he had to keep it to himself for fear of incurring any wrath from his family. One or two times when he had tried to avoid serving her refreshments when she visited for music lessons or to meet his senhora's children, stating that he was busy tending to weeds in the garden, Lisette had reproached him. So he became silent and sullen around her. And watchful. And now she had done this. Taken his beloved brood off to do God-alone-knows-what-and-where.

As quickly as he had arrived, like a monsoon wave, Eugenio had exited the house to attend to some business at the fazenda. He left instructions with Tomas, Lisette and Mushu to stay packed and ready. They were going to catch a steamer before sunset at the Mormugao harbour bound for Lisbon. He wasn't sure, but perhaps, once the war was over, they would return for the rest of their things. For now, the government was evacuating anyone who wanted to escape the situation in Goa for Portugal.

Mushu couldn't believe his luck! A free passage to his beloved Portugal. His Portuguese would improve dramatically there, and he would be one of them. All that caste rubbish would be left in the trail of water that separated the continents. In between packing with his Senhora Lisette, Mushu ran out of the main gate and searched for the familiar figures of the young Araujos with his keen eyes. That Quarachim girl had better not make us miss our steamer, he thought.

He was relieved and overjoyed when the missing children were dropped back in the Governor-General's personal Cadillac. No doubt they had been up to no good, but he didn't care. They were back just in time before Eugenio returned home.

Within the hour itself, the family had piled into the official car given to Eugenio by the fazenda for one last drive through the streets and on the ferryboats of Goa in the direction of Mormugao. They drove past familiar rivers and streams, mineral-rich hillocks and paddy-bright fields towards the harbour. Mushu made sure everything and everyone moved on time, not forgetting Lisette's precious music books or the box of Checkers Eugenio had brought all the way from Lisbon for Ana. The family retainer ensured that there would be no reason to turn the car around.

And he finally drew in a deep breath of relief, feeling an uncontrollable happiness when he was on the deck of the largest barge he had ever hoped to be on. As it pushed away from a palmy shore, he vowed never to return to the backwardness of the past.

42

The men of the Sikh Regiment were slapping each other on the back. They were the first of the Indian Army soldiers on Goan soil to find themselves in such close range of the capital. Once this was over and they were narrating the tale to their friends, they would have full rights to brag about being the 'winning' regiment.

The Mandovi looked so inviting after a long, hot day on the road to the bank at Betim that it took Aphonso all he had not to tear off his clothes, plunge headfirst into the water and allow its coolness to fill every crevice of his body. The way he and Clinton escaped the heat of the days in their village stream during elongated summers. They would sit still, and when a fish came around nuzzling in curiosity . . . sluppp! They'd catch the freshwater delicacy with their bare hands. Then, after they wound up from their Radio Romeo activity for the day, a delicious xit kodi, rice and fish curry, would await them for dinner.

But that day, Aphonso simply sat on his haunches at the water's edge like some of the others and splashed his face, wetting the front of his civilian shirt.

Once refreshed and nursing a chai handed to him, distracting himself from how he'd have to go about setting Clinton free from the Aguada prison, he noticed that the ferryboats in the water around him were grounded. They sat unused, with no locals queued up to board them. He rotated his head to see Major Kapoor booming instructions to his men. A few brightly painted fishing boats sat bobbing near the banks, as forlorn as their grounded owners. He watched as one fisherman was ordered to haul in his net by a couple of soldiers. Aphonso walked under a banana tree and sat to smoke a leaf-rolled cigarette, sending smoke rings rising through the leaves. He finished his cigarette, stood up and went over to Major Kapoor.

'Okay, Major, I have done my part and helped you and your men reach here. Now we need to infiltrate the Aguada as you promised. There are lives in there that need to be freed before the government does anything drastic or holds them ransom to negotiate with your army.'

'Ulfanze, yes, my brother . . .'

'I'm not your brother, Sir!' protested Aphonso a little too quickly, by now disdainful of the Indians. Even though he looked like he could be related to any one of these men, he saw a clear separation of himself from them—their manners were too loudmouth for his taste, their little habits too crude, and their body odour offended him. But he had to be careful, diplomatic, Clinton's life depended on it. 'Major Kapoor,' he said in a more settled tone, 'I cannot stress the importance of this. Even if you win this invasion, and the Portuguese give up Goa to India, my sources tell me that there are bombs planted strategically all over the place, including the prison. As they declare the truce, they will set off these bombs! Do you understand, Sir?' Aphonso raised his voice and Major Diljeet tried to match him.

'Yes, Ulfanze! We are . . .'

'Major, if you don't give . . .'

'. . . aware of the situation . . .'

'. . . the order now, their blood . . .'

'. . . there is protocol!'

'. . . will be on your hands!'

'You cannot dictate terms to the Indian Army!'

'Your promise, in addition . . .'

Their argument was interrupted by a commotion among the men who had crowded away from them around the water's edge. Major Kapoor, snapper-red in the face, whipped his head around and strode with authority toward the centre of the hullabaloo.

'What is the matter here?' he demanded.

The men pointed to the waters of the Mandovi that lay between them and the Panjim bank. A fisherman had deliberately ignored the warnings of the soldiers and was rowing towards the centre of the river where the evening's catch would be plentiful. As his boat glided downriver, he looked back at the noise he had created on the shore left behind. He saw his fisherman friends egging him on while the army men shouted and waved at him, indicating his immediate return.

Suddenly, some loud shots were fired, and the cocky fisherman dropped his oars to cover his head with his arms. A few seconds later, another round of shots exploded into the air and into the wooden hull of the boat. The fisherman lifted his head a few seconds later, glad to be alive as his boat started filling with water. He threw a rope towards the shore he had barely left, then jumped in the water and made his way to the group of his drunken, cheering fisherfolk friends waiting on land.

The sun was setting into the horizon, beyond the confluence of the Mandovi and the Arabian Sea. Its molten descent illuminated both the sky above and the water with flaming resplendence. But as Major Kapoor put his gun away, he missed the glorious sunset worth the paean of poets through the ages for a sight that was as incredible as it was perplexing across the river on the other bank.

Almost as a direct response to the firing, the Portuguese flag was being lowered on the flagpole at the Panjim riverbank and a white flag was fluttering its way to the top.

43

Shirly heard the sound of distinct, loud cracks outside and went to the window. Her mother had closed all the shutters, fearing that a bullet would shatter through them.

Shirly decided to risk the scratchy sound to peel the window's double shutters apart. Using all the delicacy she could channel, she cracked open one side. Just enough to allow the late-evening light to create slats of shadows on the russet tiles. She peered between the wooden shutters and through the glass pane with an eye that roamed like a searchlight.

From her first-storey window she could see the neighbourhood and the city she knew intimately but no longer recognized. An invasive silence hung about without a crease. The boulevard where Ana had once soothed her fears and where she had found the moonlight reflected in Joao's eyes—and which had been crawling with soldiers that morning—was strangely empty, devoid of streetlights. The statue of Abbé Faria in the small garden—no longer *hers* now but *theirs*—under her window looked stonier than ever. The Mandovi looked up at her quietly, unmoving, appearing destitute without any of the usual scattering of dhows bobbing on its surface, watching.

And then it happened. The ritual show that was as faithful to her as the sunset. Only this time, there was a variation that told her something town-sized had changed. The four guards in uniform marched out from the Idalcão palace and came to attention at the flagpole on the riverfront. They pulled down the fabric, which billowed with Portugal's coat of arms, unhitched it, and wrapped it deftly. All the while, the gleaming bugle lay mute, held at the fourth guard's side. Then a white flag was hoisted up the pole.

Shirly was the sole witness to this quietly dramatic scene. At least on the southern bank of the Mandovi.

Barely three hours ago, as Shirly, Ana and João were deposited home in the Governor-General's personal Cadillac, she had noted that the streets were completely deserted, save for a commotion around a large bonfire near the Gaspar Dias shore. Ana and João were dropped off first. Just before Ana disappeared within the gate of her house, she had told Shirly that her father had returned from Portugal the previous day and gifted her a new game of Checkers. Perhaps when everything got back to normal again, she could come over and have a match. If Checkers with Ana made her anticipate normal like never before, there was more to look forward to. João took her hand in his and turning it over tenderly, placed a crumpled piece of paper in her palm. Shirly was amazed. This wonderful to-be husband (who didn't know that he was her to-be yet) had swiped the switched telegraph sheet. There they were, the words 'Save Goa. No Scorched Earth.' Underscored by Salazar's signature. All in his handwriting. How marvellous life was! She would most definitely take his hand and jump over the fire at Carnaval, scorched underwear and all.

'For my girlfriend,' João said, the smile in his eyes mingling with Shirly's. 'See you tomorrow.'

When Shirly reached home, as expected, Mamtu was hysterical. Her exceedingly pregnant mother alternately shouted at her and hugged her, and cried until she gave herself a headache. A couple of hours or so later, before she went to have a lie-down to soothe herself, she instructed Shirly not to open any of the windows, reiterating that there was a war going on outside.

After being shaken more by Mamtu's teary-fiery welcome than her escapades earlier in the day, Shirly went to her room and tried to read an overdue library book. She couldn't concentrate and found that her eyes kept trailing the same page over and over again. That's when she heard the sounds on the water and became the very first resident of Panjim to witness the surrender being flagged.

'What are you doing, Shirly? Stand back!' Mamtu had come into the bedroom, and taking her daughter by the shoulders, turned her from the glass. 'It's not safe to be near the window. I told you, no?'

Her daughter retreated from the shutters, not wanting to further fan the parachute of her mother's concern.

'Mummy, they put up a white flag,' Shirly said. 'What does that mean?' After the tide of the last twenty-four hours, this was an unanticipated event that confused her.

'A white flag? Are you sure? A white flag . . .' Shirly watched her mother's visage change from worry to incredulity as she went over to the window to check for herself. 'A white flag!' she cried, and then to Shirly's surprise and consternation, she broke down and sank on to the bed, sobbing. New feelings of responsibility and dependability unfurled like a flag within Shirly, and she put her hand on her mother's shuddering shoulder.

'It's all right, Mummy,' she consoled, wrapping her arms around a gently heaving Mamtu.

Shirly could feel her mother return the embrace with her own weak grip, speaking through her tears, ironically consoling her daughter in turn, 'Don't worry, dear,' she said, gripping her belly and closing her eyes. 'Everything will be fine. Now go and find your sister. Go.'

Ignoring her mother's instructions, Shirly practically leapt out of the house to tell Ana and João the news, to make sense of it with them, and perhaps with some mingled-in hope to break in the new game of Checkers earlier than scheduled. She ran out past the surprised eyes of Sukkoo and Bukkoo in the courtyard, out the front gate and on to the sidewalk, where once she and Ana had egged on their paper boats in the drain skirting it. She reached the door of the Araujo home. When there was no response, she rang the bell once more. And once more. Not a movement. Nothing.

Where was Ana? She had seen her a couple of hours ago. What about the rest of her family? Shoulders slumped, Shirly walked back in baffled disappointment and looked at the white flag fluttering above the flagpole in the riverine breeze. The four men who had hoisted it minutes ago were now nowhere in sight.

Perplexed, Shirly slowly walked back to her gate. The streets were empty. She felt alone, abandoned. From an ache too deep to fathom within her, tears welled up. They pierced her cheeks as they streaked down her face.

Wait. She told herself to rationalize. Perhaps, like her own mother had done at their home, Dona Lisette had instructed her friend and her boyfriend—her very new and the first boyfriend of her entire life—not to open the door because there was a war going on. Yes, that made sense. That's why they hadn't answered the door. And perhaps she should be more responsible and not be out here herself. After all, she was a role model as an older sister to Devika. Wiping her tears bravely, she negotiated with herself. She had a boyfriend, so it was doubly important for her to be mature and level-headed. Yes, she was a woman now and had to act the part. She looked up and saw the form of Abbé Faria. He was loftily silent and unresponsive. Unable to hear the thoughts in her head. How much he had changed too. Oh, but how she wished he could tell her what was going on. What did he know? What had happened to the currents under the water and the tide of life on her land? Did he know anything about Ana and João, the two veins that had so recently entered her heart but forever enlarged it? His silence only amplified the ghostliness suspended like a fishnet over the town. No matter how she tried to console herself, the ache wedged itself further and further into her, squeezing out her tears helplessly.

And then his limbs shifted. No, no. That wasn't right. Shirly blinked back her tears to look clearly. She even stopped her heaving breath to be sure. There was definitely motion. But it wasn't Abbé Faria. A breeze blew in from the river, stirring the leaves, shaking them like a multitude of jazzy palms near the statue. As a figure in the near distance took a familiar shape, Shirly took a large gulp of air. She forgot everything, and the sky of all her bombarding thoughts, rational or irrational, started to clear away. Checkers could wait. Was it due to Saint Catherine or Goencho Saib or the ever-growing cross? Was it because of the old guard or the newest conquerors of the land? Was it for the iron in their blood that pulled on similar soils to itself? She ran and ran for her life and leapt into Deepak's outstretched arms.

He kissed her wet cheeks. His own were dewed with the tears that rolled down from his tired, haggard eyes. 'My beautiful Shirly . . . I'm so happy to see you again . . . I am never letting you go . . . How I missed you . . . I want to spend the rest of my life, every moment, breathing in your mother, your sister and you . . .' Shirly exulted in the comforting familiarity of her father, and at the same time was astonished at his gaunt, prison-haunted frame. As the wetness of his tears smeared her skin, the opposing feelings that he was the same and yet so different crossed paths within her. Deepak felt his heart rushing out with his words to greet his long-awaiting daughter. He wept, for she was his first sighting of land, his greatest achievement, his flag and country and his joy all rolled into one.

At that moment, Goku appeared, looking frenzied and harried. 'Baba! Shirly Baby! Baby coming! I bringing midwife . . .' And she ran out.

'. . . and the baby!' added Shirly.

'Yes, and the little baby!' her father laughed and cried. The salt of both their tears clung to the wrinkles around their eyes, as Deepak rushed into the gate of their house while carrying his daughter, the air now punctuated by the loud wails of Mamtu in labour.

With her head on her beloved father's shoulder all the way to the threshold of their home—her father, who had been returned to her with the tide—Shirly didn't know just yet that she would never play the promised game of Checkers in the spirit of discovered sisterhood with Ana. Or that her heart would be dragged over the ocean in her newly beloved João's pocket. But for now, her lungs were intact, safe. She would breathe, if not sing. Like her earth.

EPILOGUE

'And then there was a huge fire. I thought why let so much go to waste. So I just took off my petticoat, there only on the road, and filled it with escudo! So much of it! With Mother Mary's help, I felt like I was saving poor Goa!'

The lady who ran the seaside shack at Candolim never tired of narrating the story. 'See, the Patriarch had gone to meet Govner-Geral at the Palácio do Cabo on that day. He was there trying to convince him not to make bomb. But Govner-Geral had already decided not to make bomb. He was a good man. We cannot take money with us after we die. I tell Mother Mary to bless him every day.'

The moment she found out that the woman who had come to her shack accompanied by her husband and young daughter was once a former resident of Panjim, she began the tale of how she had acquired her fortunes. She told her that she had started the first shack at Candolim Beach to cater to the thirst of 'these hippie peoples' who made their way overland to deposit themselves at the virgin shores. When she referred to the hippies, she said it like it was a distasteful word. Locals like her viewed them as displaced, wayward foreigners who had thrown off most of their clothes with their culture, and who just sat there baking themselves all day in the sun, darkening their white skin in their sheer ignorance. But since they kept her in business she had learnt to smile as she served them. 'They are all nudie in Anjuna, shameless,' she said conspiratorially, implying that she preferred to serve hippies with some modicum of clothing rather than the ones who roamed around the beach further north. 'Not even bikini they are wearing . . .' she said to the woman in the black swimsuit who had begun to dig into the fried fish served to her and her family.

'Rosie!'

'There! My useless husband. What does he want now? All fisherwives singing sad mande for husbands to return but till today I have to kick him out to go in the boat and catch the fish. The food is good?' Rosie asked, slipping in some grace at the end of her rancorous complaint.

'Yes, very good, thank you,' the husband said as his wife nodded in agreement. Satisfied with their answer, Rosie walked to the rear of the shack to deal with her not-so-better half.

The family sitting in the shade sipped on their sodas, grinning at each other now that Rosie, with her comical conversation, was gone. The empty bottles stood on the rustic wooden table, each with a marble that sat inside, like the eye of a fish. Before them lay a stretch of sand fronted by the glittering, waving muscles of an ocean. On all sides of the beach, the fringe of trees sat like a bushy eyebrow, bursting with the lushness of undiscovered terrain. At one end lay the ramparts of Fort Aguada jutting out into the sea.

Later that evening, when the family returned home, they all took turns to wash out the salt in their damp hair and the sand in their swimsuits. Refreshed, the little girl went out to play before dinnertime. After the horizon had swallowed the sun, spreading its yolkiness across the estuary of the Mandovi at Gaspar Dias, the woman stepped out to fetch her in for supper. The traffic had increased these days, with cars and scooters vrooming dangerously as they passed. The woman had instructed her daughter beforehand not to cross the road without the help of an adult. She cast a quick glance around. The drain around the house needed upkeep and the walls of the buildings around her were flaky and crumbly. There were a few potholes in the road from the last monsoon, which had never been there before.

The woman saw her daughter sitting on the bench in the small garden outside, engaged in a rather engrossed conversation with no one in particular. When she called out to her, the girl took a moment to say goodbye before coming over to slip her little hand into her mother's outstretched palm.

'Who were you talking to, Ana?' asked her mother.

'Mummy, that statue man wanted to know my name and what it meant,' said the little girl.

Shirly smiled indulgently at her daughter, and the two walked in silence past the gate and up the courtyard stairs for dinner.

THE END

ACKNOWLEDGEMENTS

My mother Mridula Harchandrai for taking me to the library ever since I remember and for sparking the idea. This book isn't this book without her, and without her, this book isn't.

My late father Ashok Harchandrai, who let me be who I need to be.

Kusum Harchandrai Nairi, Padmini Harchandrai and Minal Nairi—for sisterhood. Nephews Soam and Shyam for allowing me to revisit the clear-eyed worldview of a child.

My uncle Haresh Melwani for being a firm root in Goa in every way. For being a treasure trove of ground-level stories, myths and facts.

Late former governor of Goa and literary well-wisher Mridula Sinha for hosting me and offering a special glimpse into the still-glorious world of the bygone Palácio do Cabo, and Aide-de-Camp Himanshu Tiwari for so generously and patiently taking me on a tour through its historic corridors. Sujay Gupta for being the bridge to the Raj Bhavan.

Maria de Lourdes Bravo da Costa Rodrigues at the Goa State Central Library for abundantly piling books and stories on my table during my days in a corner there. To all the writers, too numerous to name, whose books on Goa have passed through my hands over the years, for inspiring me with the fruit of their understanding and knowledge.

My literary agent and formidable dreamcatcher, Kanishka Gupta, for being a fortress of trust and encouragement, for propelling the show on the road. Amish Mulmi for his thoughtful insights and editing.

Friends and family who have graciously gone through pages and drafts at various stages—Priya Sarukkai Chabria, Mrinalini Mitra, Aditi Makim, Sucharita Dutta-Asane, Sharon Irani, Pierre Lanthier, Medha Singh. Ana Paula Chagla, who keenly patrolled through the spellings of Konkani and Portuguese words.

Boman Irani and Anosh Irani for enlightening sessions during the lockdown years.

Commissioning editor Prerna Vohra for connecting with the book and reeling it into its Bloomsbury home.

Mekhala Moorthy, my editor at Bloomsbury, for tempering quick expertise with intuition, for knowing how to ameliorate the breath of a text, for bringing forth its sheen.

My sincere thanks to Krishan Chopra and the entire team at Bloomsbury.

ABOUT THE AUTHOR

Mrinalini Harchandrai's poetry has been longlisted for the erbacce-prize 2022. She was a finalist for the Quarterly West Poetry Prize 2021 and Stephen A. DiBiase Poetry Prize 2019 and received an Honourable Mention for the Cid Pearlman Performance Project 2021. Her short fiction has been longlisted for the Commonwealth Short Story Prize 2018 and shortlisted for the *Columbia Journal* Spring 2020 Contest. Her first novel, *Rescuing a River Breeze,* was longlisted for the McKitterick Prize 2021.